Mac's Land
A Sequel to Mac's Way

Reg Quist

CKN Christian Publishing
An Imprint of Wolfpack Publishing
6032 Wheat Penny Avenue
Las Vegas, NV 89122

Print ISBN: 978-1-64119-317-7

Mac's Land

Reg Quist

1

MAC AND MARGO WALKED hand in hand to the top of the low hill in back of the ranch house. Resting on the bench that Mac built many years before, they were just in time to sit silently as evening fell upon them. The outline of the Sangre de Christo range was back-lit by a fading sun.

The bench was placed in the shade of some willows that sucked life-sustaining water from a small hill-top pond nearby. The pond, never large but also never dry, seemed to be fed from a trickle of underground water that somehow rose to the crest of the small hill.

Mac was quiet as he watched the last of the day's light fade away, moving west, always west, to bring light to lands he knew nothing about.

From his many miles of riding over the country through the years, Mac knew that the now darkening mountain slopes held a richness of cottonwood, aspen, pinyon pine, ponderosa pine, junipers, and a wide variety of smaller bushes. Although he found it necessary to harvest several hundred ponderosas for the building of the Bar-M ranch buildings, he was careful to take only as much as the project required.

As families moved in and the land filled up he feared for the future of those beautiful, green slopes. He had worried over these thoughts many times before. They came to him now, unbidden and subconsciously.

Margo had long ago accepted the fact that her husband was not normally a wordy man. Some thought he was sullen or moody, but Margo knew this wasn't true. The constant work and hardships of his youth followed by the years of war, surviving the dreadful conditions suffered by the losing side, the long struggle and desperately hard work gaining a financial foothold for his young family, left him with little patience for bunk-house chatter and the like. But when it came time for serious thought and well-considered planning, Mac McTavish was the man you wanted riding beside you. Margo understood all of that, had seen it working itself out over the years, and respected the truth of it.

With the waning light holding the promise of the soon-to-come, full dark, he slowly waved his hand towards the vast grass lands of the Bar-M. "Tell me what you see."

Margo looked at her husband with some concern, knowing there was serious intent behind the simple request. Margo was a fully active, working partner in the Bar-M. She knew the highs and lows of ranch life. She knew cattle prices, calving rates and range conditions. And she could discuss these matters intelligently.

Margo could, at times, be abrupt and a little cutting with her words, belying her inner beauty. Also beautiful of both face and figure, time had changed the youthful beauty that attracted Mac to her, for a more mature look of grace and stability.

She and Mac rubbed each other the wrong way for the first year of their acquaintance. Secretly afraid that she might be falling in love, Margo became defensive to the point of being abrasive towards Mac. Mac responded by becoming silent and remote. Over time they had, for the most part, worked themselves through these issues. But Margo still, on occasion, would pour out strong words where gentleness would have been more appropriate.

She sensed that this was the time for gentleness. She moved her gaze over the dry valley. "I see a lovely green valley that a strong and courageous man led a small group of hopeful people to. I see wealth that the group never dared dream of. I see ranches and homes alive with growing families. And I see trouble in my husband's eyes and I wonder what he sees."

Mac was quiet for some time. Then, speaking slowly, he said "What you see is what we all saw at one time. I admit it's a fond memory. But it's little more than a memory. What I see now is a mistake. A long series of mistakes. And the hard thing is that I'm the one that made those mistakes. Me and our friends and families and the other ranchers. We grew our herds too big. We asked more of the land than it could deliver.

"Rightly, this country is semi-desert. It's not the same as the green-grass country back east. It's a dry country compared to Missouri, where we had our small farm. But it's a good country. When we first rode up to it, what we saw was a world of dusky green. Desert green. Green as far as the eye could see. A green, high mountain plateau that someone called a valley, there for the taking.

"We took that lovely green valley and we killed it. There just ain't no denying it! This valley is dying, and I'm the one that killed it!"

Margo was silent for a long time, not denying her husband's words, and then gently asked, "What do you intend that we should do about it?"

Mac seemed to look over the land as if seeing it for the first time. He was slow in answering. "Do what has to be done to bring it back to life."

"I'm sensing that you've given this considerable thought. What has to be done?"

"We're going to start again. We're going to start again and we're going to do it right. I don't know if the other ranchers will go along. I suspect most of them won't. But for the Bar-M, we're going to start again."

Margo, a sometimes stern, but loving and supportive woman, was silent as her husband outlined his plans, asking just a couple of questions along the way. It was well after sunset before the two of them finished talking and headed back down the hill, stepping carefully on the dark trail.

Margo checked the sleeping children once more and then went to bed herself. Mac lifted the veranda lantern from the hook it rested on and took his last turn around the ranch yard. He had repeated this tour of their homestead every evening since they first pitched their tent all those long year before; two young newlyweds accepting the tent as their first home on solid ground. After the months living out of the back of a rolling wagon, the tent seemed like paradise. Now the tent was long gone, and in its place stood a beautifully designed and built home and an established, prosperous, ranch headquarters.

Rounding the back of the big corral, Mac met the first-shift guard, a rider named Buck Travers. The cowboy was leaning against the top rail of the corral, rolling a smoke. He watched Mac approach. "Evening, Boss."

"How goes it, Buck? Everything quiet?"

"Ain't seen nor heard a thing, Mac. Indians, they can move almighty quiet, or so I've heard said by them that seem to know. I've never had much truck with them my own self. But I've listened and watched the best I know how, and so far as I can tell, you and I are alone out here."

"Let's hope it stays that way. I look forward to the time when we won't have to stand watch of a night, but that time is not yet. Stay alert Buck. Someone will be out to relieve you in a while."

Buck blew smoke into the air. "Good night, Boss. Don't you worry about a thing."

2

MAC AND MARGO LIVED in the weather-worn tent for the first year after their move up from Texas. Traveling west from where they first entered the valley, they moved closer to the foothills before settling down to build their ranch, naming it the Bar-M. Cutting and peeling logs for the new cabin was a long and arduous process, even with a crew to help with the work. Mac, busy with the cattle, and with enough cash saved from rounding up Texas longhorns and selling them into the Northern market, brought carpenters out from Denver to build their long, low, ranch house. The same crew built the barns, sheds and bunkhouse, all from native logs hauled down from the nearby mountainsides.

Family and friends who had travelled west with Mac and Margo claimed their own portions of the valley, staking out larger claims than they ever dreamed possible. Someone called it a valley when they first rode up to it, seeing it from the raised lip of the small plateau. The title stuck although, rightly, it wasn't a valley. It was more properly a huge, high elevation plain, cut here and there by rivers and smaller streams, as well as ridges of rocky up-thrusts, gently sloping towards the foothills.

Mac's group was barely a year ahead of the westering ranchers who were gambling everything in the hopes of finding new grass for their herds, and a place to settle down, free of the conflicts that seemed to follow them after the war. These men, mostly Texans trying to put the bitter memories of war's defeat and the Reconstruction government behind them, combined with others from New Mexico and Indian Territory, along with a few Easterners, soon had every acre of the valley staked out, claiming the land as their own.

Legal ownership was not the issue in the first years. Ownership was based on possession. There was considerable pushing and grasping for the first few years, but the conflicting land claims had finally settled out, allowing a tender peace to reign.

One enterprising rancher drove a herd of breeding animals over the trail from Oregon, looking for a sunny home for his rain-hating wife. He claimed land to the East of the Bar-M. The Oregon animals were a mixture of Eastern breeds, the offspring of those driven over the long and arduous trail west, decades before. Mac purchased a small group of heifers from the Oregon herd. Still, most of the animals in the valley were longhorns.

Within two years of Mac marking out his Bar-M, every acre of grass in the valley and the surrounding foothills was entirely claimed, under one brand or another.

A small band of Ute that had hunted buffalo where the ranchers now raised their cattle, retreated into the high mountain valleys. Mindful that much of the tribe had been forced onto reserves, these lived quietly and peacefully among their hills, avoiding contact whenever possible. Mac, with the help of Jimbo, a footloose wanderer who seemed to have seen the entire West at one time or another, made friends with the local Ute, led by Chief Runs His Horses. When he was much younger, Jimbo took a Ute girl to wife. She eventually wearied of his months-long travels and moved to another's lodge. Jimbo never saw her again.

The Bar-M experienced no Indian trouble except for the loss of a few beeves that nomadic tribes took for the cook pot. Mac ignored the loss, not wishing to begrudge a few meals for the wandering souls who lost everything else, including their pride and dignity.

By the second summer on the ranch, with their first-born; a quiet and reflective boy named Jarrod, in memory of a good friend who died on the trip west, Mac and Margo were settled into the new house. The Bar-M herd grew, flourishing on grass that formerly fed thousands of wandering buffalo. By the fourth spring, the Bar-M ranch was well established with the first calf crop sold and delivered to the Denver cattle pens. Although some stock would be shipped east, most would go towards feeding the miners digging their way through the mineral bearing hills to the west of Denver.

Mac hired more riders. In a land with no fences, hard driven men were constantly scrambling for grass, threatening the prevailing peace. Patrolling the borders of the claimed spreads required relentless vigilance. Although Colorado passed a fencing law, most of the newly arrived Texas ranchers believed in the open range concept and let their animals wander at will. Mac and his crew worked hard to hold his own animals on the Bar-M range while keeping others off his grass. It was a constant battle; the cause of long hours of work and many miles ridden by the hard-working cowboys.

On a blistering hot day in the July of their fifth year, Margo delivered twins; a curly haired boy they named Adam and a girl named Jerilyn, shortened to Jerry by everyone except the baby's mother. The babies were snuggled into a pair of homemade cribs with both Mac's and Margo's mothers close by to help,

A few days after giving birth, Margo and her mother were sipping tea in the shade of the roofed-in veranda, seeking relief from the relentless summer sun. Margo, fanning herself with a turkey wing, looked over at her mother, "I don't know as I would want to do that all again tomorrow but even so, this heat might be bothering me more than bringing those babies into the world."

Her mother gave her a long, questioning look, took a sip of tea and said, "My memory of that process might be fading with time, but I don't know as I was ever that strong, or all that troubled by a bit of heat."

Ten years passed since that time. The log house took on the comfort and patina of age and familiarity, while the ranch prospered. The family grew with the addition of three-year old Becky and one-year-old Luke.

Jerrod was seldom out of Mac's sight. Serious and studious, he was tall and thin, but with wide shoulders and arms and chest showing the growing strength that would be his in maturity. He was the image of his father in looks and habits. The twins were as wild as their Indian neighbors. They spent hours each day riding their ponies wherever the notion took them, scaring their mother half to death. Getting them to sit at the kitchen table doing their numbers or puzzling out the big words in the progressively more difficult books Margo laid before them was a daily struggle.

The prosperous years saw calf crops maturing into market beef. Together with the animals the neighbors cut from their herds, the beef was driven to the Denver buyers. With each beef sale Mac renewed his praise for this new land and was careful to express his thanks for all the circumstances that led them there. But in the past couple of years he had become troubled as he rode his vast acres, studying the land.

The morning after Mac and Margo had climbed the hill to discuss their future, the hollow drum of hoof beats on the packed and hardened two-track ranch road competed with the rattle of trace chains and the crunch of wagon wheels. Mac and Margo both looked up from where they were repairing the garden fence, readying it for spring planting. Margo pulled the brim of her Stetson down a bit to shield her eyes from the summer sun and studied the oncoming wagon. "That's Bill's rig, I wonder what he's doing over here in the middle of this sweltering hot day"

Mac squinted his eyes under his hat brim and nodded in agreement. "Someone in the back of the wagon. Looks like Little Flower. Ain't like Bill to make her ride in the back of the wagon, although I've often thought that others of us could learn a thing or two about marriage from watching Bill." His tone of voice and the slight grin on his sun darkened face hid his concerns about the grazed-out range conditions and gave way to his normally good humor.

Margo turned and gave him a friendly punch on the arm. "Watch what you're saying, or you'll learn a thing or two about marriage yourself."

"I'm just saying that Bill appears to be doing alright. Little Flower was raised to believe a woman's place was to walk a step or two behind, and she seems to be at ease with the situation." Mac said it with an even bigger grin.

Margo pointed a withering look his way. "You keep this up and you'll find yourself sleeping in the barn until you have a grey beard hanging down to your knees." If Margo was smiling she was hiding it well.

Mac grinned again and hung his hammer on a fence board. "Well, let's go see what this hurry is all about."

3

A SLOW MINUTE LATER the wagon pulled to a rattling stop in front of the ranch house. The trailing dust cloud billowing behind the arriving wagon settled over everything in its path. As Bill hauled the team to a stop in front of the house, Mac stepped to the rear of the wagon. There he was startled to see a bloody blanket covering a man laid out on a pile of hay. Little Flower was holding one of the man's hands, bringing some bit of comfort.

It never failed to amaze Mac how Bill, who was Margo's brother, seemed to be careless of life, casual almost, taking his Christian beliefs, but little else seriously. He never once mentioned a desire to find a wife. And then he came up with a most attractive young girl, chosen from a wagonload of mission school students. The school year was at an end and the students were heading back to Runs His Horse's village. The Band moved from time to time, following the movements of wild game, and sometimes just because they took an urge to move. But they could always be found somewhere in the high-up foothills of the Sangre de Cristo Range. They caused no trouble and the army chose to leave them alone.

The missionary took shelter at the Bar-M ranch for the night, bunking the children down in the loft of Mac's small barn. Bill, living in a simple, one room cabin he built for himself on the ranch, met Little Flower. At sixteen, she was the oldest of the students. She spoke excellent English. She and Bill must have found enough to talk about because, much to the chagrin of the missionary, and over his strong caution, the worried and befuddled man married the couple the next morning. The missionary took word back to the tribal village and the newlyweds settled into married life as if their actions were completely normal.

Bill claimed a sizable piece of land when they first arrived from Texas. He staked out his land further west. The chosen grasslands were higher than the Bar-M acres, with the western edge rising well into the forested foothills. The location suited Bill's wilder nature. Although he didn't live on the land at first, he kept a goodly number of cattle growing and multiplying on the expanse of foothills grass.

After their marriage, Bill and Little Flower dismantled the cabin on the Bar-M and moved it to the western claim, naming the ranch the U.T.E.

To say that Little Flower was beautiful would be nothing but the truth. She knew her beauty would be short lived in the village, under the constant stress of primitive conditions, extremes of weather, hard work, smoke filled lodges and continual child bearing. Life with Bill, on a cattle ranch, with a warm, modern cabin would be a different situation altogether.

Although a few of the Ute traditions were maintained on the U.T.E. ranch, Little Flower settled in and worked alongside her husband in the building up of a typical western ranch. The larger family all came to love and appreciate Little Flower and she seemed to fit into ranch life as if she was born to it.

11

Bill turned on the spring seat and casually waved his hand at the bloody burden in the back of the wagon, "Brought you a house guest, Margo. I wasn't sure of his welcome, all things considered, but he insisted that this was where he wanted to be, so here he is."

Mac moved closer and lifted the corner of the blanket to reveal the face of his old friend, Jimbo. "This your blood ruining this blanket, Jimbo?"

Jimbo, normally a story teller and a man of many words could only nod his head weakly.

Margo pushed her way in front of Mac and removed the blanket entirely. Jimbo's shirt had been cut off to reveal a purpling bullet hole just above his left hip bone. A blood-soaked rag was tied around his upper arm. His pant leg was split open and a crude bandage covered a bloody wound in his thigh. All three wounds were on his left side.

"You been shot just the three times Jimbo or is there more I haven't seen yet?" asked Margo, never showing much patience for the old frontier wanderer.

Jimbo's lips moved, but no sound came out. Little Flower answered for him. "Three. I think that is enough for one day."

The twins, seeing their uncle Bill had arrived, ran their ponies across the ranch yard to see what was happening. They pulled their animals to a dusty stop, one on each side of the wagon. Leaning over and peering into the wagon box, Jerry helpfully said, "Whoeee, Jimbo, you're a mess. I bet that hurts."

Adam added, "I'm thinking that's going to leave a mark Jimbo."

Jimbo lifted his uninjured arm a few inches, in a weak response. The old man and the twins had developed a special relationship based on story telling, with each participant pretending to believe what the other said, no matter how ridiculous. Margo often felt Jimbo was more kid than the kids were.

Margo said, "You kids get out of here and stop raising dust. And put those ponies in the shade, you've got them all lathered up in this heat."

"Aw, Mom, these are Ute war ponies, they love running and sweating."

Little Flower smiled at them, but their mother turned and gave them a look they had no trouble understanding. They walked their ponies to the shade of the small barn.

Mac spoke to Bill and Little Flower together. "Were you there to see what happened?"

Bill nodded. "Our milk cow decided to go for a walk. I suspect she's hidden a calf somewhere in those brushy hills. We were out looking for her when we came up to a small group of Indians we never saw before. Just as they came in sight we heard a shout and the warriors lifted their carbines. The result is what you see here. I expect they would have finished the job if we hadn't come along. Even so, if I'd been alone they might have done for Jimbo, and me too. But they backed up a bit and took notice when Little Flower spoke to them."

Mac gestured to Bill. "Pull the wagon over closer to the house. We'll get him inside and then see what we can do."

"Be quiet about it," warned Margo, "You wake those kids up from their naps and you'll be in worse shape than Jimbo." Margo seldom allowed herself to be misunderstood.

The two men gently carried Jimbo into the house and laid him on a home-built cot in the back room.

Little Flower grasped the halter of one horse and walked the team over to where Mac had been burning some brush that he had been cleared from the house yard. With the side of her foot she scraped the bloody blanket onto the now-cold pile of ashes. She then did the same with the damaged hay. Pepe Fernandez, the ranch wrangler walked over from the barn and led the team to the water trough and then into the shade beside the kids' ponies.

Little Flower walked up to the house and stepped onto the kitchen porch where she found water, soap and a wash pan. It took several minutes to clean the blood from her hands and arms. The splatters on her dress would have to be dealt with later.

Margo built up the fire in the already sweltering kitchen and put on water to heat, while Bill and Mac pulled off the remainder of Jimbo's clothing. Jimbo's eyes filled with fear and panic when Mac started to cut off his long handles.

"Lay still old friend, I've got no choice here. You're going to have to be cleaned up and have those wounds treated. It's going to be the women who do it, so you might just as well grit your teeth and make the best of it. I'll find something to cover your honor with if that's what's setting your teeth on edge."

Mac spoke to Bill again. "Bill, I'd take it kindly if you'd drive your wagon down to Mex village and bring Mama up here. Some are calling her a curandero. That may or may not be true. In any case, she knows more about doctoring and such than we do."

Jimbo was finding it nearly impossible to speak in his weakened condition but when he heard Mac talk of getting Mama, he looked panic stricken and found the strength to whisper. "Mac, don't you bring that woman in here. I'd rather die than have her see me this way."

Mac chuckled. "Everyone has a little stress in their lives old friend, but mostly we live through it. If Mama don't die of laughter when she sees your scrawny self I expect things will work out just fine. Of course, she'll have to dig out that lead. I don't know if she'll enjoy that or not; I doubt as how you will. But none of these holes are anywhere near the heart so with some doctoring and the Lord's blessing I expect you have a pretty good chance of seeing more country from the back of that appaloosa. May take a day or two but I'd say you have a pretty good chance."

Little Flower, leaning on the doorpost watching the men work on Jimbo, spoke up. "He may live to see over another hill or two, but he won't do it from the back of the appaloosa. I expect that animal is on its way back to Idaho by now. Having that 'borrowed' appaloosa is what caused him to gather up this lead."

Mac looked from Little Flower, back to Jimbo, a suddenly serious expression on his face. "Well, well. This is not a totally settled or safe country we live in Jimbo. Lots of Indians still hiding out, failing to recognise the benevolence of the government or the kindly intentions of the army, and resisting the attractions of the reserve lands. If you've brought down some unwanted attention on yourself, you maybe should tell me about it, in case we have to prepare for visitors who have a different view on borrowing horses than you have. With the problems we already have, I'm not sure we would welcome any more."

Jimbo squirmed on the cot, looking for a more comfortable position. He tugged on the blanket Mac had covered him with, pulling it up to his chin and holding it like a shield in front of him. He took a sip of water from Mac's offering hand and felt a little better.

It seemed to take all of Jimbo's strength to whisper, "It's that chief I told you about. The one from way back. The one that took my gifts, including the best Green River knife I ever owned, one I truly admired. He was well paid, but he still wouldn't part with that horse, even though, rightly, we had a deal agreed on.

"He showed up. Must have ridden all the way down here from Idaho. Don't rightly understand that. I tried to explain that I'd just taken the borrow of the horse and that I'd borrow it back if he felt strongly about it. Turns out he takes a narrow view on life. The concept of holding to a fair deal seems to be missing from his Mama's training."

Jimbo took a deep breath, squinted against the gathering pain and continued. "I tried to explain that after so many years the horse had forgotten him, and that the animal and I had become partners. I offered to pay him again, although the gifts I gave before were more than enough payment. Said I had nothing he wanted, except the horse, and maybe my life. I wasn't altogether taken with his attitude. Still, I was just getting set to borrow the horse back to him, when three of his warriors up and shoot me. I took that as unfriendly."

Little Flower shook her head in amusement. "Perhaps the chief misunderstood your intentions when you turned the horse away and spurred him into a gallop."

Jimbo had nothing to add.

Mac looked truly worried. He asked Little Flower, "Do you think the chief took the horse and left out for home or should we expect a further visit from him? I don't know as I'm prepared to risk my ranch and family over an old horse."

Jimbo showed true concern as he waited for Little Flower's answer. "He was headed generally north the last we saw of him. But that's no guarantee. He may take the horse back to his camp and then return. I didn't sense any humor in the man at all, or any tendency to forgive and forget."

Mac asked, "Where were they camped?"

"They headed out north and west, up that coulee just west of the trading post. The one that leads into the higher up hills," answered Little Flower. "I don't know how far away their camp is. We didn't follow. We were a little busy trying to keep Jimbo from leaking all his blood out."

"Did you hear any of them speak English?" asked Mac.

"The chief and Jimbo seemed to have a lot to say to each other but we were too far away to hear the words. When we talked to him the chief said many words about Jimbo's thieving ways and his family heritage," answered Little Flower. "A mixture of poor English and his own tongue. I understood most of it, although I wouldn't want to have to repeat it. It would be a fair guess that the chief understands enough English to make his meaning clear."

Mac struggled between his friendship with Jimbo and his concern over the intentions of the Nez Percé chief who rode the many miles down from Idaho looking for an old horse. He finally came to the only logical conclusion: "I better try to track him down. See can we negotiate a peace. We simply can't afford to have him surprise us in the early dawn if he decides to pursue this matter any further."

After explaining to Margo, Mac went to the barn and saddled his horse. He then slipped a rope through the lead ring on the halter of a fine looking black gelding in the corral. Stepping into his saddle he rode from the yard, leading the black, heading for the coulee Little Flower described. An hour later he was in rough country, a country of rock and stunted trees, with the poorly marked trail soon fading out to nothing more than some trampled grass. It took him the most of two hours, riding through dry washes and around pear covered hillsides, before the rising smoke from the Indian camp came into view. He slowed his horse to a gentle walk and moved forward. Two Indian riders stepped their horses out of the brush and took up positions on each side of him. Although they were both well armed Mac saw no threat. Not so far anyways.

Mac pulled his horse to a stop a respectful distance from the camp. He turned to one of the riders and asked, "Do you speak English?"

The rider pointed and said, "Chief."

Mac stepped down from his horse and walked slowly, leading the gelding towards the chief, who was sitting with several other men drinking what Mac guessed, judging by smell, was coffee. Mac thought, 'They're doomed. Their women have metal cooking pots and sharp knives. The men have rifles and coffee. There's no going back.' He chuckled a bit to himself before he sobered, remembering the seriousness of his errand.

Mac stopped twenty feet from the group of men and waited for the chief to speak. It took a painfully long time.

Finally, "That is a good-looking horse. For white-man horse."

Mac pulled his eyes away from the chief long enough to take a loving look at the gelding he had raised and trained. "It is a gift for our neighbor from the north, to welcome you to this good land and to help make your long ride home more pleasant.

It is a gift from my friend who borrowed your horse." Mac pointed to the old appaloosa that was tethered a short distance away. "He is sorry that he did not ask you first if he could borrow it. He is also sorry that you had to make a very long ride to ask for it back. He says he would have gladly brought the horse back to you if he knew you wanted it. He says that he wishes you a long life and hopes that you will ride this black in good health."

"There are no spots on your black. White man horse. Spotted horse better. Black maybe make good stew."

Mac had no idea what to do next. He couldn't judge if the chief was serious or making sport of him.

Mac said, "The black is a gift to the chief. You can do what you wish with him. Before you make stew perhaps you should ride him. He is a very good horse. Maybe too good for stew."

The chief stared at Mac for a few moments and then looked around, saying a few words to the men in the circle. They all burst into laughter and pointed at Mac. He decided that perhaps he would never understand these people.

Mac was again unsure what to do next. He finally passed the lead rope to one of the riders who had escorted him into camp. He walked the few feet to his own horse and stepped into the saddle. He turned to the chief. "We have always heard that the Nez Percé people are a people of peace. It is our hope that you will take this gift and return home with good thoughts of your visit to our land." He emphasized all of this with arm gestures toward the hills and the horizons visible through the small valleys.

"We are happy that you have come in peace. There are other tribes that are sometimes not friendly. We are always on guard in case one of them visits us in the night. We would not want to mistake your friendly visit with one of the other tribes." He spoke slowly, trying to pick his words carefully. He wanted to warn the chief without giving insult or challenge.

"I have heard of your beautiful Idaho valleys and your safe villages. Your wives and children will be watching for you. It is our hope that you will make a safe trip home."

Mac was not sure if the chief spoke enough English to grasp the veiled threat or not. He hoped so. He also hoped that he had not insulted the man.

'I could sure use Bill right now,' thought Mac. 'Never saw anyone get along with Indians like Bill does.'

Mac was allowed to turn his horse and ride from the camp. Riding slowly, he resisted the temptation to look behind him, and did his best to ignore the cramped muscles in his shoulders. It was as if his body was involuntarily expecting a rifle shot. None came, and he was soon around the bend in the coulee and on his way home. Along the way he found the wayward milk cow, a newborn calf nudging her udder, wishing to be fed. Mac took careful note of the location. It would be a help when Bill and Little Flower came back for the animal.

Arriving at the Bar-M, Mac turned his dusty, tired horse over to Pepe and walked to the cabin. The women were sitting around the kitchen table drinking tea. Unwashed lunch dishes were piled on the counter. Mama was with them. Bill was nowhere to be seen. "How did it go with Jimbo?" asked Mac.

The women broke into undignified giggling. "Well," answered Margo, when she got control of herself, "I expect Jimbo would rather be shot dead than go through that again, but he should survive if he doesn't do anything stupid. He has a fair chance of escaping infection now that several layers of dirt have been scraped from his hide. But before he was to ever again let anyone give him a much-needed bath, I believe he would shoot himself. You never heard such squallering in all your life." The women started giggling again.

"That's fascinating Margo, but I was really more interested in the bullet holes than the bath."

"Bullet's gone."

That slight bit of information from Mama seemed to be all Mac was going to learn, so he nodded his head at the ladies and walked into the back room. There he found Bill holding a cup of coffee for Jimbo to slurp from. Judging by smell alone, Mac figured Bill had found his small stock of snake-bite remedy to lace the coffee with. That was typical for Jimbo but not for Bill. Mac let it go.

"Well," said Mac. "I learned almost nothing at all from the women. Am I going to learn any more from you two or should I go back to fixing fence?"

Bill answered, after taking a look at Jimbo to see if the old man was going to speak. "Two of those shots went right through. Mama dug the one out of Jimbo's leg. It bled some but it's all settled down now. I expect you have a house guest for a few days. Of course, I could load him back up and take him out to that Indian camp and let them care for him. That way you'd be rid of him. What do you think, Jimbo?" he asked with a smile.

Jimbo was several moments answering. "I think I need to get me some new friends. That's what I think, if you really want to know. This has been the awfulest day of my life. And I've had some to compare to. I lose my ride and my saddle and gear. I get shot and nearly bleed to death. Then the men I most trust in the world turn me over to the likes of those giggling women. And with me in no shape to protect myself. Cruel. That's what y'all are. Cruel. No milk of human kindness anywhere that I can see."

He turned his face to the wall and shivered down a deep breath. "And then to top it all off, whatever dignity I once had is gone."

Mac smiled a bit at Jimbo. "The good news is that I believe those Indians are on their way back to Idaho. Don't rightly know how they found you, old friend, or why they bothered after all these years. I didn't sense anything that would lead me to believe they'll seek more revenge. I think they're heading for home with your Ap. Or at least I hope they are.

"Their leaving cost me that black gelding I've been working with. Gave it to them as a gift. But I think they're going home. We'll stand an extra guard for the next few nights. But I don't expect to see them again. They're a small group. Seemed like an overall friendly bunch, now they have their horse returned. I doubt as how they'd team up with a more troublesome band and come back for a shooting visit."

Jimbo nodded and made a small, guttural sound, which Mac figured was about as much verbal thanks as he was likely to get. Jimbo would find other ways to show his appreciation. "I've been pondering on the situation. I doubt as how that bunch were here for the horse or even knew where we were. Just an accident. Bad timing, you might say. I happened along and there they were. Anyway, tell me about these other Indian troubles you're talk'n about."

Mac answered, "It's not Indian troubles, it's grass troubles. I suspect that's going to lead to white man troubles when I do what I have to do. Rancher troubles. But it's not your problem. You rest now, and we'll talk after supper."

Margo had the kids up from their afternoon naps when Mac headed back out to the fencing job. The day was nearly done but Mac figured to put a bit of fencing work behind him before he called it quits. One-year-old Luke was kept safely under his mother's watch-care. Three-year-old Becky Sue ran to where Mac was back at the garden fence. She liked nothing better than following her dad around the ranch yard. Nothing more, that is, than sitting bareback on an old mare Mac and his partners used for a pack horse. Like her older twin siblings, her antics on horseback terrified Margo, but Mac let them go, all the time keeping a close eye on her.

"That old mare walked all the way from Texas with us, Margo. And that's after going up the trail twice, following those bellering longhorns. I don't believe she has a mean bone in her body and I doubt as how she has any run left in her either. She didn't have much run in her when we bought her for a pack horse and she's a good many years older now. Your baby will be alright."

Margo had some doubts but kept her peace.

Mama took one more look at Jimbo's wounds and wrapped clean dressings on them. He mumbled a grudging thanks, still fighting his embarrassment. Bill and Little Flower drove her back to Mex Town and then turned to the trail for their two-hour ride to the U.T.E. they would pick up the milk cow on the way, giving the calf a wagon ride.

Margo served up the evening meal.

Jimbo insisted on being helped to the table. "Never ate a meal lying a-bed in my entire life. Don't figure to start now."

It would have been easier for Mac to simply pick Jimbo up and carry him to a chair, but he let the old man shuffle along, hanging on to his last shred of dignity.

After supper, sitting on the veranda with Jimbo's leg resting on a small stool, he again asked about the troubles. "I've been away for some time. But I'd admire to know just what's been happening."

The two men talked long into the evening, joined by Margo after the kids were settled in bed.

Mac and Margo, taking turns with the telling, outlined the problem of the grazed-out valley, and the Bar-M's, as well as their neighbor's desperate need for grass. Mac and Jimbo, drinking yet another pot of coffee in the gathering darkness, discussed Mac's proposed solution and how his plan might work out, and the troubles it might cause.

Margo checked the kids once more and then went to bed herself. After helping Jimbo back to his cot, Mac lifted the veranda lantern from its hook and took his last turn around the ranch yard. This night Mac doubled the guard, taking no chances on the intentions of the Nez Percé who shot Jimbo. Buck was back on duty along with another rider named Willy Williams. The two cowboys were leaning against the top rail of the corral. Willy was rolling a smoke. They seemed to find the corral, with its dozing horses, a comfort during the long nights.

They watched Mac approach. "Evening, Boss."

"How goes it Buck, Willy? Everything quiet?"

Willy looked around and nodded, as if indicating the entire ranch yard. "Ain't seen nor heard a thing.

"Let's hope it stays that way. Stay alert, boys"

Buck blew smoke into the air. "Anyone sneaks around, we'll see 'em."

4

MORNING COMES EARLY on a high-country ranch. The night's full dark was just beginning to turn to grey. The sun, rising far to the east, pushed just a hint of the day to come across the grass lands. Smoke from the stove fire in the cookhouse greeted the morning. Mac was up and ready for the day. Margo was taking the last of her night's rest, determined to lay abed until the kids awoke, demanding her attention. Mac had long been in the habit of taking his morning meal in the cookhouse with the men, so there was no real reason for Margo to rise early.

There were seventeen men on the payroll of the Bar-M; fifteen riders, one cook, and Pepe, the yard man who doubled as the horse wrangler and occasional dish washer. Pepe was the first to rise each morning. He was expected to have enough horses corralled for the day's work by the time the cowboys were up and ready to start their day.

Each cowboy would stroll out at first light and call out his ride for the day. Pepe would then rope the animal and lead it to the gate. The rider would saddle the animal and tie it to the outside of the corral before going in for breakfast.

As day was breaking, Brady, the sunrise shift guard, broke off his vigilance, waving across the yard at Pepe who was crossing the dusty path to the barn, still tucking in his shirt. Three hours of yard patrol produced no Indians, but it left Brady with a strong need for coffee.

Pepe kept his own animal in a stall in the small barn, ready for his early morning chores. Stepping to the door, he lifted the night lantern from the hook above the door and entered. As the lantern's feeble light broke the gloom of the barn he stepped towards the row of stalls and stopped in his tracks. He reached for a hay fork, the closest thing to a weapon he could think of, and carefully looked around the barn and into each stall, holding the fork ahead of himself, like a lance. Only after he satisfied himself that he was alone did he put down the fork and approach the stall next to his own horse.

He slowly stepped into the stall, gently gliding his hand along the back of the saddled appaloosa that was tied there, talking gently to the animal. The old gelding stood quietly, showing no fright. Pulling the tie rope loose, Pepe led the horse out of the stall and into the yard. There were a few cowboys, fresh from their bunks, gathered around the wash stand, waiting their turn to clean the sleep from their eyes. Mac established a washing-up rule with the very first crew he hired. No one was allowed into the cook house until they visited the wash stand and put the lie soap to good use. A few grumbled, but they soon got over it.

As Pepe approached, leading the appaloosa, one of the men called out, "Whatcha got there, Pepe? Ain't never seen but one animal like that around here and the news is that it was stoled by the Indians."

The men gathered around the horse. A shout went out to the bunk house and cook shack. More men arrived. Among them was Mac.

The men's comments stopped as Mac walked up to Pepe. He looked first at the animal and then at Pepe, questions forming in his mind. It took a good half minute for him to ask, "Where did you find this animal?"

Brady arrived, carrying his coffee mug. He too, waited for Pepe's answer.

"Tied in the stall right next to my animal, Boss. Just standing there by himself, no sign of anyone else."

Mac turned to look at Brady. There was no need to speak the question aloud.

Brady hunched his shoulders and spread his legs a bit, letting his high-heeled boots take a firmer grip in the dust. "Boss, I never once dozed off, nor even sat down. I walked the perimeter of the yard and listened into the night the whole time I was out here. I done just like you said to do. I walked through the barn maybe a half hour before you came from the house. That horse was not there, nor anywhere around. I know my job, Boss, and I done it, just as you asked."

Mac looked again at the horse, then at Pepe and then back to Brady. "I have no reason not to trust you on this Brady. Where did you go after you left the barn?"

"I hung the lantern back over the barn door. Toby was partnering me. I waved him away to get his coffee. Then I walked around back of the bunk house, then the kitchen, and on up and around the big house, making my final inspection. I was just back from that when you came out."

Mac look all around again. Taking the lead rope from the wrangler he said, "Alright men, we'll leave the mystery for now. Go get your breakfasts."

Leading the animal, Mac walked towards the house. He tied the appaloosa to the hitch rail outside the yard fence and stepped up onto the veranda. A sleepy Margo opened the door. She took a long look at the tied animal and then at Mac. "Is that…?"

Mac just nodded his head. "Don't ask, 'cuz I don't know." He walked past his wife and stepped into the back room where

Jimbo was bedded down. The old man was half awake and struggling into the pants Mac loaned him. By the look of the tangle of clothing that Mac could just barely make out in the dim early morning, there was some doubt about the success of the venture.

Mac bent and untangled the leg of the canvas pants and separated it from the bed clothes. Jimbo showed his appreciating by saying, "Don't guess I really need any help getting dressed. May need some help getting to the outhouse though. That has to happen pretty soon so I'm glad you're here."

Mac had long been familiar with Jimbo's ways and took no offense at his grumbling. "Got something you might want to see. Step into those moccasins. I ain't got all day."

Mac helped Jimbo limp through the house and out the door, onto the veranda. The wounded man was looking at the floor, watching where he was placing his feet, being careful not to stumble over anything. Finally, at the bottom of the steps, he lifted his head, saw the horse, and let out a cry. He shucked Mac's helping hands away and rushed across the pebbled walk and out the gate, the outhouse and his pain forgotten.

Mac and Margo stood silently, watching as the old man wrapped his arms around the horse's neck and buried his face in the grey hair of the gelding's mane. Jimbo, ever the cynical wanderer, seeming to never need anything or anyone other than his freedom, stood, his back to Mac and Margo, with his shoulders shaking and his quiet sobs stifled as they filtered through the mane. A few cowboys began wandering from the cookhouse to see what was happening.

Margo watched Jimbo for a half minute. "Well, maybe there's one thing on this earth that old reprobate values almost as much as himself."

Mac lifted his arm and gave her a hug around her shoulders. "Everyone hides a bit of themselves from others. I'll push the men away. Why don't you go see to the kids? We'll leave Jimbo alone for a while."

Mac led the men back to the cookhouse and detailed off the day's work to Taz Johansen, the ranch foreman. As the men filed out, gathering in the yard, Taz assigned each riding pair a task for the day. From the beginning, it was the practice on the Bar-M that men didn't ride alone except in unusual circumstances. That practice had saved many serious injuries and a couple of lives as the partners were able to come to each other's aid while working with half-wild longhorn cattle, in a land newly settled. Now, with a potential Indian issue to deal with the men all went armed and wary. Mac also warned them not to look for trouble.

Mac then made his way back to the house. He was in time to see Jimbo struggling down the path on his return from the outhouse. Mac figured it was a combination of toughness, stubbornness and pride that kept the wounded man upright. Mac stood beside the appaloosa waiting for his friend. "Can you make it to the cookhouse or do you want me to get the wheelbarrow?" Mac's smile cut the edge off the remark.

Jimbo continued his slow shuffle. "I can make it if there's coffee at the end of the trail. But first I got to show you something." He staggered the last few steps to the horse. Holding the horn for support he reached into the off-side saddle bag, He pulled out a big knife pushed firmly into a beaded and tasseled leather sheath. Holding it up to Mac he said, "The sheath is new, but the knife is the very same Green River piece I put up in trade for this horse all those years ago. You can see this nick on the upper of the blade. That happened when I... well, never mind that.

"Thought I knew something about Indians but there's no figuring this deal. Let's get that coffee."

Mac closed in, so his friend could grip his shoulder in support. "I'll take you to the wash stand and bring you a bucket of hot water from the kitchen. Nothing like a good scrubbing to get you up and shining in the morning." Mac managed that comment without breaking a grin.

Jimbo kept walking. "Tried it a time or two. Never could see the benefit."

Seated at one of the long, home-built tables the two men cradled their coffee cups in their rein and work-scarred hands, as if it was the middle of winter, while they waited for Cookie to put together some side meat and eggs for Jimbo. Mac knew by the clanking of metal pans on the iron stove that he wasn't happy about having to prepare a late breakfast. He'd do it though. The long-time cook would do most things for Mac and anything at all Margo requested of him.

Without looking at Jimbo, Mac said, "What's your best guess on all this?"

"I don't know. I really don't. I doubt as how that bunch came all this way looking for a horse that's been gone for so many years. But they're known as a wandering people. Taken all together it's not really all that far from Idaho to here if you can keep out of the way of the Mormon settlements on the sunset side of these hills. I suspect they were just a bunch out seeing what they could see, happy to be free of the winter snows, when what they saw was me and my ride. My bet would be that they were as surprised as I was. Then it just kind of got out of hand. Sorry about that black you at your heart set on riding, but I do appreciate your help."

After a pause he continued. "Can't explain the knife. They've always been known as a friendly bunch but mayhap no one really understands them as well as we thought we did."

Jimbo ate his breakfast and then went back to the little cot in the back room of the house. He made every effort to stay out of Margo's way.

5

THE COMMUNITY-WIDE SPRING roundup was just a couple of weeks from starting. Mac and Margo worked together at the kitchen table to make a list of supplies that would be needed for the roundup; new ropes, a tub of axle grease, repairs to a branding iron that was horse stomped and bent, salves and whatever medication was available for cut or injured animals, new work pants and shirts for Mac, a rain slicker, and a few other odds and ends. To this list he added the longer list Cookie gave him for cookhouse and chuckwagon provisions.

Mac then jotted down a note to gather up some new clothing for Jimbo. Mac's oversized cast-offs kept the old man covered but not much else good could be said about the arrangement.

Margo wrote her own list for kids' summer clothing and family groceries, plus seeds for the garden. She kept this list separate. She would do her own shopping.

Mac decided that this was probably the last roundup on the Bar-M. Feeling that Jerrod was old enough to go along and wanting the young man to at least have a feel for what roundup was like, he said, "Pick out what clothing you think you'll need. Ask your grandpa to advise on putting a bedroll together. Don't forget a new rain slicker." Jerrod warmed to the idea and flashed one of his rare smiles.

Ad Adkins, Margo's father, along with his wife, plus their son Bill and the younger children, trailed west after joining up with Mac and his two partners, Jerrod and Luke. After many months and thousands of miles of bawling cattle, dust, storms, rustlers, rattlesnakes, and just about anything else a man could come to dislike, Ad lost his desire to ranch. Following much discussion with the family, he opened a trading post on fifty acres of flat land he claimed and fenced, alongside a small river, well above the highest flood line.

He called his first modest adobe building, "Adkins Trading Post and Smithy". Luke suggested he might have to build a bigger store just to accommodate the name he hand-wrote across the front in big black letters. Dry goods trade-stock had arrived from the east and business was good, almost from the start. Following on the heels of Mac's group, land hungry men, mostly fresh from the big war, spread across the west in large numbers, settling every piece of land they could lay claim to. The ranches were big, in keeping with the land and the attitudes of the ranchers. The valley was soon the home to some of these wanderers.

Ranch homes were often miles apart. With land being opened in all directions, but especially into the foothills of the Sangre de Christo's, Ad had chosen a spot about ten miles north-west of the Bar-M, more central to the farm district that was spread along the big river to the north.

The ranches tended to lie to the south and east of the true foothills, although a few, like Bill, were attracted to the more remote, challenging grass and forest lands. The many farmers growing hay and grain were to the north and west on the more fertile lands close to the river and some of its tributaries.

Most of the vaqueros who helped drive Mac's original herd from Texas developed a liking for the Colorado country and stayed on. They established Mex Town about three miles from Ad's store. There they built their homes and grew amazing market gardens, watering them from a small stream that flowed into the big river. Most of the vaqueros were riding for the ranchers.

The farmers outnumbered the ranchers by some dozens of families. Ad stocked supplies for both groups.

The small trading post offered the only supply point for many miles in any direction. Within five years, Ad built a bigger store and had the only outlet for the mail for many miles around. The Post Office demanded a name for their records. They called it Adkins, and soon that became the established district name.

Pepe put a team to the wagon and soon Mac and Margo were headed for Adkins for their spring shopping. Planning to stay a couple of nights, they loaded bedding and a change of clothing into the wagon, along with a deep bed of dry hay. Four of the kids were riding horseback. Margo knew Becky wouldn't make the entire ten-mile trip without tiring out. When the little girl started to fade they would tie the trusted old mare to the back of the wagon and Becky would continue the trip napping in the soft hay. Mac promised to wake her in time to complete the trip on horseback.

The twins raced ahead, exploring one side coulee and then another, putting double the distance on their sweating mounts. Jerrod rode beside the wagon, never wandering far from what he saw as responsibility.

Before they left, Mac told Margo, "Moved Jimbo out to the bunk house. He'll take his meals there too, so you're shut of him. He probably won't say anything to you, but he told me how much he appreciates all you done for him."

"I expect that useless old fool would choke before he actually came right out and showed appreciation."

Mac said, "He's been a help over the years Margo, you know that as well as I do. He just got crossways in your mind and there he stays. Anyway, none of that matters. Let's get on the way or those kids will be miles ahead.

Ad, working in his store, heard what sounded like Indian war cries. He stepped onto the veranda in time to see the twins riding their ponies at a lathering gallop, with Becky far behind, kicking the old mare in a vain attempt to keep up. The twins were standing in the stirrups and screeching at the tops of their lungs. They rode down the dirt street of Adkins, dropped into their saddles and pulled their ponies to a dust swirling halt. "Howdy, Gramps," yelled Adam, "We come for a visit."

"I see you did," answered Ad. "And it's God's own mercy that you didn't kill yourselves in the doing of it. Or kill your ponies! I swear, you kids are a throwback to another time. Can't you see how those ponies are heaving?

"Aw," answered Adam, with his standard answer, "These ponies love to run. They're Ute war horses, raised in the hills and given to us special by Uncle Buffalo Killer. If we didn't let these warrior ponies run, why they'd feel so bad they just might run off one night and go back to the Band. We wouldn't want that, would we?"

Ad figured there was no use pressing the issue. "Seems like I've heard all that before. Well, get down and go say "Hi" to your Grandma. She's in the kitchen making donuts, so don't you take her from her work! And leave a donut or two for me!"

"We have to take care of these animals first, Gramps," said Jerry. Else Pa will give us a hiding."

Ad waved his arm towards the back of the store. "You know where the water trough is. You might want to tie your ponies back there in the shade too." To himself Ad said, 'I don't think those little terrors even know what a hiding is.'

The slow-moving wagon and the old mare carrying Becky finally arrived. Jerrod, showing responsibility far beyond his years, rode dutifully beside the wagon. Ad lifted Becky down and received a big two-armed squeeze as thanks. Welcoming hugs were given and received, and the horses cared for.

The kids tied into the wash pan full of donuts. Mac and Margo were welcomed for a family visit with coffee and donuts and many questions.

When the long work day ended and the lamps in the trading post were blown out, the adults sat in the evening shade for a long-awaited visit. Mac outlined his fears and his plans to his father-in-law as they sat in the cool of the evening. Ad listened in silence. The women went to check on the kids and then found chairs and joined the conversation.

At one time or another, Ad had done business with most of the ranchers. He had a pretty good handle on the natures and drives of the men Mac would be dealing with. Choosing his words carefully, he said, "I agree with your analysis of the situation, and I think you've probably hit on the only long-term solution. Some will object because they hate change. Some will object because that's their nature. Some will object because they don't see the problem or because they're busy blaming something or someone else. But many will agree, even if they let you go first to see how it works out."

The discussion ranged far into the evening with no serious ideas for other solutions presented.

On the return trip two days later, Mac swung off the trail for a visit to his own parents, who kept a large market garden on a river flat five miles to the north, Mac led a discussion on the same topic.

Mac and Margo both listened carefully to the concerns and advice from the older generations. The younger children played in the yard while Jerrod sat with his parents listening to the discussion.

Margo could sense that the slow wagon ride towards home was more than a return from shopping and visiting for Mac. It was one more opportunity for the rancher to grit his teeth at what he was seeing along the way. The encroaching sage brush and dried out, struggling grass seemed to fill Mac with an inner rage made worse by his own sense of failure and responsibility.

On the days following their return to the Bar-M, Mac was as restless as a springtime wind. He seemed to be working all the time, charging from one task to the next, with still more work waiting.

The ranch was twenty-five miles from north to south and over fifteen miles east to west. The eastern border was reasonably straight, with only the normal small, rocky hills and damp swales. The western border followed the crooked and winding hills and washes of the rocky up-thrusts that warned of the foothills not many miles further west. It included dozens of small canyons and gullies plus three sizable streams and several springs. By strict legalities, Mac owned only a portion of it, although he purchased whatever was freed up from other claims as the land became available. Through lease contracts signed with the Mexican land grant agents and hand shake agreements with the Ute, the land was his to use. Neither the land grant nor the Ute agreements were any sure thing. The government had yet to come up with firm answers on these.

Through his early arrival and long use, and by ranching convention, he enjoyed the use of the land without challenge. All the neighboring ranchers worked under similar agreements. The fact that some ranchers allowed their animals to wander at will did not change the accepted range borders, but the loose herding managed to create considerable tension between ranchers over the years.

Mac, at one time thinned out and toughened up by war, hard work and poverty, had filled out and settled back in at his original two hundred pounds, every pound as hard as the sun-soaked caliche in the dry creek bottoms. As strong and capable as Mac looked, Margo worried about him. He seemed driven. His every thought was directed to the saving and prospering of the Bar-M, and all that might include.

Love for the land itself and his love for the Bar-M were seen as one in the rancher's eyes. Over the years he was often heard to say, "The Lord loaned us this land. He expects us to care for it." Even with that thought firmly in his mind, Mac still allowed the grazing to get ahead of the land's ability to produce grass. The guilt he heaped on himself was a hard burden to carry.

The late evening talk on the hillside convinced Margo that the ranching country was in serious trouble that few could see or cared to do anything about. She knew Mac was going to try. But at what cost?

The prosperity of the early years was a grateful memory. The frugal nature of both Mac and Margo assured that a considerable portion of the ranch earnings went into accounts spread among several Denver banks. But regardless of the prosperity of the good years, even a casual glance with half opened eyes presented the inescapable truth; the grazed-out miles of grassland and the encroachment of weeds, sage brush and cactus showed clearly that the prosperity wouldn't be there for the next generation unless something was done to control the overgrazing.

The rancher prowled his holdings like a man possessed, spending hours sitting on one hillside and then another, studying the land. He filled three notebooks with thoughts and sketches.

The valley looked dead for most of the year. He sent his crew to fall roundup the previous year, wondering if it was to be the last one, and fearful for the condition of the animals.

Several small, struggling ranchers came to Mac for loans and advice. He gave small loans but was sparing on the advice, still unsure himself what the future would hold or what actions he might be forced to take. Even the loans were given with little hope of recovery. He expected most debts would be re-paid with grazed-out land and half-starved cattle.

6

MARGO WAS JUST PLACING the latch back on the chicken yard fence after gathering eggs when Mac rode up to her.

"I'm riding over to have a visit with Luke. I'll try to get home tonight, tomorrow at the latest."

Margo just nodded. "Say hello to Dorit for me."

Mac nodded his head and spurred his gelding into a trot. He stopped and turned around. "Make sure those twins don't saddle up and follow me."

Margo just waved him off. Jerrod stood beside her saying nothing. Margo knew how the young man longed to ride with his father. "I'm going to make myself a cup of tea. I've still got a couple of cinnamon buns left we might lay claim to before those twins eat them all." Margo took advantage of every opportunity to show Jerrod a gentle nature.

Luke, Mac's old riding partner from their trail driving days came west as a single man, settling on a hilly piece of foothills grass that bordered the Bar-M for several miles. Luke named his spread the Lazy L, which branded out as nothing more than a big L lying on its back. Even with the ranch land joining the Bar-M along one side, the Lazy L headquarters was nearly twenty miles south-west of the Bar-M.

Luke started ranching from a bachelor cabin Mac and Bill, assisted by Mac's two young brothers, Bobby and Jeremiah, helped him put up. Luke, Bobby and Jeremiah rode down into New Mexico to purchase cattle. Manuel, Mama's son, and their friend from the cattle driving days, who would rather fight than work, accompanied them, as much for safety on the trail as for his language skills.

Luke started with a smaller herd than Mac and Margo but with good calving years, enhanced by the purchase of better bulls, there was soon a solid number of animals grazing the Lazy L. Luke's start toward true prosperity was guaranteed when his first calves reached market size within three years and Luke shipped into an eager market, largely fed by the demands of the many enthusiastic souls digging up the mountainsides in search of gold.

Luke hired three cowboys and a cook, all Mexicans.

Not a handsome man by any stretch, and a little rough around the edges, Luke found a natural fit in life as a Cavalry Sergeant. In battle, he was fearless. Among men of his own kind he was trusted, followed and quickly rose to positions of leadership. Among woman he was uneasy, tongue-tied and awkward.

He had thought of himself as a lifelong bachelor. But riding the vast ranges of his Lazy L, working dark to dark in searing heat and miserable cold, Luke started wondering why he was working so hard to make money he had no real use for. He, too, had a considerable stash of coin saved from their trail driving days. Driving longhorns up the trail with Mac and the others gave all of them the kind of financial start most ranchers only dream about.

Prosperity aside, the truth was that he was alone and often lonely. A man shouldn't be alone. It's true that there are those rare individuals, hermits and loners, who choose to live apart.

But they are few in number. Luke couldn't be counted in that number. He was alone, and he was lonely.

Lying in a hard cot in the little cabin, listening to the snorts and snores of the crew, Luke found himself longing for more; something more and something different. Something better. He needed a wife. He wanted children.

He took to writing letters to Denver newspapers that showed up at Ad's post office, answering advertisements placed by women, mostly widows, who were looking for a new start in life in the west. The war had been over for some years but there was still a wide choice of struggling widows. Perhaps there was one woman somewhere who would see past Luke's rough exterior and make a home with him.

Bill found out about the enquiries when his mother asked him to deliver an answering letter that arrived at the store. Bill was merciless, as only a good friend has the right to be. He suggested that Luke might be better off just to capture some girl from an emigrant wagon, since he was not likely to win a girl's heart, as rough as he was.

Then the vaqueros got into it, offering to find a senorita down south and moving her to the ranch, her and her ready-made family, children to grandparents. It didn't stop until Luke threatened to fire them all. He sounded like he meant it and the men backed off.

The cook, hoping to get back into the good books, brought Luke a bigger than usual piece of dried apple pie, hot from the oven, trying to console him. With his Sergeant's voice in full bloom Luke responded, "You ain't bribing me with my own pie, bought and paid for with my own money, and all the while you're working on my wages. Get back in the kitchen and let's see an end to you for this day. Let's see, do you remember how to wash dishes"

It was not clear how much of the rapid-fire English the man understood, but he beat a hasty retreat, leaving the pie behind.

In due time, Luke welcomed a widow named Dorit, who arrived on the Lazy L with her two children, a boy of seven and a girl of five. Rather than being a war widow, she was alone as the result of a long bout of pneumonia that her husband was unable to fight off. Luke answered her advertisement in a Chicago newspaper.

Dorit sent a photo and a letter. Luke wrote back, "You and the kids look just fine to me. I ain't a handsome man myself but I'm not a drinker and I would never strike you or the kids. The Lazy L is a right pretty place with lots of room to grow and for the kids to run around. The ranch owes no mortgage and I have money set aside for a proper house. We only have the cabin bunk house at this time, but I've hired a crew to build a new house. If you were to get here before they start you can show them what you want included."

There was more writing but before long an understanding was reached, and Luke sent train tickets. Luke drove his wagon and team over the long trail to Denver to meet the lady and her children, fear and anticipation wrestling for first place in his mind.

As Dorit stepped to the door of the passenger car and looked around at the crowd on the platform, Luke ran his finger under his uncomfortable collar. More frightened than he had ever been on a cavalry charge, he stepped forward. "Dorit? I'm Luke. May I help you down?

He said this with his hat in one hand while he held the other hand out to the lady. She stood there with the kids clinging to her dress, one on each side. The three of them slowly took in the busy terminal, the cacophony of sound, the unfamiliar sights and, finally, Luke himself.

With just a bit of a smile, Dorit let go of the railing at the top of the steps and laid her hand in Luke's. "Mr. Black?"

Luke assured her that he was, indeed Luke Black. She stepped to the platform, the children following closely behind. They both started talking at the same time. Dorit showed the half smile again and said, "You first, Mr. Black."

Luke returned what for him was a grin but might have been mistaken for a grimace. "I thought we might walk over to the hotel dining room for lunch. We can talk and get to know each other a bit while they unload the baggage."

Despite the initial awkwardness, the more casual introductions over lunch worked out fine. The marriage went ahead and the four of them spent a week in Denver. Dorit bought furniture and household items and Luke arranged for their shipment to the ranch.

After three years the family grew, with the addition of a boy they named Rolly. Dorit found her home, while Luke found more contentment than he ever hoped for.

Mac scouted the range as he rode towards Luke's fence line. Only a small part of the land was fenced with the new barbed wire, just enough to keep the herds somewhat separated. Mac and Luke hoped the hills and dry washes along the border of the two ranches would discourage the cattle from leaving their home ranges. And mostly it did. The twice-yearly roundups would sort out the wanderers.

Mac built a gate into the fence at the easiest point of travel between the two ranches. On a small hilltop, a couple of miles into Luke's range there was a fresh-water spring under a small thicket of brush. Below the overhanging cluster of branches was a small fire pit, blackened from frequent use. On a stub of a branch hung a much-used coffeepot and a pair of tin mugs. Tucked into an empty five-pound coffee can tied sideways onto a couple of branches was a sack of coffee beans, a box of sulfur matches and a bit of dry kindling. Mac and his old friend drank that pot dry many a time, squatting on their heels while they waited for another pot to boil.

Mac filled a canvas pannier with dry wood for the fire before heading out, tying it behind his saddle; wood that would be stacked against the next time a fire was wanted. He would stoke up a fire and wait a while, hoping Luke was somewhere close enough to see the smoke and ride over for a visit. If that failed, Mac would ride the rest of the miles to the Lazy L ranch house.

Rounding the last turn in the gully he was following, Mac could see there would be no need to light a fire or go further. A faint plume of grey smoke was already rising from the fire pit and there was a black gelding picketed a short walk away.

Stepping off his horse and dropping the reins to ground hitch the animal, Mac said, "You been sitting right there since the last time we met?"

Luke gestured towards Mac with his tin mug. "Mostly. Went back to the house once for some clean socks, but otherwise…" He paused and looked around. "Kinda like it up here. I ever get put in the dog house for permanent I just might build me a little squatter's hut up here."

He stood up and stepped over to shake Mac's hand. "You just out for a ride to escape some work?"

Mac paused and looked around at the small draw he had just ridden through, and then further away towards the spread-out acres of the Lazy L. From the hilltop he could see for miles.

Luke squatted back down and poured the second tin mug full with the dregs of the coffee pot. Passing the poisonous brew to Mac, he said, "Bite into that while I put on another pot."

Mac took a sip and squinted his eyes, while his lips puckered. He said nothing, accepting Luke's hospitality, just as he had for so many years. He remembered Margo saying 'It's a good thing Luke hired that Mexican cook and now has Dorit. I never knew a man that could destroy perfectly good grub the way he can.'

Settled back down, squatting on their heels, cradling their coffee mugs as if they were gold, and watching the coffee pot, Luke waited. He knew that eventually the reason for the visit would come out. Finally, Mac tipped his hat brim back, looking through the smoke of the camp fire. "Thinking hard on making some changes. Thought I'd run it all past you and get your drift."

Luke nodded and waited.

Mac stood to his feet as if this telling would require a more formal posture. "Going to sell off the most of the Bar-M herd. Keep those pricy white-face bulls and the white-face heifer calves as a start towards re-building the herd in a couple of years, and to justify holding the lease land. Keep the feeder animals until they're of a size to drive to market. Sell off every longhorn and just raise the white-face."

He then went on to talk about the dried-out miles of range, the encroachment of cactus and weeds, and the rest of the things that were troubling his mind.

Luke listened without saying a word.

When Mac was finished talking the two men sat in **companionable** silence for a long time, each worrying over his own thoughts. Luke tipped the coffee pot towards Mac. Mac swirled the last of his cold brew and tossed it into the grass beside him. After re-filling both cups Luke put the pot back on the coals and stood up. He turned and studied his own spreading acres of grass, just like Mac did when he first walked to the fire.

"I hadn't thought of going that far but it's been clear something has to be done. The Lazy L is mostly a bit higher than the Bar-M. Get a bit more rain up here. Some early and late snows. Grass has a bit more moisture to work with. Still, your plan bears some thought. How long do you figure we'd have to be off the grass for it to regain its foothold?"

Mac stood and looked back towards his own dried-out Bar-M. "Depends on the rains and the winter snows. Two years at least. Three? Won't know until I do it."

After a long pause, with both men studying the dying fire, Mac said, "There's one more thing. Might upset some of the cattle men who can't see past a curved horn. There's that hard to reach hillside land of mine, just to the west of the creek. Hills too steep for cattle to graze and all in all, pretty much unusable, but there's a lot of it. It's a big space. Sweeping down-slope, that whole mess of hills and rocks borders up to both you and U.T.E.

"So, what I'm planning will have an impact on you both. I'm going to put sheep on it. Sheep do well on that scrub land. There's good profit in woolies. I'll bring them in from down south, animals, herders and all. They'll be isolated up there and won't bother a thing. Might bring them down to the ranch for lambing and shearing and winter feed, then back to the hills. We'll have to see about that. See what the sheep men want to do."

Luke couldn't hide his surprise. "You're right on one thing. Some of those Texas boys will have an opinion."

The two friends spent the next hour examining possibilities and then Mac rode for home. He was home in time for dinner and then more coffee on the veranda with Margo as he told her about his talk with Luke. He hadn't seen Dorit, but he sent Margo's greetings home with Luke.

7

AFTER A HOT, DUSTY DAY of hard work that brought the spring roundup to an end, the men turned their horses over to the wranglers who were responsible for the remuda. One of the wranglers was Jerrod. Although he knew he was proving his worth wrangling horses, he longed to be working cattle with the men. Mac promised there would be lots of cattle work right at home on the Bar-M.

The cowboys wiped their hands on their pant legs and lined up for chow. They took their tin plates of steaming stew and a handful of biscuits and found a place to sit. Mac worked the branding fire for most of the day, heating irons and marking the calves as the riders dragged them, bawling and kicking, to the fire. Wearily, he sat on a wagon tongue, a tin plate balanced on his knee, a cup of coffee sitting in the short grass at his feet.

He sat, looking out over the familiar work grounds on the Flying W, the neighboring ranch owned by Willard Wallace. He saw the same grazed out land that he saw on the Bar-M.

The roundup crew moved camp three times as they worked their way across the range, starting far to the south. In every location the main features were desperately over-grazed land and dust.

The complaining crews, the chuckwagon with the predictably grumpy cook, the bawling cattle, the half-wild horses, the stink of burned hair and hide from the branding; all the requirements that make roundup what it is, were there in abundance.

Mac's crew worked hard year around to keep his cattle on the home range. Few Bar-M's wandered to the neighboring ranches. The Bar-M branding iron saw little use on the roundup. The few wandering animals would be driven back to the Bar-M to join the main herd.

Taken together, the cows, the calves and the feeder steers of the Bar-M represented more wealth than the McTavish family, struggling on their little Missouri farm, ever dreamed of possessing. Texas and Colorado had been good to them. Looking at the condition of the range Mac knew it couldn't last.

Mac sipped his coffee while looking over the gathered cowboys and ranch owners. He knew them all, although he knew some only slightly. Glancing among the group he tried to fit it all together. So much was changed since he first arrived in the valley.

Bill and Little Flower joined the roundup together. With two or three of the old Ute widows ever in attendance at the U.T.E. home place, there was never a need to wonder who would care for the kids. Little Flower called all these women 'Grandmother'. Only one was her real grandmother. The title was one of respect. With these grandmas ever in attendance with the children, Bill and Little Flower were free to travel as they wished. Two Ute riders came with them. Dressed as cowboys they were indistinguishable from the other riders, without looking closely at their faces. By agreement, the ranchers ignored the presence of the Indians who were supposed to be on the reserve.

Bill's Ute in-laws, with about twenty of the extended family, spent the winters at and around the ranch, coming and going by their own will and plans. Bill and Little Flower built their cabin and ranch headquarters in a remote corner of their range, preferring hills, timber and solitude plus easy access to the hills where Little Flower's small band could be found. It was an area not altogether safe from roaming bands of Apache and Comanche. Bill took the addition of the Ute family as a safeguard against the unforeseen.

At one time, this was Comanche country and the Ute avoided it. But that was long ago. In more recent years the Ute made their way through the mountains from what was now Utah. Now they thought of the valleys and green hillsides of the Sangre de Christo's as their own. As a tribe more dependent on deer and elk than of the buffalo, the Ute were willing to share the more easterly valleys with the ranchers. No one was sure what would happen if another wave of settlers pushed further into the high-up hills.

Between roundups a few of the young men helped with Bill's cattle, riding alongside the U.T.E.'s four hired hands. They refused any work that didn't involve horses and riding. The younger women kept busy under Little Flower's directions. Little Flower's father seemed to be happy doing nothing day after day. He sat by his lodge and smoked, watching the activities of the ranch. By spring's arrival, Bill was showing some frustration at the continual crowd of visitors. Uncharacteristically, he let his frustration be known. "Ain't they supposed to be on the reserve? Does the army know they're here?

"The army does not need to know everything," was Little Flower's answer. Muttering under his breath, Bill wandered over to the corral.

Bill traded the Indians a few head of beef for their work and even though the work done was slight, with beef easily come by, he felt he might have the better of the bargain. Still, he was glad when springtime came, and the group headed to the hills for the summer, leaving the widowed grandmas and one or two men behind.

There were approximately twenty ranches within riding distance of Adkins. There were also thirty or so farmers working much smaller land holdings, growing hay and oats that they sold to the big ranchers. There were even more small farmers spread out along the big river to the north.

The warm valley bottoms were good for garden vegetables and the farmers grew these in abundance. A few were experimenting with fruit trees. Smaller acreage farms were being claimed and opened up on a regular basis, some experimenting with whatever form of irrigation they could devise.

Most of the further west ranches and smaller farms were within easy riding distance of the Adkin's store. They were the mainstay of Ad's business. Some of the further away ranchers only came to what was called 'town' twice per year, spring and fall, stocking up on large quantities of supplies.

Mac's father, Hiram McTavish, had long been a lay-preacher in their little Missouri town. He continued that practice after arriving in the shadow of the Sangre De Christo's, meeting in the brush arbor he built beside his house. As weather permitted, farmers and ranchers came in from miles around to sing the songs and hear Hiram preach the Word in his gentle manner. Most Sunday mornings concluded with lunches brought from home being shared around the tables Hiram built and placed in the yard, providing one of the few opportunities to visit with neighbors.

The available ranch land was all claimed by one cattleman or another, although from time to time a newly arrived crew would push their herd onto the range. Several times in past years this led to gun trouble.

The ranchers and farmers came looking for opportunity; the thought that there really might be a pot of gold at the end of the rainbow ever in their minds. Like Mac and the original settlers, they saw untold miles of grass, unused since the buffalo fell to the hunter's guns. All in all, the ranchers developed a system of land use that most could live with. Water was the issue. As long as no one closed off access to major water sources the remaining disputes could be dealt with.

But now the valley was green for only a couple of weeks after the spring rains washed the last of the winter's snow off the land. The mid-summer sun burned hard against the stubs of grass the thousands of ranging cattle left behind. The herds grew until the ranchers were forced to search out every blade of grass. Nor did the grass have time to recover. The grazing was relentless. The result was half-starved cows and a reduced calf crop. The finished stock no longer had the edge the market was looking for.

Roundups were carried out in a swirl of dust that never seemed to end. Little more than fifteen years has passed since Mac first saw the valley. The change was heartbreaking; the destruction almost complete. The general thought was that the rains were less frequent and that all would be well when the rains returned. Mac knew that to be untrue.

Some smaller ranches borrowed to keep their brands alive; an action that had only one possible ending. Two ranchers gave up, with the owners moving on after taking a much-reduced price for their stock. Other ranchers pushed their hungry cows onto the vacated grass and nothing really changed.

With less income available to cover expenses, some ranchers reduced the number of riders. With fewer riders the cattle wandered more freely. Rustlers, never before a problem, started working along the edges of the hills. Before long they were emboldened to make advances into the hearts of some ranches. They left Mac and Luke alone, knowing any incursion onto Bar-M or Lazy L land would be dealt with quickly and definitively.   But some of the ranchers with fewer riders suffered considerable loss.

Formal law was chancy at best and unavailable much of the time. The ranchers were forced to take valuable time away from other work while the cowboys searched for lost stock and patrolled the perimeters of the ranches. Two rustlers were caught and hung but the thefts continued.

The rustlers hit Bill's herd just once. It was rumored that a few young Ute painted their faces and saddled up. They found the rustler hideout and had a talk with them, and the rustling stopped. Bill wasn't sure if this was the whole story or not, or what exactly happened. He felt he was well off not knowing everything.

With all this information causing worry in his mind, Mac was again wondering if this was the last roundup in the Adkins district.

8

BEYOND TALKING TO FAMILY and Luke, Mac kept his silence about his plans until this last day of roundup.

With the day's work done and the dinner time over, the riders sprawled on bedrolls or leaned against the stunted trees and bushes surrounding the camp site. Mac called his ranch foreman over. "Taz, I wish you'd call the men over here. They're about finished their dinners. I want everyone here, owners, cowboys, the two cooks, everyone."

Taz gave Mac a questioning look but Mac just waved a hand, indicating that the young man should get about the task assigned. As Taz made the rounds, the men looked up at him and then over at Mac. The owner of the Bar-M was on a wagon tongue, drinking the last of his coffee. One by one the men dropped their tin plates into the crash buckets and sauntered over to stand or squat in front of Mac.

Standing up, Mac looked the group over and spoke, lifting his voice so everyone could hear. "Luke, I wish you'd pick up a handful of what your standing on and tell us what it is."

Luke looked questioningly at Mac and then seemed to understand. He bent over and scooped up a handful of dirt and dry, short, grass. He held it up. Then he opened his fingers, holding his hand up where everyone could see, and let it sift through. Grey, dry dust was carried away by the wind. The bits of grass fluttered to the ground. "That there is dust, Mac. Dust and a bit of half-dead grass. Got a lot like that around these parts."

"If you'd done that back at the beginning Luke, what would you have picked up?"

Luke grinned, understanding where Mac was going with the talk, and played along. "Why, I guess I'd have come up with my hand full of green grass, Mac. And maybe a dry buffalo chip or two."

"Grass is gone," said Mac. "We killed it, and it's gone."

"Just don't rain like it used to," offered a rancher named Jenkins.

"No such a thing," answered Mac. "I've been keeping track of rains and snow fall for years. Got a whole book full of numbers I could show you. It ain't a shortage of either rain or snow. We just grew too many cows. We have more cows than this valley, or any other valley can provide for. I ain't blaming any of you, leastwise the cowboys. You cowboys just done what you were paid to do. But some of you are bound to lose your jobs as conditions get worse so I wanted you to listen to what I have to say. Rightly, the blame is mostly mine. I grew my herds as fast as I could, trying to put the bitterness of poverty behind me. Well, I accomplished that, and now the wealth of this valley is in my pockets. And it's in your pockets. But we killed the valley getting it there.

"The reason for the dried-out ground is that there's no grass to shelter it from the sun. There's no grass because we let our animals graze it all off."

"I sense you have a plan, Mac," said Luke. "Spit it out. I'm listening."

Mac slowly looked over the gathered cattlemen, wondering what the next few minutes would bring from these hardworking but stubborn men. "I'm selling out."

There was a general gasp among the men and a muttered round of comments, one rancher to another. "That's hard to believe, Mac," offered Bill. "This valley is all you ever wanted. You sure about this?"

"This ain't the valley I always wanted," answered Mac. "It's the valley we used to have that I wanted. It's the valley we saw when we rode over that rise across yonder and looked over the lip of the rim. Near took my breath away, the sight of this valley. I remember a bedraggled bunch of weary travelers, beat up with work and eye-sore from riding into the westering sun for weeks at a stretch. Clothing wearing out and women in serious need of settling down. Wagon teams about on their last legs. Cattle bawling morning to night, needing water and rest. Whole families running on faith that what a wandering old man said was the truth. Did the promised green valley exist? I remember wondering if there really was such a valley, here or anywhere else.

"We'd heard the promise, but until we looked over that river bank rim it was all just a distant hope. And I remember the group of us standing there. The only sound was the wind and a crying baby. None of us could find the words to tell what we were seeing.

"We drove our herds down into the valley and across the river and we were home. Home in a lovely green place that only God could have created.

"But that place don't exist anymore. And I want it back. I'm hoping you do too.

"Now listen up. I ain't selling my land holdings. Fact is, I've bought and paid for all the land I can get my hands on. I'd buy up the leases too if they could be bought. But the leases are tied up with the Mexican land grants that the government is still undecided about. The Ute ain't altogether sure about their claims either.

"No! I'm not selling out the way you might think. I'm selling my cattle. Every last hoof, except the top-grade white-face bulls, a smattering of young white-face heifers, and the feeder animals. I'll keep the nursing cows until weaning time and then they'll be gone too.

"The dry cows are going to market along with the market ready steers. The yearling calves are going into feeding pens down by the home ranch. The calves will be weaned just as soon as possible, and the cows will go to market. The calves will go into feeding pens.

A week from now there won't be one hoof of Bar-M stock kicking up this here dry valley dust. Those animals that we keep will be held down by the main ranch and along the river flat."

The ranchers and cowboys were silent, fidgeting and standing on one foot and then the other. A few were rolling tobacco into thin white paper. Here and there smoke was rising above the heads of the listeners. Ranchers and cowboys alike were trying to get their minds around what Mac was saying.

"This land needs a rest" continued Mac, "I'm going to see that it gets it. The Bar-M land anyway. Starting right away. The feeder calves will be fed up on hay and grain bought from the farmers down the valley. They'll be taken to market next spring or whenever they reach their weight. The white-face bulls will be kept close to the ranch headquarters. The longhorn bulls will go to market. This land is going to rest. It's going to rest for two full years, praying all the time for rain, and then we'll see, will the grass come back in strength, or does it need even more rest."

"This is all open range", shouted Baxter, a rancher whose land joined the eastern limits of the Bar-M for just a couple of miles. "How you hope to rest your land with thousands of other cattle spreading all over the country?"

"It's not open range." answered Mac. "It never has been. That's Texas thinking you've got to put behind you. I just told you. I've bought it and I own it. Either bought or leased. The little bit I don't own I've held under the Bar-M brand for fifteen years. Before any of the rest of you were even here. I'll hold that land as mine until the government sees fit to put it up for sale. Then I'll buy it if I can.

"A surveying crew will be here next week. They'll mark it all out. Then I'm going to fence the whole place, every last mile of it."

The ranchers were aghast. No one had ever strung wire in the valley or anywhere close to the valley, except in a few critical areas. They knew it was being done in some states further east but believed it might never happen to them.

"That ain't friendly," said Baxter, who was always ready for a fight. "That ain't friendly at all. Looks to me like you got your share, and a bit more, and now you want to block out us smaller ranchers. I say this is open range and it will always be open range. And the water has always been available to all. I'm prepared to stand up and fight for that!"

Mac chose to ignore the challenge, although there was a grumbling of agreement from several of the ranchers.

Murphy Cox, one of the smaller ranchers, and a neighbor to Baxter, said "You can't hold your leases, lessen you got cattle on them. Your leases nor your open range, neither one. You give up your cattle, you give up your leases. Might be I could lay claim to some of that lease land. I always wondered how you seemed to get the best of the land, Mac, you and your friends. Maybe now's the time to share some of it up."

Cox was ever the follower. Mac figured that taking his lead from Baxter would prove to be a mistake for Cox.

Luke's usual grin disappeared. His grin fooled a lot of men over the years. Ever the warrior, Luke was quick to rile up, losing the grin in the blink of an eye. He took several steps towards Cox and, pointing his finger almost into Cox's eye said, "We was here first. We came when others were saying we couldn't raise cattle this close to the mountains. They said it was too cold and the cattle wouldn't survive. They said there was too much snow. They said it was too far from the markets.

They said the Indians would drive us out. They said a lot of things.

"Well, we came. We came years before you and your kind. We came, and we stayed. We learned how to live with the snow and the cold and we made friends with the Indians, those that were left, anyway. We gathered the buffalo bones and we put our cows onto new grass. We worked harder than any man should ever have to work. We froze our feet and we near died of thirst, animals and riders both, when the summer sun dried up the water holes. But we stayed. And not a whiner among us! You want something, Cox, you work for it. Don't you go to thinking you can take it from a better man than you'll ever be."

He pointed back at Mac. "You listen to that man, you might learn something."

Cox and Baxter both held silent, although everyone there knew they would eventually have more to say.

Mac walked to his horse and lifted into the saddle. He stepped the animal close enough to the gathered men to be easily heard. "Men, I'm hoping you'll give serious thought to what you're doing. If you won't let your land rest for a couple of years at least sell off half your animals. And as far as the Bar-M is concerned, not one foot of it is available to you. Anyone crossing animals onto Bar-M grass will deal with me. Don't any of you think to bother the survey crew or the fence builders. I'm hoping for peace but know this; I'll not tolerate any foolishness."

Mac waited until the grumbling faded out. "One more thing you need to know. Some of the Bar-M extends into the higher up rough country to the west. Into rough grasslands that we've never been able to use. It's too steep and too rocky for cattle so it remains unused. I'm going to fence it and run sheep on it."

There was a general gasp of unbelief. Traditional cattle men, especially Texans, held a deep-seated loathing for woolies.

Again, Mac outwaited the shouts and grumbling. "Now hear me well. The sheep will be set apart in that isolated jumble of rocks. They'll have shepherds and herd-dogs with them at all times. There will be no sheep on my cattle range although in many parts of the country it's been proven that they can graze together, and both do well.

"What I'm talking about with the sheep and the rest of the Bar-M lands are my decisions. None of you has anything to say about it. But understand me clearly. I was hoping you would all see the condition of the range and agree to do something about it. That doesn't seem to be the case. I urge you to re-think that. As for the Bar-M we are going to protect our range and regrow the grass. I'm a man who desires peace. My crew are all peaceful men. But make no mistake. I will protect the Bar-M and everything about it."

Cox shouted out to Mac, "How we going to get our animals to market if everyone fences up?"

Mac had a ready answer. "We'll be holding our fence line fifty feet back to allow for roads. We'll also be putting a gate in every couple of miles. No one will bother you if you're just driving across the Bar-M. But if you poke along, taking advantage of the grass you will find my crew driving your herd for you.

"I'm not closing off the land or the water. You can drive your herds to market. You can go for supplies to Ad's. You can drive through on a Sunday morning if that shortens your trip to church. None of that will change."

Mac turned his horse and rode for home. Jerrod was riding beside him. The men gathered in groups, discussing what they heard.

The roundup came to an end with each rancher driving his own stock towards home range. Some of the ranchers were carefully considering Mac's plans but most were hostile, angry. They were angry at Mac and Luke and they were angry at the weather. They were angry at everything but themselves.

They knew Mac was right about the grass. Anyone could see there was no grass.

But in a land where success is counted in numbers of animals under a brand, to cut back would strike hard at a man's pride. Most of the owners just couldn't face that loss of pride or own up to their own complicity in the overgrazing.

Mac had his drovers direct the small Bar-M cut directly to the ranch headquarters. The next day the entire crew was sent to the furthest reaches of the Bar-M. From there every mile of the flat land, every gulley and wash, every fold in the hills was scoured. Not a single animal was left on Bar-M range. The animals, in their thousands, were driven to the river flats beside the ranch headquarters. The herd was sorted out and joined with the animals already there. It was a large gather.

The market ready steers and the few dry cows were driven to the eastern end of the Bar-M and held for the drive to the railhead. Luke and Bill both added some market animals to the mix. A few days later Wallace drove a cut of Flying W stock to join the drive. Three other small ranchers showed up with animals within the week.

Back on the Bar-M the chuckwagon was outfitted and manned by the ranch cook. The largest wagon Mac owned was loaded out with gear and supplies. It was a two-week drive to market, with the return ride taking just a few days.

Margo, with the help of a couple of ladies from Mex town, would feed the crew staying at the home ranch.

The number of small farmers along the drive route was increasing year by year. With the small property owners needing to protect their crops, the farmers found a ready acceptance of the new barb wire fencing. Detouring around the fences slowed the drive and made it more difficult as the years went by. The counties were slow in developing established roads.

Before the drive crew left, Mac spoke to them in the cookhouse after breakfast. Mac was more comfortable with silence than with speechmaking, but as owner he sometimes had no choice.

"Men, I know most of you don't like these changes. I can't help that. Without the changes the ranch will cease to exist. I know you're wondering about your jobs. There's still work to be done. In fact, we'll be hiring more men. But most of that work won't be cowboy work for the next couple of years. We're going to build fences and corrals and feed pens. That means cutting and trimming fence posts for large corrals and pens. We're going to try to hire a fence contractor, but he'll still need our help, protecting his crew if nothing else. We'll be stringing wire. Miles and miles of it. We're going to drill wells. We're going dig water ditches and holding ponds. We're going to care for the feeder stock. We're going to cut hay and we're going to break some river flats and plant grain. Most of the work will be done on the ground, working from a wagon. But if you wish to stay you'll be paid regular wages."

Mac paused and looked over the crew, every man of which had been with the Bar-M for several years.

"I figure we can restock the range within two years, three at the most, and then you can be cowboys again. Some of you, at least. A fenced range won't need the crew that open range needs but there will be work of some kind for those that wish to stay.

"If you decide to move on, I'll understand. Take your personal belongings with you on the drive and Taz will pay you off at the railhead. Thank you for your work and God bless."

Taz set out on the drive with ten cowboys, plus the chuckwagon and the cook.

9

WITH MOST OF THE CREW GONE on the drive, mornings were quiet around the Bar-M ranch yard. Everyone's attention was drawn to the north access road where the barking of the yard dog announced the early morning arrival of a two-seater wagon with a canvas cover stretched over bent wooden bows. The canvas was rolled up and tied back, revealing three passengers plus the driver. Hitched to the rear of the wagon was a combination hoodlum wagon and chuck wagon. A fine roan gelding was tied off the rear. The teamster, clad in typical western wear topped off with a once-white Stetson, leisurely turned the rig in a wide arc and hauled the team to a halt in the shade of the barn. Three men stepped to the ground, stretching the kinks out of their travel weary bodies.

Mac, fresh from assigning the day's duties to the skeleton crew, stood on the cookhouse porch studying the new arrivals. The teamster, a man of average height with the look of a rider about him, was an easy read; old enough to know what he was doing but young enough to still see life as an adventure, dressed boots to hat as a western raised man and handling the rig like he was born to it.

Idly, the thought entered Mac's mind that the young man had taken whatever work was available and was happy to have it. He looked over at Mac and grinned. "Morn'n Boss. I take it this fine-looking establishment is the Bar-M."

Not waiting for an answer but gesturing at the wagon he asked, "We alright here for a while?" Still not waiting for an answer he hooked his thumb over his shoulder and said, "Put the team in there?" Mac guessed that 'there' was the small corral that was still enjoying the morning shade cast by the barn. He also idly wondered if he looked so much like the boss that the kid didn't see the need to wait for confirmation.

Seeming to have taken Mac's silence for an answer the young man stepped to the ground, going first to the roan gelding. Removing the lead rope from the halter he turned the animal loose. It immediately walked towards the water trough. As the gelding dipped his head to drink the young man returned to the team. In just a matter of moments they were stripped of their harness. They joined the gelding at the trough. None of the animals showed any inclination to wander away. The young man carefully straightened out the harness and hung it on pegs attached to the wagon hoops.

Just as the teamster put his hand to the corral gate Pepe stepped from the barn. Hands on hips he sized up the situation. He nodded to the driver and moved towards the horses as if to lead them to the gate. "Don't bother", the kid grinned. With the teamster's sharp whistle, the three animals lifted their heads from the water and obediently walked to the corral. The gate was closed, and the horses quickly found the manger with its supply of hay waiting for them.

Only then did the kid turn to Pepe. "Shep Trimble." He held out his hand and Pepe shook it. "Pepe." The two men were content with that amount of familiarity. Pepe sauntered over to the wagons. Silently he looked over the unusual caravan. Shep watched, smiling all the time at Pepe's questioning look.

Pepe glanced at Shep, indicating the chuck wagon, with the pointing of his thumb. On the side of the wagon was a wire cage suspended from hooks on the chuck box, with a canvas tarpaulin protecting it from the sun. "Chickens," said Shep. "These boys purely love their eggs of a morning. So, I whipped up this little rig. Works pretty good too. Chickens, they don't much care where they are, and the bumpy ride don't seem to bother them none. We stop for the work I lift the cage down, shelter them under the wagon. Throw them a bit of wheat from a sack we carry, a bit of water and there you have it. Eggs. Every day, rain or shine."

Pepe shook his head but said nothing.

The three surveyors made their way over to Mac. Canvas pants tucked into knee high lace-up boots, tough canvas shirts that seemed to have pockets sewn onto every available space and bulging with pencils, small note books, and gadgets that Mac couldn't make out, identified these men as the contracted survey crew. The Stetsons were for shade more than identity.

Without offering to shake, Mac waited. The older of the three lifted his hat and brushed dust off his pants. "Mr. McTavish?" At Mac's nodded assent the new arrival, indicating the men standing beside him with a wave of his hat said, "Web Hanson. Jack Jacoby. I'm Lod Anderson. You need some surveying done."

The three surveyors, slim and broad shouldered, skin burned by the sun and with sun-squint lines around their eyes, were different only in height.

Mac felt there was no need to answer the question about the surveying. "You must've got an early start. Had breakfast?"

"Rolled our beds in the full dark of night. Campsite wasn't all that attractive anyway. Planned to get here in time to try your cookhouse. Hope we're not too late. We avoid our own cooking every chance we get."

The teamster walked up in time to hear, "The kid there sold us on his cooking abilities, but we've some reason to regret believing him. Breakfast sounds good if we could impose."

The kid teamster just grinned at Mac and lifted his hat. Long blond curls fell in every direction. He brushed them out of his eyes and held his hand out to Mac. "Shep Trimble. Cook and wagon master. And a better grub hustler than these three pilgrims appreciate. Good to be here." Mac couldn't refuse the handshake, marveling at the good-natured forwardness of the young man.

After breakfast Shep returned to his horses. A good wiping down with a rough piece of a burlap sack Shep saved and washed over and over, followed by a workout with the curry comb, had them looking like show animals. He borrowed a bucket from Pepe and washed down the horse's legs, removing any sign of road dust. Checking for loose shoes or small pebbles that could lame the animal, completed the daily ritual. He then made his way back to the kitchen and helped himself to more coffee.

Mac and the surveyors were hunched over crude maps that Mac had drawn, comparing them to the more official military maps the surveyors brought with them. This went on for maybe an hour. Shep drank his fill of coffee and wandered outside, taking a seat on the cookhouse steps.

The door to the house burst open and the twins, freed from their daily schooling, let out what they had come to think of as Ute war cries. They charged across the veranda, leaped down the stairs and headed for the barn at full speed. Shep laughed out loud at their antics. Adam saw the young teamster for the first time and ran over. "Don't know you. You come to work on the Bar-M?"

Shep grinned at Adam. "Come to guide some surveyors around. Look after their horses. Cook their vittles so's they don't waste away to nubbins. Generally, keep them out of trouble. What's your name?"

"They named me Adam on account of I come first, before this here girl. Jerry, they call her. Not much of a name but good enough for a girl I guess."

Jerry gave him a push on the arm and they both ran off screaming towards the barn. Shep watched them go with a grin on his face. When he turned back Jerrod was standing looking at him "Whoa. You move quiet young fellow. Didn't even hear you com'n up. You come near to giving me a fright. What's your name? I'm Shep."

"Know your name. Heard it before." He tilted his hat back just a bit and said "Jerrod".

"Well Jerrod, come sit here and tell me all about the Bar-M."

About that time the twins came racing out of the barn atop their horses. Shep watched them tear across the yard. "They ride pretty good."

Jerrod acknowledged the point with a nod of his head and said, "Pa will skin them if he sees them mounting those animals inside the barn. They've been told many's the time."

The two young cowboys visited in the shade of the cookhouse until Mac came out. Jerrod rose to his feet. "You going out to the herd Pa?"

"Just for a bit. Be back shortly."

Jerrod walked along with his dad. Shep said, "Mind if I drag along. Nothing else needs doing here."

The three of them were soon on their way to the holding grounds, Shep riding his own gelding. Arriving there, Shep was amazed at the work being done. With the crew not yet returned from driving the market herd to Denver, Mac hired additional help from Mex Town and a few of the smaller farms. The men were busy digging postholes, laying out fencing planks, skinning bark off trees that would be turned into fence posts, and a myriad of other chores.

The extra crew was hired to assist the Bar-M cowboys with preparing the feed pens, corrals and the calving yard that would be put into use for the next fall and spring. Several loads of green, rough-cut lumber arrived from a foothills mill run by a cantankerous Kansas transplant. The old man never seemed to tire of telling folks that, "This would be a pretty good country if it weren't for these danged mountains spoiling the view."

Most people learned not to press the old man on his opinions. When questioned about his decision to deal with the complainer Mac simply said, "Don't care about his talk. He can sure turn out the lumber and that's what's needed."

In the early spring Mac made a circuit of the farmers. He purchased all the hay the men could spare from the previous year's cut. Luke and Bill did the same closer to their home ranches. The farmers included delivery in their selling price. Three wagons, loaded with hay stacked and kept dry since the past summer were just arriving at the Bar-M hay yard, ready to add their loads to the mountain of cured grass that was already there.

A well-drilling outfit from New Mexico was hired and brought in. The feed grounds would need more water than the small creek could provide. Mac also intended to dig wells across the vast acres of Bar-M range. The key to success was grass and water. The country naturally grew grass in abundance, but the water wasn't always exactly where it was needed. Mac figured to help a little with this oversight of nature.

Until the pens and corrals were completed the animals were close herded on what grass was available. A couple of early spring rains helped with the greening of the countryside.

Shep folded his hands on the saddle horn and looked long at all the activity. He shook his head. "Ain't never seen the like."

Shep rode over to watch the well drilling. The noise of the steam engine and the drilling gear was enough to hold him at a distance. The busy workers had no time for talk.

Jerrod stuck to his father like a shadow while Mac talked with the corral builders. They then moved on to the cowboys herding the cattle. "Any trouble boys?"

"Nothing a touch with a ten-pound hammer on a couple of these bunch-quitt'n ol' mamas heads wouldn't fix."

Mac took his time answering. "Well, try to remember that you're supposed to be smarter than the cow."

He then rode on to the east. Shep took one last look at the drilling rig and then rode along. The trail followed the creek on its winding path. A couple of miles east of the herding grounds the creek opened out into a large flat area that looked as if it might be wet for part of the year. Looking towards the curve of the low surrounding hills Shep couldn't see how far east the flat went. But on the west edge of the flat he could see two four-horse hitches pulling plows, breaking up the bottom land for the first time, turning the grass under and exposing the rich loam hidden beneath.

A two-horse hitch followed along pulling a set of harrows. The turned-over soil was black and rich looking. Having figured out that Mac was not an easy talker Shep simply looked a question over at the man.

Mac picked up on the unspoken query. "We're hoping to grow barley on maybe fifty acres down there this year. More next year if it works out. We're a little late starting this spring so we may switch to oats for this first year. We have a lot to learn yet about growing crops in this country.

"The rest of the bottom land we'll reserve for hay. We've been cutting hay there for some years. Our calves will go into feeding pens with hay and grain. Our goal is to have only mature breeding animals and sucking calves on the range.

They all returned to the cookhouse for lunch and Mac had another long talk with the surveyors. Again, they hunched their heads over the maps. Mac's property lines and rough measurements were penciled in on the military maps. The surveyors also studied the little bit of information on the Bar-M property titles and lease documents, transferring it all to the maps.

Lod Anderson said, "We can't start just anywhere. We have to establish longitude and latitude lines that will mesh with the surveys being done in the rest of the country. The official surveys have established north/south and east/west survey points. The sixth principal meridian, over in Kansas is the north/south line and the east/west line, called the base line, runs at 37deg. North, which is the southern boundary of the state. We have to calculate as close as we can to establish your boundaries on one-mile increments from those measurements. This close to the border there could be some confusion with the Ute and New Mexico calculations, but we'll go with this until someone says different."

Mac looked bewildered, staring at the map the men were pointing at and the confusion of crisscrossed pencil lines they had drawn on it. "Just so's you can establish our rightful boundaries. I don't need to understand the how's of it."

The cook-wrangler had the rig loaded and the team harnessed by the time the surveyors finished breakfast the next morning. Mac followed them out of the cookhouse. Pointing to a young cowboy saddled and ready beside the wagon he said, "This is Clete Harbin. He'll ride along and show you the lay of the land, stay with you for a few days, then I'll send out another man to replace him. He'll help where he can and keep off any boogers that show up. There's them that don't want the country surveyed or fenced, either one. Keep your weapons handy but don't fight unless to protect yourselves. Any trouble you head back here, and I'll deal with it."

The crew followed the trail to Adkins. There they stocked up on foodstuffs and camp supplies, charging it all to the Bar-M. Shep had the wagon loaded and was just about to return to the store to get the last small sack of supplies when the door opened and Clara, Ad's twenty-year-old daughter came out carrying the sack.

Shep stopped so fast he came near to falling over his own feet. He whipped his hat off and flashed his most appreciative smile. His blond curls reflected the early morning light. His smile was enough to set smiling records if there was such a thing. "Well now, you're just about the purtiest helper this here old boy ever did see. Brightens my day considerable, yes it does. I didn't see you in the store."

Clara pushed the sack into Shep's arms. "I just brought this out so's you could load up and get on your way more quickly. Don't need you hanging around when we've all got work to do. And you have miles to go."

One of the surveyors laughed out loud and said. "He's a cheeky one miss. Pays to be careful of his type."

Shep gave him a hard look and Clara flounced back into the store. Was there just a bit of exaggerated movement in the flouncing? Shep immediately convinced himself that there was and that it was for his personal benefit.

Clete Harbin pointed out to the group. "This here's where the Bar-M's west boundary is at. Or near enough. You start lay'n out a fence line right about here and ol' Mac'l be smil'n 'n thank'n ya'll.

Shep laid out the camp at that point

The survey crew set up their instruments and readied themselves for the task ahead.

Mac and Jimbo rode out a few days later. Jerrod rode along with them. Jimbo was hurting from his run-in with the Nez Percé but he gritted his teeth and said nothing. As they rode up to the camp Shep hollered a greeting. "The boys are over that way a-way. Across that hill and down some." He pointed his thumb to the north west. "Time you get there and back I'll have grub ready. Might even wash up a plate or two just for you fellers. Don't bother with the wash'n for those others."

Jimbo grinned at the man.

Jerrod gave Shep a questioning look, hoping the cook was simply making sport of the surveyors.

The three riders arrived in time to see Web Hanson pile the last few rocks onto a stone cairn. Jimbo watched a moment and then offered, "Seen such as that up Denver way. Corner post?"

Lod Anderson took over the explanation. "Took a while to establish the true boundary but from here on it goes pretty quickly. You were off about a half mile from where your man showed us as your boundary. That's pretty good for a seat-of-the-pants land stakeout. The iron rod you see sticking out of that cairn is our bench mark. Everything measures out from there. We told you the job would take a couple of months. If that misbegotten cook don't poison us first we should wrap it up in that time or perhaps a little less."

Mac walked over to the cairn and looked along the southerly and then the eastern reaches. To the west, beyond another grass plain cut with gullies and rocky ridges were the steep slopes leading to the Sangre de Christo peaks. Mac indicated the southern line with his pointed arm, "What are those flagged posts off there?"

Lod turned to look south, where Mac was pointing. "Those show true south and these others show true east, starting from the bench mark. Those will be your perimeter fence lines."

The two-track trail that led to the U.T.E. and the ranches and farms beyond was about one quarter mile north of the projected fence line.

Jerrod was standing with his father, looking first south and then east. He took it all in without saying anything.

The three riders were back on the Bar-M in time for evening dinner.

10

THE FIRST SIGN OF RANGE trouble came just three weeks after the roundup. The herd was on the trail to market and the Bar-M crew left at the ranch was down to just a few riders. The crew from the drive was expected back within a week.

Keeping three Bar-M riders plus five riders hired from Mex Town at the ranch to work with the keeping animals, Mac assigned two riders to patrol the perimeter of his range. "Don't you boys get yourselves into any scrapes, shooting scrapes nor any other kind. You watch and report back to me. Stay out no more than one week. Then ride back to the ranch and two others will take your place. There's provisions enough in both the line cabins. If anyone pushes animals onto the Bar-M you ride back and tell me. I'll deal with it myself. Peacefully if possible."

But Baxter, Cox and a few of their smaller neighbors weren't in a waiting or a peaceful frame of mind. Desperate for graze and water, their own land long abused, with the fear of a long hot summer still ahead of them, the men pushed animals wherever they thought a blade of grass might still exist. They made their boasts at the roundup. Now they had it to do. The recently vacated Bar-M grass was a temptation and a challenge that Baxter couldn't resist.

His mind closed to other options, Baxter bulled his way forward. With his land joining the eastern end of the Bar-M for a couple of miles it was a simple task to push his herd north onto Mac's grass. Cox and the others drove across several grazed-down ranges and finally pushed onto the Bar-M to join Baxter's X-O animals that were already there.

Mac's crew reported back with the news and Mac rode out alone, heading towards his south boundary, still hoping to reason with the encroaching owners. With the distance to ride he would be gone overnight, making use of the line cabin. Jerrod followed Mac to the barn and reached for his saddle. "Not this time son."

The young man watched until Mac rode into the distance and could no longer be seen.

It was a long ride across the Bar-M. But Mac didn't have to go the entire distance before he started to see cattle. A mix of brands told him that Baxter wasn't alone in his determination to encroach on the Bar-M. Seeing no riders, Mac started gathering cattle and heading them south. The half-starved animals bawled and balked at the pushing. After circling back to their straggling calves, a couple of times they finally stopped altogether, their heads hanging low under the unrelenting spring sun. A couple of very young calves refused to stand. Mac figured the youngest and weakest of them would be dead by the next morning. He left the animals where they were and continued his ride.

Although the spring grass was making a try at growth it was easy to see there was no chance that it would compare to previous years. Five miles further south he discovered the main herd. He saw four riders sitting their mounts off to one side. He headed that way.

Ignoring the other cowboys, Mac spoke to Baxter's foreman. Cray Dobbs was a big man, heavy through the shoulders and neck. The big hat covered his head of black hair but the three-day growth on his cheeks and chin only added to the sense of size and strength.

Looking directly at the Baxter man he said, "Cray, you're a good man. A cattle man. You understand range condition. You know better than this. You also know I meant what I said at roundup. And you know that I'm not about to look the other way. Baxter knows all that too. There's nothing here for your animals to eat. They're half starved. I'm asking you to drive them off the Bar-M and take them home."

Cray stubbed his cigarette on the top of his saddle horn and then rubbed the ashes on the palm of his work hardened hand until all the heat was gone from the tobacco. Like most of the local riders, Cray respected Mac and the Bar-M. He hunched his shoulders and folded his hands, one on top of the other, on the horn. Somewhat guiltily he said, "Don't matter what I think Mac. Following orders. Even if I wanted to, I don't take orders from you. We're here, and from what I'm told, the owners of these animals intend to stay, challenge you on the leases and the open range you claim rights to. You're right about the grass but it ain't my decision."

Mac looked over the four riders, judging their determination. Finally, knowing he had to make his play, Mac said, "You can't win this one Cray. Baxter and the others are in the wrong. This is my land. Your cattle will die just like this land will die if we don't give it a rest. They can't eat dust. Men will die too if you and your crew follow foolish orders, making a hopeless fight. And in the end the land will still have to be rested. We could fight until there's no one left standing and there still wouldn't be any grass. You need to take these cattle home."

A young rider that Mac had never seen before said, "Could be you're the one to die. Always did want to watch a rich man groveling for his life." With this he lifted his Colt and leveled it at Mac. For a split second everyone froze, unbelieving. Cray reached his hand towards the hot-headed youngster and started to say, "No…" but his voice was cut off by the sound of the shot.

Mac left the saddle the instant he saw the rider pull his weapon, diving head first under Cray's horse. The dive saved his life when the bullet that was meant for his chest took him, instead, in the upper arm, after grazing a couple of ribs, entering above his left elbow and exiting below his shoulder. As he was falling Mac drew his own weapon, belted butt forward on his left side, set well for a cross draw. Rolling to the far side of Cray's terrified horse, he saw the young shooter trying to calm his spooked animal.

Cray was working to get his own horse under control and hollering at the young shooter to stop. The prancing horse managed to step on Mac's wounded shoulder. Mac screamed in pain. The young rider was getting his horse under control. He was taking aim at Mac as Cray's mount hopped aside. Mac was flat on his back with his gun pointed up at the shooter. The two men squeezed their triggers at the same time. A shot plowed dirt beside Mac's head, showering one side of his face with dust and small pebbles. As Mac cleared his eyes he watched the shooter fold from his saddle and tumble headfirst to the ground. His horse skittered aside and ran off. Mac's shot took him under the chin, leaving a gory mess where it plowed upward and exited through the man's filthy hair. His soiled Stetson floated to the ground.

Cray managed to stop the other riders from entering the fight. The men looked at their dead riding partner and were clearly ready for a foolish fight for their brand. Cray barked orders. "Stop. No more. Drop those weapons back into their holsters. We didn't come out here to get into no shooting scrap."

One of the Baxter riders, a man named Bo Wilson, said, Tell's dead. We can't just let that go."

Cray pointed a finger at Wilson. "You're under my orders Wilson. My orders are to back off. You lift that gun again, I'll shoot you myself. Tell was a hot-headed fool and Mac clearly shot in self defence. You fools have no idea at all what an explosion Tell just lit fire to. There's not a better or more respected man in many a mile than Mac McTavish. The country won't stand for what's happened here this day. The Bar-M is liable to come in force and you'll all be hiding behind rocks, begging for your lives. Fools. You're all fools, working for a fool.

"Now you two load that idiot kid onto his horse and take him back to the ranch. And no arguments." Cray aimed a frightening look at the two riders. "And don't you be telling any wild stories back at headquarters. That idiot kid started this ruckus. Mac was doing no more than defending himself. Trying to be reasonable. You tell it otherwise and you'll answer to me. Now get with it. And pick up those Cox riders and the others on your way past. Leave the cattle and get yourselves off the Bar-M while you still have the chance."

With that, Cray dismounted and went to Mac. Mac was sitting up by this time, although he was a bit wobbly and clearly in pain. He was trying to pull his shredded sleeve away to get a look at the wound. Cray squatted down beside him, turning so that he could watch what the other riders were doing.

Pulling his knife from the sheaf attached to his belt, he lifted Mac's hand away from the wound. "Hold still. I'll cut away this sleeve. We've got to get the bleeding stopped."

After cutting away the sleeve he shook his canteen to see what water was left. Holding the half full container in front of Mac he said, "Sorry, Mac. I've got nothing stronger to clean those holes with." He then poured the tepid water over Mac's arm and shoulder, dabbing them dry with the remains of the bloody shirt sleeve, hoping to cleanse the worst of the dirt off. Mac sucked a deep breath and gasped as the water entered the wounds, but he made no other response.

Cray lifted the cut-off sleeve and started wrapping it around the wound. There were bits of grass and what-not forced into the wound by the horse's hoof.

Mac gasped through clenched teeth. "Clean shirt in my saddle bag."

Cray discarded the bloody, sweat stained and dirt embedded shirt sleeve. Rising, he went to Mac's horse and found the clean shirt. Using his knife, he cut off both sleeves. He then cut two large patches out of the remaining material and folded them for padding. Wrapping one bandage around each wound Cray said, "In just these few minutes you already lost a lot of blood. I'll tie these tight. Got to stop the bleeding or you won't finish the ride home."

Cray completed the bandaging and then sat back on his haunches, watching the two riders as they finished tying down Tell's body. One rider picked up the reins of the dead man's horse and the two men started for home with no further words, the X-O cattle forgotten.

Cray rolled a smoke and offered it to Mac. "Never took up the habit." Cray lit the cigarette for himself and watched Mac as he smoked it down, wondering what his next move should be. Mac took a drink from the canteen, cleared his throat and said, "Got no choice here Cray. You ride for the Baxter place and see if you can talk some sense to anyone there. I'll ride for home."

Cray again mashed his cigarette ashes on the palm of his hand until they were cold. "No Mac. That's not how it's going to be. I'll ride along and see you back to the Bar-M. Baxter ain't going to listen to me nor anyone else. He's desperate for grass and greedy for more range. That, plus he's blind to the truth. I'm better to see you back safely. You're going to need some doctoring that I don't know how to do."

Mac said, "Appreciate it. Could cost you a job though."

"There's other jobs."

He studied Mac for another few seconds. "Hot out here. Long way to the Bar-M. You sit a saddle?"

Mac nodded and answered, "Never saw the day I couldn't."

"Long ways to the Bar-M." Cray said again. "I hope you're really up to it. Don't see any other option. There's sure no help out here."

After another pause Cray stood and took Mac by his good arm. "Let's get you on your feet."

With that accomplished Cray held the man steady for a few moments and then let go. "Can you stand while I get your horse?"

Mac just nodded, using his good hand like a sling to hold the wounded arm. Cray noted what Mac was doing and said, "Should have thought of a sling. Sorry about that Mac." With that he picked up the scraps of Mac's shirt and started to fashion them into a sling. After a few moments he threw the cloth on the ground and went to his own saddle bag. He pulled out his own clean shirt. "You're going to owe me a shirt."

Mac grinned a lopsided grin through his pain. "Buy you a store full of shirts, you get me home."

With considerable help from Cray, Mac rose to the saddle. Without asking Mac, Cray picked up the reins to Mac's animal and started for the Bar-M. Mac gritted his teeth with every movement of the horse but said nothing. Cray looked back after a few minutes. Mac had his eyes closed but there was a determined look on his face. Cray could see that the wounded arm was still bleeding, with blood seeping out of the bandage and weeping down the sling. He didn't know what else to do except keep moving north towards the Bar -M.

A half hour later Mac spoke for the first time. "Line cabin right over there, just past those cottonwoods. Find some supplies there."

Without comment Cray swung the two animals that way. Riding around and then under the towering cottonwoods the riders pulled up in front of the rough-built cabin. Cray swung down. "You want to get down and rest a bit?"

Mac was speaking a bit more clearly than he was at first. "No time for resting. I'll get down though. Should be some salve and some towels and such we can use to bind this arm a bit tighter. Maybe stop the bleeding. Fill our canteens too. Water the horses."

Before Cray got a chance to help, Mac swung his leg over the saddle and went to step to the ground, misjudging his weakness. Missing his grab for the horn with his right hand he lost his balance, his body swinging to the left like a one-sided pendulum. It was too late to stop his downward momentum. His right foot stepped off into nothing but air. He lost the bit of grip he had managed to get on the horn. He fell, landing on his bleeding arm and shoulder, his left foot hung up in the stirrup. Mac's scream of agony startled the horse and brought Cray running. The horse shied and took several steps sideways, dragging Mac with him. Mac screamed again, rolling onto his right side and grabbed the injured arm. He clamped his teeth tight and shuddered, determined to prevent another scream from escaping.

Cray moved swiftly past his own animal and grabbed the bridle of Mac's frightened horse, talking quietly to it and trying to settle it down. When he had some confidence that the animal would stand, he loosely held one rein while he pulled Mac's booted foot from the stirrup, laying it gently on the ground. Mac let go of the injured shoulder and pushed himself into a sitting position but couldn't hold it. With teeth still clenched tight against the pain Mac fell back onto his right side. He pulled his legs almost up to his chest and simply lay there.

Cray said, "Best you stay right there while I do what has to be done." Mac nodded, still gritting his teeth.

Cray led the animals to the small trickle of water that flowed past the cabin and let them drink from the small pool dug years ago. He then led them to the tie rack in front of the cabin. Picking the canteens off the two saddles he went back to the creek and filled them with fresh water from the pipe that directed water from the stream to the hand-dug pool. He hung his own canteen back on the saddle and held Mac's out to him. Mac took it and nodded his thanks. He didn't drink. He simply held it to his chest, his pain preventing any other actions.

Only then did Cray enter the cabin in search of what was needed.

A half hour later, fortified by two cups of quickly made coffee and his wound re-bandaged with the supplies found in the cabin, Mac again allowed Cray to boost him into the saddle. Cray asked, "You alright for now?" Mac nodded. "Don't do anything but just sit there and grip that horn. I don't want to have to re-do those bandages again. I think the bleeding is stopped. Slowed down to a trickle anyway. But you lost a site of blood just the same. I'll be in front leading your animal. You feel woozy and think you might fall you call out."

Without waiting for Mac's agreement Cray swung aboard his own ride and they moved out for the Bar-M.

The going was slow in the extreme. Only once did Cray put the animals into a trot and then a slow lope. Mac held on with all his determination, but it was no good. Finally, through clenched teeth he called out, "No good. Let em walk. Best I can do."

A slow three hours went by judging by the movement of the dimming sun. It would be dark soon. Mac offered no words in that time and Cray asked him no questions, only looking back from time to time. Finally, Mac spoke. His voice was so quiet Cray had to stop and let Mac's horse catch up. Leaning close to Mac he said, "Say it again."

Pointing feebly with his chin Mac said, "Another line cabin. Up that little draw if I have the location figured right. A few horses held in a small trap between the hills. Get some fresh mounts."

Cray turned the small cavalcade and was soon dismounting in front of the cabin. "Sit tight Mac. Don't you try anything foolish."

Mac nodded his head and continued holding the horn. Cray helped the injured man to the ground and led him to the cabin door. "You need to lay down for a bit. I'll fire up some coffee and a bite of something to eat."

When the fire was going in the little cast-iron stove and the coffee pot filled with water Cray said, "You lay there a while. I'll change out the horses and be back soon as ever I can."

By the time the coffee water was boiling Cray was back. "Horses are ready. We'll get some nourishment in you and get back on the trail. Going to be full dark before we see the ranch but there's nothing to be done about that."

Cray pulled a frying pan off the shelf beside the stove and put it on the heat. In the screened-in pantry he found a slab of bacon and a few potatoes. A dozen slices of bacon were soon sizzling in the hot pan. The potatoes were cut into small chunks, without being peeled, and added to the bacon grease. What he dished up on a tin plate wouldn't make mouths water in anticipation, but he figured it was probably edible. He walked over to Mac's bunk. "Got a bit of grub and coffee. Best you try to eat. Gain a mite of strength back. We've still got a long night ahead of us."

Mac groaned and tried to sit up. With another cry of pain, he fell back onto the straw mattress. "C'mon Mac. You got it to do." Cray took Mac's good arm and started lifting. He finally got the man's feet on the floor and his back against the wall, half sitting and half lying down. He figured that was probably the best he could do. He managed to help Mac take a few bites of the badly burned supper.

Mac's hands were trembling with pain and weakness. Cray passed him a cup of coffee. After shaking coffee out of the cup and down the front of his shirt, Mac gave it up. He put the cup down in defeat, spilling even more coffee in the doing of it.

Cray took the mug and held it up to Mac's mouth. With a few swallows of coffee and a bite of food, Mac was showing just a bit of recovered strength. Cray doubted that it was enough. It was still a far way to the ranch.

Mac managed to say, "You want to come to the Bar-M there's a job waiting for you. Won't be in the cookhouse."

Cray chuckled at the thought. "No, I suppose not. Never starved out yet though."

Mac fell into a troubled sleep and slid back onto the bunk. Cray looked on in dismay, not knowing what the next step should be.

The Baxter foreman drank his own coffee and ate most of the bacon and potatoes directly from the pan while he studied out what to do next. Finally, he made a decision.

He shook Mac awake and said, "Listen up Mac. I'm going to leave you here. You stay and rest. Try to stay awake if you can but I'll be a while. I'm riding for help. That wound isn't really all that serious. Mostly painful I think where the bullet took out a chunk of bone. Being horse stomped and then falling on it didn't do even one good thing for you either. Not sure I got anywhere near all the dirt out. But you can't ride any further.

"I'm no doctor but I'm thinking you lost a small bucket of blood and its weakened you. I figure about ten or twelve miles to the Bar-M. That about right from this cabin?"

Mac stared with glassy eyes. "Mite closer to fifteen."

"OK. So, by the time I ride there and gather up some help and get back with a wagon, some time's going to pass. You'll be alright here. I'm leaving your gun right there on the bed beside you. I don't figure those others will be coming along but just in case. Now you sit tight. You'll hear the rattle of a wagon just as soon as ever is possible. I'll leave this lantern lit and turned down low. You can reach it from the cot but don't knock it over and burn this shack down."

Mac nodded his understanding. "I owe you. I'll be fine."

After losing his direction once and wasting time in the darkness getting his bearing again Cray rode into the Bar-M ranch yard shortly before midnight. His first thought was to find the night man. That proved to not be necessary. He was pulling up beside the bunk house when a voice commanded, "Stop right there and identify yourself."

Cray said, "That you Clete? I seem to know the voice. Cray Dobbs here. Need some help for Mac. Can you roust out a team and a wagon? Mac's shot and bad off. He's at the line cabin."

Clete was suspicious. "That for true? You ain't trying to pull something are you?"

"Ain't doin nothing but trying to save Mac's life. Now shake out some help and let's get a move on. I'll go wake up the house."

There was no need to wake up the house. Margo was sitting on the veranda in the darkness, wrapped in a blanket, waiting for her husband to come home. She was familiar with his many overnight stays with Luke, or Bill or, on occasion, in Denver on business, but this was different. He rode out alone to confront the encroaching ranchers. That didn't seem wise to Margo, but Mac insisted that a show of force might start something no one could stop. She knew he might stay over in the line cabin but still she sat in her rocking chair hoping to hear him ride in.

She couldn't hear the words down at the bunkhouse, but she heard Clete and Cray talking and went to find out what was happening.

With a demand from Margo the entire skeleton crew shook themselves awake and went to work. Lamps were lit and the yard. The buildings took on an eerie, shadowy glow. Horses were saddled, the wagon was rolled out and a team harnessed. The wagon bed was layered deep with hay. Several blankets were piled in a corner. Margo was shouting instructions.

Jimbo limped out of the bunkhouse. "If someone will saddle me a horse I'm ready to ride. Need a younger animal than old Ap."

Margo doubted the old man was healed enough from his shooting but said nothing at first. After a moment's reflection she said, "Jimbo, if you really feel you can ride you can be the most help by taking a couple of messages. Go to Mex Town and roust out Mama, tell her we really need her. Tell her we'll be there shortly with the wagon to pick her up. Tell her to bring everything she has that might help with a bullet wound and loss of blood.

"Then ride past Mac's folks place and ask them to come here to look after the kids. Jerrod can take responsibility until they arrive.

"Go past the trading post and tell my folks what happened and then ride for Bill's.

"Tell Bill I'd like if he'd go tell Luke. The two of them will know what to do that would be most helpful. Tell them to try not to start a war. They can't help Mac tonight, but they could maybe get those cattle off our land. And tell Bill that no matter what happens, to keep his Indians away. The last thing we need is some rancher shouting about an Indian uprising."

Pepe led out an all black gelding Jimbo could hardly see in the dark of midnight. The animal was rigged out with Jimbo's gear. The old man swung aboard from the off side with surprising agility. His intent was to protect his injured leg but as he swung it over the animal and hit the saddle he shuddered in pain, grabbed his leg and bit down a groan. No one noticed in the darkness. He spoke to Margo. "I'll do all that and then I'm going to get the boys. I'll be a while. Don't know anyone more welcome, a time like this. Bobby's still lawing down at Las Vegas, last I heard. Jeremiah will be close by. Those two are never far apart. Be a few days but we'll be back just as quick as ever we can."

After a short pause he said, "Ain't no nonsense with them boys when they see a need. We could use them about now."

He looked down at Margo, repeating, "I'll be back just as soon as ever I can."

Margo stopped him with a raised hand. "You tell the boys we could use another dozen riders. We're not starting a war, so we don't want any misunderstandings. But we want to be ready if someone else does something stupid."

Jimbo didn't wait for further comments or argument. With a small psst from his lips he jogged the horse into action and rode into the night.

Margo spoke to herself. "The old fool doesn't even have a bedroll or a slicker."

With Cray leading, the wagon and three outriders chosen from the remnants of the ranch crew were soon at Mex Town. Mama stepped onto the wagon seat beside Margo. Margo lashed the team into action. The fifteen miles to the line cabin was quartered by gullies, low lying hills and several small water courses. The going was slow. The first grey of dawn was peeking over the eastern horizon and the wagon was still a couple of miles from the cabin when just a shadow of a horseman drew into sight.

Margo pulled the team to a halt on the edge of a gulley. She figured the horseman would be Mac. His animal could scramble through the gulley more easily than the team and wagon. She turned the wagon around, pointing it towards home and stepped to the ground, waiting.

Cray and the outriders galloped forward and surrounded the rider. Mac was slumped over his saddle, his hands firmly gripping the horn. His eyes were closed, and he didn't see the riders until one of them spoke. The horse was walking on its own, guided only by its desire to be back at the Bar-M.

One of the riders picked up the reins to Mac's horse and led out. Cray and another rider took up positions on either side ready to catch the wounded man if need presented itself. Within fifteen minutes Mac was helped out of the saddle and laid in the wagon. One of the men lit a fire, placing a pot of water on to heat. Margo lit a lantern. Holding the light high she watched as Mama peeled off the sling and the filthy, blood-soaked wrappings below. Margo helped Mama roll Mac over a bit, so the exit wound could be seen better. Pulling Mac's arm closer to where the lamp would cast its light on the wound, Mama said something in Spanish, speaking so quietly that Margo couldn't pick up the words. But it was not difficult to pick up Mama's head shake, nor see her as she crossed herself.

It took a half hour before Mama completed her ministration and gave the signal to head out. There was more to do but this wasn't the place.

Cray said to Margo, "If it's all the same to you I'll head back to the line shack and get a few hours of shut eye, then make my way to the X-O. Don't know if I still have a job or no but I better report in.

Margo nodded to him. "I can't thank you enough for all you've done Cray. If you no longer have a job you come to the Bar-M. Come anyway if you feel you want to change jobs. You take a message to Baxter directly from me. You tell him that Mac was easy to deal with, always wanting peace. If he has to deal with me he'll be sorry he ever heard of Colorado. You tell him if my man dies there is no country big enough to hide in. You tell him every mouthful of grass his animals eat on Bar-M range will come right out of his miserable hide. In case he doesn't understand that…"

Cray laughed and held up his hands. "I'm thinking he'll understand the message. Whether he believes or takes the proper action is another matter. He's not a particularly smart man and some of those siding him are dumb as door posts. But he's scared. He knows Mac's right and he knows his range is eaten off. The spring growth is slow, and the heat of summer hasn't even shown itself yet. No telling which 'away he'll jump. I'll tell him though."

It was approaching noon before the slow-moving caravan pulled into the Bar-M yard. Facing up to her exhaustion, Margo finally turned the reins over to one of the cowboys. She was seated in the hay beside Mac, her eyes closed, her back propped against the jolting side of the wagon.

Jarrod rode out a few miles to meet the in-coming group. The sober young man took up a proprietary position beside the wagon, forcing a cowboy away. Riding silently, he never took his eyes off his father. Margo gave him a grim smile that wasn't returned.

Margo was surprised to see a group of riders from Mex Town armed and patrolling the perimeters of the Bar-M.

Mac's parents were sitting in the rockers on the veranda. Hiram's carbine was leaning on the railing beside him. Della was cradling a double barrel shotgun. The twins were sitting on the steps, their elbows on their knees, their chins supported by cupped hands, strangely quiet.

Mama supervised as the men moved the wounded man to the cot Jimbo had recently vacated. With just a bit of help from Mac, Margo and Mama stripped his filthy and blood-spattered clothing off. He was soon wrapped in oven-warmed blankets on the cot. Only Mac's left arm and shoulder were exposed. Even in the full light of day Mama had Margo hold a lit lamp with a shiny reflector on it, as close as she dared to Mac's shoulder. Mac rolled on his side, so the exit wound would be fully exposed. Margo stuffed several pillows under his back and side to ease the strain of holding the position.

Margo understood that in other surroundings no one would die or be in serious trouble from the wound, as ugly as it was. But the loss of blood and the filthy range conditions that could so easily lead to deadly infection were a whole other matter.

Jerrod was standing at the foot of the bed looking serious, saying nothing. Margo sometimes worried about her eldest son. His silence and intensity could drive a young man into unwelcome directions if something should happen that overcame his good judgment. She went out of her way to show him extra tenderness as often as he would stand for it.

Mama was kneeling on the floor, her head bent over the wound. She washed the area with hot water and then with some disinfectant she brought from home. Margo idly hoped the smell emanating from the disinfectant bottle didn't kill them all. There was a small hissing and some bubbles rose from the raw meat of Mac's arm and shoulder as the disinfectant was applied. Mac, stoic until that moment, gasped and shuddered. Mama seemed happy with the result.

Mama pulled herself up and sat on the edge of the bed, still studying the wound. "Bueno, Bueno, good."

Margo took a careful look. "Did you get all the dirt and filth?"

Mama shrugged her shoulders. "I think Bueno. All I can see. Much dirt from horse step on. I think Bueno."

Mama had come a long way in her use of English but many of the more subtle expressions still escaped her.

Knowing what came next, Margo brought another pot of hot water from the stove and set it on a wooden chair next to the bed. In it were a small collection of needles and a coil of thread. Margo then brought another supply of clean towels.

Mama washed her hands again and poured some of the dreadful smelling disinfectant over them. She chose a small curved needle and eased a foot length of thread through the eye. Back on her knees, Margo again holding the lamp close, Mama very carefully stitched up the wound, first the inner layers and then, using a larger needle, the surface skin. The smaller entry wound, just above the elbow, was an easier task. The bullet-grazed rib left just a flap of skin to sew.

Some years earlier, a group of travellers stopped to rest their animals and themselves while they replenished their supplies at Ad's trading post. They were lost and well off the trail.

Among the travellers was a young doctor hoping to set up his first practice when the group reached Santa Fe. Ad made a deal with the young man to teach some modern doctoring to Mama while the group rested. They would be more than a few miles backtracking to the shortest wagon trail south. The rest and restocking of supplies would help them weather the extra miles their mistake had caused.

The doctor was more than happy to share his college education and Mama was an apt student. With Imelda, her English-speaking daughter-in-law to help with translation Mama was soon fully immersed in the learning process.

When the travelers were again on their way, the doctor stopped in Mex Town. He found Mama and held out a box of supplies to her. "You take these Mama. I can get more. There's needles and a scalpel and some stitching cord. Some disinfectant too and a few other things. Good luck and God bless."

Mama held the box like a golden treasure. The contents of the box as well as Mama's knowledge were put to good use over the years. The box was refilled more than once with supplies Ad ordered in from the east.

Mac gritted his teeth for so long and hard during Mama's ministrations that Margo was afraid he would crush them down to the gums. Margo wiped the sweat from her husband's face and spoke softly. "It's over. You can relax. You did real well. The wound isn't wrapped yet so don't touch it."

Mama packed up her curandero supplies and left the room. She was soon back with a concoction of herbs that were boiled down into a paste. Mac's mother supervised the boiling pot while Mama worked on Mac. As soon as the paste cooled enough Mama applied a liberal covering on the three wounds.

Margo tore up a clean bed sheet which Mama used for bandages. The bandaging done, the wounds were left while nature took its healing course.

Mama leaned back and stretched her sore back. She took Margo by the hand and crossed herself. "I will pray."

Margo nodded in agreement. "We will all pray."

As the two women left the room Jerrod stepped to the edge of the bed. "Pa?" But Mac had fallen into an exhausted and pain worn sleep.

11

THE SURVEY CREW was well underway and making good time. The western most boundary was laid out for fifteen miles with rock cairns on most of the hilltops as a visual guide to help the fencing crew that would follow. The iron pins would be their permanent markers. Shep moved the camp every day to keep up with the surveying progress. Only a couple of times had they camped within easy access of a running stream. Shep walked the horses to the nearest water source twice each day. The water barrels on the wagon were nearing empty. Camp supplies were running low. A trip to Adkins was in order.

As Shep was dishing up the evening meal he spoke to the three surveyors. "If you three city boys thought you could keep yourselves out of trouble for one day I'm thinking I need to take the wagon in for supplies. We're commencing to run out of just about everything that matters. Thought I'd drive down there in the morning. I'd try to get back by evening so's I could tuck you fellers in and keep the boogers off you when the darkness takes over the land."

Lod Anderson, stretched out on one elbow beside the fire grinned good naturedly. "Better take some bread crumbs to sprinkle along else you'll never find your way back, what with being alone and all."

"Boys, I ain't never been lost in my whole entire life. Don't expect I'll have any problems in this mostly open country. Time I get within five miles of the camp I'll just guide myself in by the supper fire smoke and the smell of burnt biscuits and beans. That's all the time assuming you can get a fire lit."

From the ground the country wasn't really all that open, with sagebrush, yucca, cholla and prickly pear crowding the rocky up thrusts. A gathering of cottonwood, small pines and other evergreens, grew here and there along the streams. On the hillsides, pinon fought for space and water.

But from the height of a horse's back or a wagon seat a traveler could see for miles.

The cheerful surveyors took the ribbing all in good humor. Web Hanson looked over at Lod. "Lod, I'm remembering all the peaceful and quiet camps we've set up in the past. Makes a man long for old times. But we were careless in our hiring. Paying the price for that now. I've heard enough noise and foolish talk to hold me for the summer. I swear, this young feller might just wear out his jaw before its time, what with all the flapping he puts it through. What say, Lod, should we tell this bowlegged biscuit burner to take his time? Maybe stay a few days. My ears have been ringing ever since he rode into camp, broke and desperate and pretending to be a teamster and cook."

Lod answered, "I expect we could get along just fine without the company of a bragging young Texan, but we do need supplies. Best we encourage him to make a quick trip."

Jack Jacoby nodded in agreement. "You happen to have a bit of venison on the hoof jump into the wagon with you, you bring it along. Ain't seen nothing like that around here."

Shep cleaned up the breakfast dishes the next morning, straightened up the chuck wagon so the men could find the fixings for their own meals, refilled the coffee pot ready for boiling later in the morning and pointed the hoop-topped wagon towards Adkins.

Ad never built a loading dock so Shep pulled the wagon as close as he could to the front door. As he was leading the unharnessed team to the water trough he was pleased to hear a female voice behind him. "I take it you've come for supplies. After you water that team you can put them in the corral and throw a bit of hay to them."

Shep turned with a smile and lifted his hat, releasing a mass of blond curly hair. Holding the hat against his chest he smiled at the lovely young lady who had spoken. Perhaps five feet four inches tall and filled out just right, the young lady stood straight and self-confident before him.

"And here I half convinced myself that you was but a dream. That I just saw you in my imagination. Like maybe I hadn't really seen you the last time we were here. Lost some sleep over that, I did. Wondering. But there you stand. Brightening the morning you are. And my eyes too. Why, just the sight of you about makes a man forget all the hardships of life on the range."

The two young people stood silently for just a few seconds before Shep spoke again. "My Ma named me some family name I can't even pronounce, let alone spell but I prefer just Shep. Tell you the story sometime of how I come by that moniker.

"I'm assuming your Ma and Pa laid some handle on you. Have to be something bright and beautiful to really do you justice."

The young lady did not offer her name. Instead she said, "You can assume anything you want. Do you have a written down list I can fill or are you planning on just wandering around the store until you see something you like?"

"Already seen something I like." He winked at the young lady. He reached into his shirt pocket and passed a wrinkled and soiled piece of paper to her. "I'd be pleased if you could fill this order. I know it's early in the year but if any fresh vegetables are available you could add those in. Maybe some rock candy too. My job is to keep those surveyors happy and working, so throw in anything you think will help. I'll be in as soon as I wipe down these animals and fill the water barrels, all the time assuming you don't mind me using the well pump."

Clara nodded and turned to go, hesitated, and then turned back. "Clara."

"Clara. That's a lovely name for a lovely lady. I'm most pleased to meet you, beautiful lady."

A stern voice from behind startled him. "And I'm the beautiful lady's mother."

Shep jumped clear off the ground in surprise and whipped around, his hat still in his hand. He recovered quickly. "I remember from our first visit and I'm pleased to meet you again, beautiful lady's mother. And I can easily see where the beautiful lady gets her beauty from." His smile was radiant.

Mrs. Adkins expelled a held breath, shook her head, walked past Shep and put her arm around her daughter's shoulders. Loudly she said, "Never met a Texan, except maybe once or twice, who could really be trusted Clara, no matter how many curls they have or how twangy they talk. They're all smiles, spouting glib talk, with their run-down boots and big belt buckles. Then they'll ask for credit in the store."

The two women laughed and left Shep standing there, curry comb in his hand. He grinned and turned to the team. He walked the team to the small river flowing behind the adobe trading post and gave the horses ample time to take their fill. With that done and the horses in the corral, Shep filled the water barrels strapped to the wagon's sides, from Ad's well pump. The full barrels would save the crew from having to rely on questionable creek water for a few more days.

Filling the order and shopping for things forgotten took far more time than it normally would. It appeared that Shep needed Clara's help or advice on just about every item he laid hands to. She didn't seem to mind.

Lunch time came, and the family invited Shep to join them. "Just common range courtesy," Mrs. Adkins assured the Texan. "Nothing more."

Ad wandered up from the smithy, washed his hands and face and looked over at Shep. After a brief pause the trading post proprietor held out his big blacksmith's hand and the two men shook. Ad seemed to be taking the young man in from boots to hat without really making a show of it. "How is the survey work coming?"

The men discussed the survey as they slowly made their way to the kitchen table.

Taking his seat Shep smiled at Mrs. Adkins. "Sure do appreciate it Ma'am. I was about to go sit in the shade and lunch on cold biscuits and river water." His smiles seemed unending.

Lunch time gave the wrangler opportunity to tell about the Texas ranch his family owned and the reason for his wandering. "Three older brothers. Two of them married. One sister married to a would-be cowboy from Tennessee. Another sister shopping around for opportunities. Every one of them crowded around the home place like a colony. Acting like barn swallows, all building their nests atop one another. Can't keep up with the number of kids running around, getting under foot and causing all kinds of upsets to man and beast. Can't remember all their names. You'd have thought someone might've moved off the ranch but there they all are, fat and sassy.

"Good ranch though. My grand-pappy started it long ago. Lots of cattle, enough work to keep everyone busy. But the ranch yard looks to get smaller every year. Seems if one woman isn't complaining the other one is. Ma just shakes her head, but Pa is about ready to go out of his mind. A time or two there I figured we'd find Pa dragging his bed roll out to a line shack, only coming home for Christmas and such.

"Don't really know if there ever was a ranch big enough to hold more than just the one woman. Figured it was time for me

92

to get out and see the world. So far, I've seen a small corner of New Mexico and this little bit of Colorado. Rate I'm going I'll be old as Methuselah before I see Montana."

After a moment of quiet, Shep said with a laugh, "We're a Bible reading and go-to-meet'n family but sometimes I think we need a little less of the Patriarchs and their nation building and a bit more common sense."

With another grand smile aimed at Clara he said, "I figure to pick through the crop of available girls, wherever my horse takes me, till I find the very best. Someone peaceful and loving. Sure do enjoy a peaceful life. I'm not moving back to that Texas ranch though. I figure one yard filled with Trimble's is lots.

"Looking over this Colorado country I started giving thought to asking for my inheritance to get me a good start on a ranch of my own, away from all those others, you know, like that story in the Bible. But then, I read that story again by the flickering light of a smoky fire a while ago. Seems like it didn't end all that well. I kind of missed that part in the first reading. Pays a man to be careful, it does. Sometimes there's another story writ between the lines. A body could miss such as that if he weren't careful."

Again, he smiled at Clara. The young lady wisely said nothing.

Ad looked on silently, thinking his own thoughts and recognizing that Shep's rambling didn't require a response.

Finally, when the conversation seemed to run itself out Ad spoke. "Major happening a couple of days ago. You and your crew need to know." He then told Shep about the incident that put Mac in bed with bullet wounds.

Shep's smile was gone for the moment. "Is he going to be alright?"

"He'll live. It's too soon to know if he'll have full use of his arm."

After a pause the surveyor's wrangler asked, "Do you think he'll want us to finish the job"

Clara spoke up. "You keep right on doing what you were hired to do. Margo's my sister. She's in charge until Mac is back on his feet. If you knew anything at all about her you'd know she doesn't have much back up in her make-up. I think you can plan on her explaining things clearly to the other ranchers."

"I'd best get along then. There's just no way at all to make good time with that wagon, what with all the gullies and rocky pressure ridges and all. A feller named Clete Harbin was sent along from the Bar-M to guide us and kind of help me keep an eye on things, but he went back to the Bar-M a few days ago. Ain't nobody else showed up to take his place. From what you told me of Mac being shot I can understand why no one else came out. Still, don't like to have those boys out there all alone. Never can tell what trouble them pilgrims I'm saddled with could get theirselves into."

By early afternoon Shep was on his way back to camp, the heavily loaded wagon cumbersome on the rough trail.

Ad returned to his smithy.

Clara was idly looking out the window when her mother walked over and put her arm around her shoulder. "I know it's lonesome out here Clara, but you have to judge a man on more than blond curls and glib talk. Truth told, there's no telling if his family are Texas ranchers or Texas share croppers."

Clara leaned just a bit into her mother's caress. "I know all that Ma. But he sure is pretty. And he seems to smile all the time. In any part of the country you want to name I'd be an old maid. All I ever see are married men and dollar-a-day cowboys in run-down boots and sweat-stained hats and every single one needing a bath. Nary a one to depend on. The best of them could pack up and ride away with the spring breeze.

"I'm not so blinded that I'm liable to saddle up and ride away with a passing stranger but if someone promising came along...."

Shep arrived back in camp to find the three surveyors hunkered down behind the chuck wagon, rifles at the ready. "What's going on boys?"

Web Hanson stood from the crouch he had been in and turned to the wrangler. "Line riders just over the ridge. Don't know if they've pulled stakes or if they're still there. Told us they'd be back. If we were still here they'd move us along. Full of lead if need be."

Shep stepped down from the wagon and whistled for his gelding who was allowed to roam at will. He threw his saddle on the animal and checked the loads in his carbine, then loosened his Colt in the holster. He slid a second Colt under his belt at his back. Swinging aboard he said, "You boys sit tight. Take care of that team if you've a mind to."

He trotted the gelding the long way around the small hill the surveyors had been working on, approaching from the off side. Riding slowly to the top, he stopped when he could nicely see over the ridge. He saw three riders sprawled carelessly beside a fire, drinking coffee. Seeing no one else around, Shep put his horse over the top and rode down toward the three coffee drinkers, the carbine held over his saddle. As he rode down the slight grade he casually moved the carbine to lay along his right leg where it was pointing at the riders, the hammer pulled back and his finger on the trigger guard, ready for whatever might happen. He stopped twenty feet away and smiled. "Nice to have you boys come for a visit and share our range, but now we have work to do so I'm obliged to ask you to move along."

The biggest of the men slowly got to his feet. He pushed his hat back away from his forehead, exposing black hair and a stiff, black, week old beard. He lowered his hand and brushed it against the Colt at his hip. "Sonny, you needs ta git along home and leave these here things ta the men. Ain't no place here for no smooth faced boy. Anyway, we ain't leavin ner goin nowhere. We was hired out ta come here and stop a survey'n and a fenc'n job and that's exactly what we aim ta do.

We tooken the money and now we aim ta git the job done. There don't goin ta be no fences on this here open range. You go help those others pack up and git along. That way ain't no one needs ta git hurt."

The other two men grinned up at Shep.

Shep stepped his horse a bit closer. Still smiling he said, "You see Black Beard, here's the problem. You got several things wrong. Firstly, this here is private land, owned and titled. No open range anywhere even close by. Second, we got a job to do and it's going to get done. Beside all that, I don't hold no fear of you nor the three of you all together. Now, I know you boys are just funnin and you don't really mean no harm. Just doing a job of work like we's all doin. The difference is that we're anxious to get back to our work just like we're gettin paid to do. You're either goin to swing into your saddles and show me your backs or we're about to commence goin around and around. I'd advise you to take the sure, easy trail."

Black Beard took a more careful look at the young man and his easy smile and made a mistake in judgement. He reached for the gun on his hip. No one would have been impressed with his speed or dexterity.

Shep, still smiling, his carbine balanced on his right hip for support, squeezed the trigger. The shot clanged off Black Beards Colt, setting off one round and destroying the piece. It then ricocheted off, taking a big chunk of meat out of the shooters hand, cutting off the thumb and one finger in the process. The injured shooter screamed and grabbed his hand, clearly out of whatever was to come next.

The other two coffee drinkers started to scramble to their feet. Shep lifted the carbine to his shoulder and emptied the gun, placing shot after shot around the two men and into the fire, showering the two with sparks and live coals. His first shot took off the boot heel of one man. The next took the hat off the second. The two scrambled for safety, tripping over each other and falling to the ground as 44-40 slugs dug up dirt and pebbles all around them.

As the hammer fell on an empty chamber and Shep's weapon fell silent the three surveyors trotted down the hill, puffing from their run. They came armed and ready. The two raiders were lying in the sparse grass, tangled in a heap. Shep started pushing cartridges into the carbine.

"You boys just lay still there now. You got four guns pointed your way. Moving could have a strong impact on your future plans." His horse stood like a statue through all the shooting.

The carbine re-loaded, Shep slid it back into the saddle scabbard.

The young man smiled at the surveyors. "It's all over boys. Good to have you join the party though. It would help if one of you could build up that fire. Throw all that gathered wood on. We need a healthy blaze."

Added to the fire that was already burning it took no time at all for the new wood to ignite and roar to life.

Still sitting the saddle, Shep lifted his Colt and casually pointed it at the two cowering riders. "You boys get to your feet. Turn your backs to me so's you won't be tempted into any foolish decisions and unbuckle your hardware. Throw it on that fire. Lod, you help Black Beard there. He might have a mite of trouble seeing as how he seems to have hurt his hand."

One of the raiders started to object. He was holding his shell belt in his hand, the holstered pistol hanging from it. He half turned to Shep and said, "You can't burn this up. I paid good money for this and I need it."

Shep kind of chuckled at the plea. "No, all's you really need is to keep on breathing. Everything else is optional. Now, you rightly ought to give thanks to whatever god you find yourself praying to. I've got every right to shoot you in the brisket and leave you for the coyotes, but we have to work here. Having your stinking carcasses lying around wouldn't improve our lot in life, even by a little bit."

Lod dropped Black Beard's gun rig on the blaze and stepped back. The other two raiders sullenly followed suit.

Shep spoke to the surveyors without taking his eyes off the gunmen. "Jack, you go see what's in their saddle bags. If there's other weapons there you bring them along. Ammunition too. And we have to step lively here boys. Pretty soon those shiny brass shells are going to start making a nuisance of themselves."

The surveyors and the raiders all started backing away, watching every move Shep made. Shep swung the gelding and followed the raiders. Black Beard was walking hunched over, still holding his injured hand, painting a trail with his dripping blood. As the first shell popped off, the three raiders turned and ran to their horses. Black Beard had trouble pulling the picket pin but finally got it done. Shep watched them mount. "Enjoyed the visit boys but do yourselves a favor. Don't come back. My milk of human kindness only has the one serving. The second time around there's no telling what might happen. My suggestion is you draw your time and ride for somewhere far away."

The three were still struggling to get their mounts straightened around and headed in the right direction when more shells started going off. Black Beards terrified animal took several leaping steps towards the fire. With a cruel yank on the bit and an even crueler dig with spurs he got the animal headed over the rise, close on the tails of his companions.

Shep was pretty sure he was in no real danger from the bursting shells, but he put his horse into a slow lope anyway. He rode along with the raiders. Safely over the hill they all slowed. Smiling, Shep said, "You boys don't come back now. You done wore out your welcome. And Black Beard, you really need to do something with that hand." He stopped and watched the three men ride away.

Riding back into camp a short while later he looked at the three surveyors, still holding their carbines and again hunkered behind the wagon. "You boys figuring on taking the rest of the day off? I'm surprised. There's an hour of good daylight left and there's all these miles to go and here you squat."

Lod was getting a bit tired of the young man's smile.

12

SHEP TURNED THE GELDING LOOSE and walked to the fire. He poured himself a cup of coffee that resembled molasses as it came from the spout. "Good looking coffee boys. Can't imagine why you felt you needed a cook. But listen up now. There's a wagon to unload and sort out and supper to make. You're on your own on that this night. I brought a slab of bacon to go with your eggs. That's an easy meal. I'm heading back to Adkins just as fast as ever that horse will take me. I figure we'll have company again come morning. I'm going to see what I can do about finding some men to side us. Might leave them short handed over there at the Bar-M but I'll find someone."

He told them about Mac in as few words as possible. "There's no playin about this. Someone means business. You boys make yourselves a meal and then put out the fire. Leave the camp dark. Stay close to the two wagons and watch the horses. They'll let you know if you're having visitors."

Lod looked at the young wrangler. "You done good there, Shep. You came along at just the right time. Come dark there's no telling what mischief those fellas might have gotten up to. You had every right to kill those boys too, but you took a better path. I admire that in a man."

For once Shep had nothing to say.

Lod continued, "You go now, but ride with your eyes open. Take as much time as you need. We'll be alright here. We'll stay in camp until you're back. We've seen this before. Some folks will fight change even if the fight makes no sense. Always before we had to fight fire with fire. I expect it'll be no different this time. You bring back some help. We can't lay out these survey lines if we're all the time looking over our shoulders."

Shep rode up to Adkins in the full dark of midnight on his sweat stained gelding. There were no lights showing. He repeated his pounding on the door several times before a slight lamp glow indicated that someone was coming.

Ad opened the door a crack. "Who's there?"

"Shep here again, Mr. Adkins. We've had some trouble. I need to talk to you."

Ad set the lamp on a store counter and stepped out the door into the darkness. "What's up?"

Shep outlined the situation and asked, "Is there anyone that can ride to the Bar-M? We're going to need that help Mac promised. I could go but then I wouldn't be back in camp until late morning."

"I'll go. Pa you saddle up for me while I get dressed." Clara had silently stepped onto the store veranda without either man hearing her.

Ad turned and looked at his daughter. "That's a long ride in the dark. You sure you'll be alright?"

"I'll be fine Pa. You go back to the survey camp Shep. Leave this to me and the Bar-M. There'll be men riding just as soon as possible. Their trail crew should be back by now. You can count on some help." She stepped back through the door and was gone.

Shep borrowed a fresh mount from Ad and was back in camp just as dawn was beginning to break.

Jack was lighting a breakfast fire while Lod dragged in more desert-dry scrub brush branches. Web lay under the wagon, rolled in his blankets.

As Shep unsaddled his gelding Jack said, "We're having a camp day. It's a chance to get caught up on the mapping and paper work. We're agreed that one of us will be awake and sharp eyed all the time while the others take some rest. Web stood guard most of the night."

Jack pointed with the stem of his pipe. "We'll set up there on the highest point of that knoll where we can see the whole country around. Take turn about. Those who want to can catch up on some shut-eye. By the looks of you and your horse both, you could do with some bunk time yourself."

Shep lifted his hat and wiped his sweating forehead on his sleeve. "That's a good offer. That animal's put some fast miles on tonight though, so I'll deal with him first."

"You hit the sack. I'll do for your animal."

13

THE YARD OF THE BAR-M was buzzing with activity. The drive crew was back. Every one of them. None drew their time. Even with the prospect of having to do work that wasn't done from a saddle the men knew jobs were scarce and they were better off at the Bar-M than they would be most other places. The men from the Flying-W and the one Luke sent along plus the three riders from the ranches that contributed animals to the drive all left for their home ranches.

Taz, the foreman led the animals to the Denver stock yards. He negotiated a deal with a buyer and deposited the sale check in the Denver bank. The crew were free in the big city for a couple of days to do as they wished. After a bath and a night in the hotel Taz went looking for a fence contractor. He found three that were available. After talking with each contractor, he hired Rocky Patterson.

Patterson's yard was piled high with cut fence posts and wire. Rocky's crew loaded four large, tandem wagons with posts and one with wire, along with four kegs of staples. Other crews and wagons were detailed off to replenish the stock of posts from the close-by hills. They hoped to add to the supply of posts by cutting what was available from the hills around the Bar-M.

It would take many trips between the Bar-M and the contractor's yard to move the supplies needed to complete the miles of fencing.

Rocky Patterson's wife and one other woman came along to cook and run the camp. It took the women the full of a day to stock up the chuck wagon for the twelve-man fencing crew.

On the third morning in Denver Taz rousted the crew out of their hotel beds. "Boys, we're riding for home. You have one hour to pack up, have your breakfast and saddle your horse. We'll meet at the livery and ride out together."

They caught up Rocky's slow-moving wagons a couple of miles south of town. The fence builders were a tough looking crew; bold riding and well armed, but casual as they sat their mounts or lazed around the wagons.

Like most truly strong men, these men seemed to feel no need to demonstrate their toughness. Rocky noticed Taz looking them over. "They're good boys and good at what they do. A couple of those Dutchmen don't speak much English, but we get along. A lot of open range ranchers take exception to our work. We ride ready for whatever comes our way. Three of these men do nothing but guard the others. We'll get your fence built alright. Up to you to keep it from falling to the fence cutters."

Mac, slowly healing but still feeling weak from the loss of blood, was seated on a chair outside the cookhouse, welcoming the returned crew. His eye glanced towards the barn's shade where another wagon team he didn't recognise was being cared for by Pepe. Taz passed him the receipts from the sale of the Bar-M animals.

Mac's attention returned to the drive. He looked the receipts over and then glanced at the bank record. He looked up at Taz, "Good job Taz. I'm glad you're back. Bring that fence contractor over here and the three of us will have a talk. I'm ready for coffee too, so we'll go inside."

"Before I do that Mac I wish you'd say hello to a couple of people we brought back with us."

The rancher turned to his right, watching as two very attractive young ladies walked up from the wagon Pepe was caring for. By appearances, Mac figured they were easing into their late twenties, maybe even into the thirties, although the cattle-minded rancher would admit he was no judge of women. He had no idea who they were. He stood to greet them, touching the brim of his hat as they came close.

A lady dressed in a tan colored, split riding skirt and a matching jacket lifted a white Stetson from her head, showing unusually close-cut blond hair, and held out her hand. "You don't know me, Mr. McTavish but you knew my fiancé. I believe Jerrod was a friend and partner."

Mac was lost for words for just a moment. Finally gathering his thoughts, he said, "You're Jerrod's girl? The one he used to talk about?"

"I am. My name is Matilda. Jerrod liked to call me Mattie. And this is my friend Gail." She indicated a darker haired woman dressed in a full length, light blue dress, holding her grey Stetson before her. "We didn't start out to come here and we didn't set out particularly to find you, although I knew you were originally heading to somewhere in Colorado. The truth is that we found ourselves craving a bit of adventure that wasn't available in Boston, so we purchased tickets on the rails, hoping to see some of the western countryside. After several stops along the way we arrived in Denver last week.

"As happanstance would have it we were in a general store buying these magnificent hats, which I truly love, when we heard someone speak of the Bar-M. I remembered the brand from Jerrod's letters. It turned out to be one of your cowboys who was speaking. Well, one thing led to another and here we are after inviting ourselves along. Taz has been very kind to us. We appreciate the invitation to tag along. I especially wanted to meet you and Luke to say thank you for your friendship to Jerrod.

"I can see this is a very busy time for you though. If our being here is not convenient we could turn the wagon around and head back to Denver."

Mac paused for just a moment. "Taz, get yourself a coffee and wait here for me. You two ladies come with me please."

Walking slowly, easing the weight on the sling with his good hand, Mac led them to the house. He opened the door and called for Margo. She arrived in a few moments, wiping her hands with a small towel. At the sight of the two women she stopped abruptly, a questioning look on her face.

Mac made the introductions and turned to leave. The three women watched him climb down the stairs. The two visitors were looking puzzled at his abrupt introduction and departure.

Margo smiled after her husband. "You'll have to accept Mac the way he is. It's a very busy time on the Bar-M and he has much on his mind. I think he may be a bit overwhelmed at meeting you two as well, after all these years. Jerrod and Mac were very close. Your arrival will have his mind going back to other times. But you are most welcome. Come in. I'll have the kids find Pepe. He'll bring in your things."

Once settled in the cook shack Taz indicated Mac's arm, still in the sling. "You fall from a horse?"

"I wish that was all it was." Mac explained the situation with Baxter and the ranchers who sided him. He looked across the table at Rocky who has listened to the whole sordid story. "Any of that liable to scare you or your crew off?"

Rocky laughed right out loud. "We're not easy to scare Mac. You send a few riders along with us. We'll get your fence built."

After a thorough discussion with the fence builder it was decided to move out the next morning. Mac wasn't one to waste time and he was pleased to find that Rocky was of the same mind. The men and animals would benefit from some cookhouse food and a night's rest before they started the big job. The fence crew pitched their own camp but joined the Bar-M crew for the evening meal. When Rocky's wife offered to help with the cookhouse chores the Bar-M cook simply turned his back and ignored her.

Well before first light the next morning Clara rode into the yard on an exhausted black mare. She ran the horse most of the distance. Tyler was on night guard. The cowboy nursed a yearning for Clara ever since he first rode into Adkins a year before. He said nothing because he was secretly afraid of her, feeling well below her station in life, and intimidated by her beauty. He was afraid of Mac and Ad too. So, he took the safe, silent route. But that didn't stop his breath from catching a bit as he watched her ride into the light of the cookhouse porch lantern.

"Miss Clara, what in the world..."

She didn't let him finish. "No time for explanations, Tyler. I'd like if you would care for this animal and saddle another for me while I raise the house. I have to talk with Mac and Margo." Not waiting for an answer, she swung to the ground and passed him the reins. The ranch house door was never locked but she pounded on it anyway, before opening it and walking in.

Margo met her in the hallway, coming from the kitchen, dressed and ready for the day. Mac slowly walked out, a cup of coffee in his hands. He had been taking his breakfast with the family since the shooting. Clara could hear talk from the kids' bedrooms but none of them came out.

"You're up early," was Clara's greeting.

"Busy times. What's up Clara that brings you here this time of day?"

After a hasty explanation the two women retired to the kitchen where Margo had a pan of bacon sizzling, with sliced potatoes browning in the grease. A pan of fried eggs sat ready for serving. They dished up the food while Mac made his slow way to the cookhouse. He raised his voice over the talk and the clattering of cutlery on porcelain. "Hold up a minute boys."

The room quieted down, and Mac outlined the situation at the surveyor camp.

He gave the crew a few moments to digest the news before asking, "Do any of you wish to volunteer for guard duty for a few days? It will mean camping out."

Most of the crew raised their hands.

Mac turned to Taz. "Alright Taz. You know what work needs doing and who you have in mind for each task. You've already picked some men to go with the fence crew. They'll be working in the same area as the surveyors, but they'll be too far apart to be much help, should someone cause trouble. You pick four men you can spare and rig them out with whatever they need to side the surveyors. Anything you're short of they can pick up at Ad's along the way. Maybe using a couple of the new men would leave the Bar-M crew home doing familiar work.

"They're to escort Clara back home as well."

He then spoke to the crew. "We're still not looking for fights men. Don't any of you start something that could be avoided. And thanks."

14

IN TIME FOR A LATE BREAKFAST the next morning, Bill and Luke rode into the yard. Cray Dobbs was just a bit behind them. Again, Mac, still looking wan and impatient with his convalescence, was riding his chair in front of the cookhouse.

Luke and Bill rode over and dismounted, turning their horses over to Pepe. Mac smiled up at Cray, "Good to see you Cray. But your being here has to have a story behind it. And these other two must be here for a reason too." He struggled to his feet, holding the back of the chair for support and shook hands with the three men, with Cray leaning from the saddle.

Ranch country convention said that a visitor waited to be asked before dismounting. With Luke and Bill, their familiarity with the Bar-M overrode that practice. Mac found his chair again and said, "Step down here Cray and tell us what's happened."

Cray started his short tale. "I was having a perfectly good sleep in your closer-in line cabin last night when these two uncivilized characters came in long after full dark and started banging stove lids and clanking fry pans, laughing and talking loud. Never heard the like. Woke me up, it did. When I spoke up from the darkness of the bunk these two nearly jumped out of their skins. Acted like they'd heard the ghost of all their past indiscretions come for an accounting. It was a pleasure to see.

"I was heading this way yesterday and decided to take advantage of your hospitality rather than ride all night or sleep on the ground."

He swung out of the saddle during this telling. He looped the reins on the gelding's neck and gave it a light slap on the rump. The animal wandered in the direction of the barn.

Stepping closer to Mac, Cray said, "Baxter's fit to be tied. I think he cared more about Luke and Bill running his cattle off the Bar-M than he did about having one of his riders killed. They buried the boy down a nice little valley about a mile from the ranch. Not much was said about him.

"Then to top it all off, the Flying-W and the Double-S kept pushing Baxter's animals until they were back on their home range. Baxter's gone and stirred up all this trouble, lost a man, got you shot, made half the country mad at him in the process, and he's right back where he was at the start of it all. He might even be worse off. He's lost considerable support. A lot of the ranchers are upset with the shooting. They expected there might be gun play. But when your name found its way into the picture, along with the details of what happened, the neighbors didn't take it well at all."

A few of the crew gathered close to hear Cray's talk.

"The X-O crew are worried. That Tell kid could have shot just about anyone else in the valley and not much would be said. But when they heard it was you that was down the boys kind of backed up and looked sober. Then when I relayed Margo's message, Baxter kicked dirt all over the ranch yard mumbling, "I can't be seen to be fighting women and kids." That really set off the crew."

Mac hadn't heard of Margo's message. Rather than pursue it in front of the men he left it for later.

Cray had more to say. "Still, Baxter probably could have held it together except when he ordered the crew to cut out another big bunch of cattle and drive them back onto the Bar-M grass. Four of the boys quit him right off, including me. Bottom line is, I need a job."

"And I need to wrap myself around some grub," said Luke.

Mac chuckled and said, "I think we can accommodate both needs. Follow me." He moved slowly, favoring his arm. Suddenly he stopped, remembering, and pointed at the big house with his chin. "We got some company yesterday Luke. That girl Jerrod used to talk about arrived with another friend, both of them riding that wagon sitting over there. Don't expect they've started their day yet. We'll go and meet them by and by."

Luke glanced over at the house and started to say something. Mac cut him off. "That can all wait. Let's get you some grub and we'll talk."

Cray watched as Mac carefully climb the couple of stairs to enter the cookhouse and slowly settle into a chair. "I see you moving slow and careful Mac."

"Weak. Feeling not too bad. But weak. Arm doesn't hurt much except where the stiches pull from time to time. Just got to get my strength back from the blood loss. If it weren't for you I'd be under the sod so I'm learning patience. And thankfulness."

After a further brief discussion of the situation and what to expect from Baxter, Luke asked Mac, "You still got line riders out? We spent a couple of days pushing cattle and riding line. Never saw a soul."

Mac shook his head. "No. It seemed better to hold them back for a few days. Kind of let things settle out. Getting the range back into condition isn't a matter of a couple of days. We're talking a couple of years. It's not worth risking lives over a few days.

"But the market drive crew is back and Taz has some boys getting outfitted for a ride to the south line tomorrow morning.

Might be best to hold them back a bit more from what you said. We aren't purposely trying to stir up trouble. We'll wait a bit and see what happens. I'm hoping Baxter will pull in his horns. He's the ring leader. The other ranchers will quit the bluff if Baxter quits."

Again, the men were silent for a few moments. Finally, Cray said, "Mac, I surely hope you're right, but somehow I don't see it working out that way. Baxter has taken a stand. His pride is on the line. I don't see him backing off until more blood flows, probably his own. I'd sure like to be wrong on that."

The four men sat in silence for several minutes, each man with his own thoughts. There didn't seem to be much more to say, so they drank their coffee in the quietness of the early morning. Luke finally stretched and stood up. "Gotta get back. Got work of my own needs doing and a wife that'll be wondering. I'll have to meet Jerrod's girl another time."

The cook paper-wrapped a cold bundle for Luke and Bill to take along for afternoon lunch. With a wave at Margo, who was standing on the veranda, they headed back to their own ranches and responsibilities. The twins started following but their Uncle Bill chased them back.

Mac called out to Taz. The Bar-M foreman walked over to where Mac was again sitting on his chair, with Cray standing close by.

"Taz, you know Cray. We're putting him on the payroll. I think it's best to hold him away from the south line for a while. Maybe find a spot for him with the keeping herd."

Taz nodded and turned to Cray. "C'mon. I'm about to ride down to the herd. Might just as well come see what it's all about."

At the survey line all was quiet. The guard riders sent out by the Bar-M rode constant patrol, remaining watchful, but no challenges came their way.

15

MANY MILES TO THE SOUTH Jimbo turned his weary horse towards a small, isolated ranch house. Getting closer he could recognize it as a sheep spread, identifiable by the size and shape of the corrals, as well as sound and smell. The adobe structure and the yard layout branded it as a Mexican outfit. A barking dog warned the herders of his coming. Two riders, looking like father and son, were holding the animals close to the home place, taking advantage of the newly greened grass on the lower reaches of the ranch. As the weather warmed they would move into the higher-up surrounding hills.

A rider wearing a huge sun and sweat stained sombrero broke away from the flock. "*Hola mi amigo*. Welcome to my humble home. You have traveled far to come here."

Jimbo raised his hat in greeting. "*Hola mi amigo*. I'm happy to hear you speaking English. I have much to yet learn about your beautiful language."

Jimbo was quite fluent in the language but he often held back that information until he saw how the land lay.

Jimbo rode up to the man. "You are correct, we have come far, my horse and I, and have yet far to go. We wish to be in Las Vegas tomorrow. I am hoping to water my horse and perhaps purchase a meal from you."

The sheep man smiled past a magnificent grey mustache. "We will go to the water first for your horse and then we will sit for a few moments in the shade while my Juana prepares food. She saw you coming before I did. She will be busy at the stove now. Always she wishes to have visitors leave thinking good thoughts about Rancho Garcia."

The two men introduced themselves before taking their places on a bench built under the wind fluttered leaves of a giant cottonwood. Juan Garcia immediately asked, "What is happening around the country? We live far from people and seldom have visitors."

Jimbo answered with a chuckle. "Don't spend much time around folks my own self. Mostly ride the country just seeing and looking. Been cattle range troubles way north of here. Friends of mine. I've come to find some hombres we think will be able to help. Deputy sheriff in Las Vegas and his brother. Want to take them back with me."

Juan sat up straighter. "This deputy. He has a name?"

Jimbo saw no problem in continuing the conversation. "Bobby McTavish and his brother Jeremiah. Brothers to the head honcho up north."

Juan clapped his hands. "The sheriff I met just once but the Jeremiah he comes this way. He waters his horse like you and others. My Juana she likes him to visit. He is much smiling and always he kisses her hand after she has fed him and when he is gone she sometimes finds a coin under his plate.

"He visits Margarita Reyes of the Rancho Reyes. Our neighbor. Just fifteen miles through the hills." He pointed to the south west. "If you take the young man far to the north my Eduardo will be much happy, for he also visits the rancho Reyes hoping for a moment with the beautiful Margarita." The sheep man clapped his hands again and smiled at Jimbo as if this was the best news he could have brought from the north.

Jimbo took the hint and slipped a coin under his plate after finishing his lamb stew and tortillas that he rolled around some eye-watering goat cheese before using it to scoop up the stew gravy.

Juan and his wife stood waving as Jimbo cantered his horse out of the yard. After one more night on the rocky New Mexico ground, rolled in the blanket he borrowed from Bill and Little Flower, Jimbo rode into Las Vegas, bone weary, at noon the next day. He asked directions to the sheriff's office and was soon shaking hands with Bobby. "You was always a wanderer Jimbo but what made you wander way down here?"

"You lead us to the closest eating house and I'll tell you a story. You're looking at a hungry and a wore-out man."

"C'mon, I always love your stories whether there's any truth in them or not." He pulled the law office door shut behind them and the two men walked together across the crowded street. A boy of perhaps ten sat whittling on the porch steps in front of the café. Bobby said, "Rolly, you see that dusty grulla over there. You take him to the livery for my friend, unsaddle him, get him some water and feed, and treat him to a rubdown and there's a two-bit piece in it for you."

The boy quickly folded his knife, snatched the flipped coin out of the air and ran off.

Jimbo said nothing until they were seated and both men had their hands wrapped around porcelain coffee mugs, waiting for their lunches to arrive. "I'll overlook your jabbering about the factualness of my stories. But listen up here because there is no nonsense about this story. Where's Jeremiah, by the way. He needs to hear this too."

"He's visiting the mayor's daughter. Pretty girl but not smart enough to come in out of the rain. Needs constant watching lessen she falls off a cliff or some such thing. Jeremiah figures it's his civic duty to do most of the watching. I saw him this morning early. He was at the general store buying some foofaraw he'll use to try to impress her with. Rides for a ranch on the south edge of town but somehow manages to find an excuse to make his way over to see the young lady ever now and then. The rancher gets a kick out of the whole thing, so just as long as it don't interfere with ranch operations he closes his eyes when Jeremiah rides out."

"Well, we can talk to him later. This story is of interest to the two of you. To get down to it, Mac's been shot."

Bobby sat up straight and placed his coffee cup back on the table. "Whoa. Now I'm listening."

Jimbo told the story in as few words as he knew how. He finished with, "The Bar-M needs you boys." He let the implications sit right there.

Within a few minutes Bobby had sent young Rolly down to the mayor's house. The message brought his brother on the run, Rolly sitting behind Jeremiah, holding onto the cantle. Pulling up in front of the little eating house, Rolly slid off the horse and Jeremiah swung to the ground. Entering the small café, without even a greeting or a hand shake he said, "Talk to me Jimbo."

Jimbo laid his fork and knife down and rose from the bench he was sitting on. He held out his hand. Jeremiah shook it and again said, "Talk to me."

A couple of years had passed since Jimbo last saw the brothers. Glancing from one to the other he could see old man Hiram's bloodline breeding true. Tall and almost gaunt in their slenderness, with slightly stooped back, shoulders, arms and hands strong and toughened by years of wrangling and cow work, the two men showed McTavish traits in every way but their seriousness. Where Hiram and Mac were serious almost to a fault, the brothers were more given to smiling adventure. Until trouble hit. Then the smiles vanished. At that point any fighting man would welcome them at his side.

Jimbo took his seat and picked up his coffee mug. He slurped back a drink and sucked his lips dry before saying, "Short story, son. Mac looked over his grass and came to the conclusion that there were too many cattle in the country. He's right about that, by the way. Told everyone at roundup that he was selling off most of his herd and was planning to fence the entire Bar-M. He's right on that decision too. But it doesn't sit well with a few of the others who remember the open range in Texas.

"One, Baxter by name, moved some cows onto Mac's vacated grass. When Mac told them to take them home a squirt too young to know much about life, or ranching, or honor, and who had yet to gain any respect for his betters, took a couple of shots at Mac. The kid won't be getting any older. They buried him back on the X-O. Mac took one bullet in the set-to.

"Mac's alright. Weak from loss of blood and some infection is all. Bullet hit a rib. Took a chunk of meat from his arm. He gets a bit more use from the arm as the days go along. Mama comes by the Bar-M most days and cleans out the wound. He'll be back in the saddle in no time.

"But there's fear the whole thing with Baxter and those siding him will blow up. There just isn't one single thing good that can come from such as that. You boys got to come home."

He paused and took another sip of coffee. "My opinion, should you be wondering; Mac's too gentle. Always wanting peace. He was trying to reason with the Baxter bunch when he was shot. Should have shot first, is my opinion."

Bobby jumped in. "The war did that to him. He never talked about it with me, but just the once. Time he finished telling me what all it was he seen and done he was shuddering, with tears running down his cheeks. On top of all that, he's his father's son. Pa's always looking for the peaceful way. Mac pretty much takes after him.

"Now you take Ma's family. Gatlin by name. Grandpa Gatlin, he was a fierce old man. Lived with us for a time until his passing.

"Even after time and age took away the most of his strength to where he could hardly walk, his eyes were sharp and clear, suspicious, watching every move a man made. Never caught him without he had a weapon on him, either his old squirrel gun or an antiquated cap and ball in a holster on his sagging belt.

"There's more than just the one or two old timer Gatlins that got themselves wrapped up in mountain country feuds. Mean, some of them were, if the stories are anywhere near true. Just plain mean.

"Ma ain't mean. I'm not suggesting anything like that. But each of us has seen a time or two where it was safest to be almost anywhere else when reckoning time come around. Ma on a tear is a sight to behold. Especially if her family's good is involved. She used both barrels of Pa's twelve gauge to blow a fella out of his saddle on the trip west from Missouri. The fool threatened Pa and Pa was a bit slow to react, so Ma stepped in."

"Ma's changed considerable from her upbringing over the years. From living with Pa, I suppose. Still, if someone don't deal with this Baxter you talk about, you might just see Ma saddle up. Baxter would regret the day that come about.

"I guess most would say that this ugly brother of mine and me pretty much lean towards the Gatlin side."

Jimbo repeated himself. "You got to come home."

Without a word Jeremiah rose from the table, left the café, swung back onto his horse and spurred out of town.

Bobby got up and left Jimbo sitting alone. His lunch finished, Jimbo sat dozing in the shade of the jail house for an hour before Bobby was back. The young man walked into the jail office, tossed his deputy badge on the desk and started gathering up his belongings. Looking down at the badge he kind of smiled. He picked up the cheap tin emblem of authority and stuffed it in his pocket.

Bobby heard Jimbo's step on the office floor. Without turning he said, "Finally found our lazy sheriff so's I could quit this job. Broke up his siesta but he'll get over it."

He stacked his few things on the sidewalk outside the door and lay two carbines on top. "Be right back," he said.

Jimbo was back on the bench outside the office. He sat silently watching, figuring the younger man could do without his help.

Within another hour Jeremiah was back with his bedroll tied behind the saddle. He swung down and tied his animal. Turning to Jimbo he asked, "Where's Bobby?"

"Gone off to get his bedroll."

Jeremiah walked swiftly to the livery and was back in ten minutes with Bobby's horse, saddled and ready to go. To Jimbo he said, "Rolly's putting your rig back together. Be here in a little bit. I'll go buy some trail fixings." He left no room for discussion.

Mumbling to himself Jimbo said, "Don't know as how one night on a hotel mattress would change things much on the Bar-M." With a fond look at the hotel across the street he went back to the shaded bench.

The three men were twenty-five miles north of town when dusk started to dim the trail. "Keep together, boys," hollered Jeremiah. "I'm not stopping till we've made some more miles. Let's don't get separated."

They pulled into the Garcia ranch on staggering animals just as dawn's first light was showing over the eastern horizon, Jeremiah still leading. "We'll change horses, grab a meal and get back on the road." He swung his horse toward the small corral.

Jimbo caught up and swung down beside Jeremiah. "Garcia going to have animals to swap? That surprises me. Ain't much of a ranch."

"He'll have at least one of his own and I keep a couple here my own self. Man never knows when he'll need a fresh mount. Got several stashed around the country."

Garcia's son strolled out from the house. Jeremiah saw him coming. "*Hola mi amigo*, Francisco, we need some horses and a bite of breakfast *por favor*."

Without asking questions the young man said, "You go to the house. I will bring in the horses."

"*Gracias*, bring my two and one other *por favor*."

As the three tired riders came in sight of the ranch house door Juan was standing on the shaded porch. "You are in much hurry, yes? Come we will eat."

Within a half hour they were again in the saddle. There were three coins left under plates and much thanks expressed to the little family. Jeremiah, sitting his saddle, looked down at Juan. "Thank you again. If we don't come back the horses are yours."

"*Via con Dios*, my friends. Ride well. We will care for the animals."

Two days later, after changing horses three more times at friendly ranches, and grabbing a few hours sleep in a lonely line shack, the weary men rode onto the Bar-M range. A couple of miles in they heard the bawling of cattle. Riding around a rocky ridge up-thrust brought them to where they could see four riders keeping watch over about three hundred animals, placidly eating Bar-M grass. Their weariness and the thought of what happened to Mac pushed all restraint aside.

Bobby pulled his carbine, tugged his hat down tight, kicked his horse into a run and rode straight at the men. He was among them before they had a chance to react.

The four riders pulled out of their careless, slouched positions and sat up in their saddles. They were too late. Bobby was already in action, with Jeremiah only a few steps behind. Bobby swung his carbine straight from his shoulder as he rode past the first man. The rider took the blow above his ear and dropped to the ground without a sound, blood pouring from his split scalp. Bobby turned and was lined up on the next rider. Jeremiah had his man down.

Jimbo pointed his carbine at the one man who was still in the saddle. The rider was frantically reaching for his Colt. "You're dead if you do it."

The rider snapped his head around. Seeing Jimbo holding that carbine caused him to reconsider. He decided he was mostly enjoying life and wanted to enjoy more of it. He dropped the weapon back into the holster and lifted his hands. Jimbo nodded. "Good decision."

Two of the men on the ground fought their way up to a sitting position, glaring at their attackers. One had blood running down the side of his face, disappearing under his shirt collar. The third rider showed no sign of awareness, lying right where he landed when he fell from his riding animal.

Bobby lined his carbine up on the man in the saddle. "Now listen up you three, so's you can explain the situation to your friend there on the ground if he ever wakes up."

Jeremiah cut in. "The first man to reach for a gun dies. You might want to remember that while my brother explains some facts to you."

A few hours later the three long-travelling men rode into the Bar-M yard on sweaty, staggering horses. Without more than a nod at Mac and the crew, Jimbo, still not fully recovered from his bullet wounds, fell into a bunk and was snoring within a few seconds.

Pepe led their horses to the barn where he would grain them and rub them down. Bobby and Jeremiah greeted Mac and the twins who came running from the house. Jerrod strolled over and watched silently from a distance until Bobby waved him over. Jerrod was embarrassed by the bear hug administered by his uncle Bobby but secretly he enjoyed it.

Margo came out wiping her bread dough covered hands on a cloth. "Thanks for coming boys. We can use a bit of help right now until Mac's back on his feet. We're all hoping too that will find a good reason to stay and settle down here."

"Why, Margo, the only'st reason we've been wandering far and wide is that we're looking for a couple of girls just like you. We've about come to the conclusion that there's only just the one ever borned. Sure is a disappointment to me and that ugly brother of mine." Bobby was all smiles, a look that didn't fool Margo for a moment.

Jeremiah wasn't listening to the nonsense Bobby was laying on Margo. His eyes were glued to the house veranda and the two ladies holding down the carved oak rocking chairs that were normally reserved for Mac and Margo.

Margo saw where he was looking and took a deep breath followed by a sigh. Speaking loud enough to be heard across the distance she called out, "Matilda, Gail, you might just as well come down here and meet these two."

The girls looked at one another, slowly rose to their feet and stepped towards the stairs. In just a few moments they were being introduced to Bobby and Jeremiah. Margo finished the introductions with, "These two have enough McTavish in them to keep them from going completely wild but that doesn't mean you should believe everything they tell you. Caution is called for when dealing with either of them."

Matilda held her hand out with a smile. Bobby gave it a slow, careful shake, tipping his hat back with his other thumb. "Would you look at that? I've been ridin all over Colorado and a big part of New Mexico tryin to find me a girl with eyes as blue as yours and here you are right back on the home ranch. Just goes to show. A body might be better off just stayin to home."

Jeremiah was shaking Gail's offered hand, seemingly tongue tied for the first time in his life.

Margo looked at the girls, "As I already told you, caution and disbelief is the order of the day."

16

THE FENCING CREW MADE a good start along the western boundary of the Bar-M, holding the fence line fifty feet inside the survey line to allow for future roads. After anchoring the largest post they could find for the north-west corner, Rocky set up a transit like the one the surveyors were using and started spotting the locations for each post hole. While four men dug holes in the rock-strewn caliche soil, and two men placed posts, tamping them firmly into place with iron bars, the wire crew started rolling out wire.

Mounting a reel of wire onto the rotating spindle attached to a wagon, a teamster walking beside his animals slowly guided the team along the fence line while two men, well protected with leather gloves, heavy leather chaps and long sleeve leather jackets, guided the wire off the spool, laying it in the grass far enough from the diggers and post men to allow them the freedom to work. At the end of the spool they loosely wrapped the wire around a post and lay it on the ground to prevent the wire from spinning back into a coil. This was repeated until there were four strands carefully laid in the grass, far enough apart to prevent tangles.

A keg of staples was off-loaded.

All the time this was taking place the Bar-M riders were assisting Rocky's guards, slowly circling the site, watching for intruders. Two of the men staked out positions on high points where they could see for miles in all directions. Their only task was to keep the fencing crew safe and to prevent the cutting of wire.

17

ON THE DAY THEY returned Bobby and Jeremiah took the afternoon and the following night to catch up on food and sleep. Jimbo slept right through, not even rising for the evening meal.

While the boys were resting, Mac called Jerrod over to where he was holding down his usual chair in front of the cookhouse. "Son, I'd like it if you'd take a ride over to your grandparent's farm and tell them the boys are home. See if they can get away from their work tomorrow morning. It's easier if we all visit here rather than the lot of us going over there." Jerrod simply nodded his head and turned for the barn.

The following morning Mac pulled Taz aside before they detailed out the work for the day. "Taz, I want rid of those visiting girls for a while this morning. I wish you would have Pepe saddle a couple of gentle horses. Then I'd appreciate if you'd detail off a trustworthy man to take them for a ride. Show them around the country a bit. I don't care where. Just don't lose them. They might wish to see the herd or maybe just go see can they find a coyote down the north coulee. Keep them gone two or three hours. And watch those twins don't follow along and lead the girls into some foolishness. I don't know how well either of those city ladies can ride."

Taz looked quickly at the house to see if the girls were ready. "I'll get right on it boss." He turned towards the cookhouse to detail off the day's work to the crew.

Earlier, when Margo suggested a ride to the girls they agreed immediately and went to put on the riding clothes they purchased in Denver. Pepe led the saddled horses out of the barn and the girls met them half way across the yard. Buck Travers sauntered over, leading his big black gelding, with an embarrassed look on his face. "I'm told I'll be your guide this morning ladies. I'm ready just about whenever you are."

Mac listened to the chirping and excited exclamations from the girls and shook his head. He mumbled something about city folks as he watched them slowly make their way out of the yard on their morning adventure.

Margo had the twins pull a few wooden-back chairs from the kitchen onto the veranda before releasing them for the morning. The men ate their breakfasts at the cookhouse and then slowly made their way to the veranda. Jimbo was asked to join them. As the men started to gather, Margo carried a big pot of coffee from the kitchen and went back for mugs. A jug of separated cream and a coffee can of sugar followed. Margo long wondered about riders that would exclaim approvingly over bitter, nearly undrinkable camp coffee, but at the ranch would expect to have copious quantities of fresh cream and spoonsful of sugar available.

Mac was watching for his parents to come down the lane. There was still no one Mac trusted or respected more than his father. He needed the older man's wisdom now, perhaps more than he ever needed it.

Just as the men were taking their seats Hiram, with Della sitting beside him, arrived with the rattle of the old wagon and the crunching of rock and caliche under steel rimmed wheels drowning out conversation. Bobby and Jeremiah rose immediately and went to greet their parents. Hiram gave each a hearty handshake and then stepped back a bit and looked at the two boys. "It's been too long boys, it's sure good to see you."

Della, who the boys only knew as Ma was wiping tears from her eyes. With an arm around each of her sons she made her way to the stairs and then to a cushioned wicker chair on the veranda. Mac nodded at her and said, "Ma."

When everyone was seated and slurping coffee, Mac spoke, flipping his thumb at Bobby and Jeremiah. "It's good to have you boys home and back on the Bar-M. We have some ranch business to discuss but before we get to that why don't you two bring us up to date on your wanderings and such.

Jeremiah found a seat between Mac and Jimbo. Bobby was seated between his parents, his mother holding his hand. The two McTavish sons took turns telling about the past couple of years. Hiram and Della both asked a question or two that the boys answered, although Mac suspected some of the answers were a bit short of the whole entire truth. He didn't push for more details though, suspecting there were things best not discussed fully.

Della listened to the various tales and then said, "Boys you're not really young anymore. It's time you settled down. Perhaps you could find yourselves each a good wife. I'm sure there must be some land around here that could be purchased if you wished to ranch."

She was all set to continue but Jeremiah grinned and interrupted her. "Ma, you know we really only set out on the road to find us a couple of girls just like Margo. Everything else along the way was just to put coin in our pockets so's we wouldn't starve out over the winter months. Seems as how there's no girls like that in these parts though. We've given it a pretty good search, but none really measure up and neither of us is ready to take second best. We've been talking about trying Montana."

Margo stood up. "I can't listen to any more of this drivel. I'll go refill the coffee pot."

Everyone around the table chuckled.

Mac waited a few moments and when no one else spoke he said, "Jimbo rode alone to Las Vegas to bring the boys home. He was still getting over a couple of bullet holes himself and should have really been a-bed. I've thanked him for that but I'm asking all of you to thank him too. "

There was a mumble of something that sounded a bit like thanks and a general nodding of heads. Jimbo had nothing to say.

Mac figured it was safe to move on to ranch business. "When that Baxter rider put the bullet in me the situation took on considerable gloom in Margo's eyes. Thanks to Mama and her medical help I'll be back a-saddle any day now. I've thanked her and now I want to thank each of you for your prayers and your standing by Margo and the Bar-M while I was out of commission." A low rumble of agreement grew around the table.

Mac continued, looking from one brother to the other. "Jimbo convinced himself that Baxter and the other ranchers were about to create serious trouble in the valley and you boys were the best bet for standing against that. He may yet be proven to be right. In the meantime, we have things to do."

He looked around the table waiting for someone to speak. When no one did he continued.

"Y'all have a pretty good idea of the goings on in the valley. You've got eyes to see range conditions. You see the sun-burned grass, the stunted growth, the bare dirt in places and the encroachment of brush and cactus. I know we could push the situation for another year or two and still get some beef off but I'm afraid we might damage the land beyond repair.

"So, I've done what I felt needs doing and I have no intention of backing down. I don't want to talk about that decision. I want to talk about how to keep Baxter and his kind from pushing cattle onto Bar-M grass. I also want to talk about keeping the surveyors and the fencing crew safe while they finish their work. And then there's the matter of fence cutting after the wire is strung."

Mac leaned forward, picked up his mug and took a drink of coffee. Everyone was silent, waiting.

"Finally, the last thing I want to do is start a range war. I don't suppose I came away from wearing a grey uniform with very much wisdom. But one thing I'm convinced of, there were no real winners in that foolish set-to. The blood letting eventually stopped but the anger and resentment didn't. I don't see that as a pattern to follow here in the valley."

He took another drink of coffee and again everyone waited silently.

"I'm wanting to hear what y'all have to say. How do we save the valley and not start a range war?"

Mac looked around the table. Silently staring back at him were Taz, the Bar-M ranch foreman, Cray Dobbs, Bobby, Jeremiah and Jimbo, plus Hiram, Mac's father and Della, his mother. Hiram settled comfortably into a wooden rocker. Margo sat in the other rocker. Jerrod took up a chair next to his father, silently taking in the conversation. The twins saddled up and went to catch up to Buck and the visiting ladies.

Bobby was the first to speak. "We left out of Las Vegas in pretty much of a hurry but not before I managed to locate a trusted friend who promised to find a dozen or so good riders and head up this way. They were to keep an eye out for your sheep herd too Mac. I must say I thought Jimbo was joshing when he told us about the sheep. But he finally convinced us of the truth of your intentions. If those riders ain't off throw'n snow balls at each other on the top of one of those there mountains, cause they're lost, I expect they'll ride in about any day now."

Della spoke up. "Son, I find it discouraging to hear you so brutalize the language I carefully taught you around the kitchen table."

Everyone laughed while Bobby fought back a comment, remembering that it was his mother who had spoken.

Margo said, "Ma, I long ago gave up any hope of holding half-wild men to any form of reasonable diction. I fear our cause is lost. I'm now hoping for the next generation. I've settled for these ones having a bath once in a while no matter what words they throw our way." There were a few more chuckles from the gathered men. Neither Margo nor Della joined in.

Mac said, "Thank you ladies but what we're dealing with here will be the same whether we're using good diction or bad. So, the question is, is a show of force along the property line the best choice or should a few of us ride over and try to reason with Baxter and his group again?"

Margo spoke up immediately. "There's one thing you can absolutely take to the bank, Mac McTavish. You are not riding over there by yourself again."

No one added anything to Margo's statement. The group drank coffee and stared out over the ranch yard for a few moments.

Della McTavish spoke up. "There was a time when a man like this Baxter would just be made to disappear." She sounded as if she yearned again for that long-gone day. Bobby took a long, smiling look at his mother.

No one broke the silence around the table. The shock at her words was complete. Hiram reached over and gripped his wife's hand tenderly.

To get the conversation back on track Mac finally said, "Cray, how do you think it really stands on the X-O?"

Cray answered, "Mac. I expect I know Baxter about as well as anyone here. I worked for him for nigh onto two years. He's a stubborn cuss and not any smarter than he really needs to be. On top of that he's got his pride bent a little.

"Some of the smaller ranchers siding him might be open to wise talk but I suspect Baxter is going to be a continuing problem. The really stupid part is that the X-O is a good ranch.

Baxter already has all most men would ask for. It's difficult to understand what's driving the man.

"Murphy Cox is a small rancher with only a couple of riders, but I expect he'll follow Baxter no matter where that trail leads. The others? Who knows? I know of at least three ranchers that pulled their horns right back in when you were shot Mac. The news of that shooting went through the country like a lightening strike. Even a few of those sticking with Baxter didn't like it."

Taz spoke up. "The Flying W borders us for a good long way. Wallace has always showed a cool head and he joined the market drive. He'd be a good one to have on our side."

The thoughts of the men were kicked around the table until everyone spoke their piece. Mac listened carefully, inserting a question or two from time to time. Hiram paid close attention, as if he was taking mental notes. His only comment was. "Be good if Ad was here. He knows all these ranchers, and the farmers too. Might have something to contribute to all this talk."

Mac looked at his father. "That's why he's not here Dad. Ad relies on these people for his living and the ranchers and farmers rely on Ad being where he is. We'll try to keep Ad neutral if possible."

It took a few minutes to loosen the conversation to where everyone felt free to talk. Every idea from waiting for something to happen before acting, to going in force to make a strong point was presented. Hiram quietly asked, "What about the law? Can we find a federal deputy marshal anywhere around?"

The table was quiet for a bit until Mac spoke. "We've thought of that Dad. It would probably mean a trip to Denver and even then, we might not find a lawman with authority in this area. I don't feel like I can be away at this time and I don't know who else we could send."

Hiram looked over at his wife and asked a silent question. She returned a silent answer with a slight nod. Like so many couples who had put the years behind them, Hiram and Della seemed to know what the other was thinking.

Hiram shifted in his chair and cleared his throat. "If you could put a man on our place for a week or so Mac, your mother and I would enjoy a trip to Denver. We could search out the deputy marshal. See if we can get any action out of him.

"We haven't seen the big city in two years or more. Haven't seen Nancy and her family in all that time either. Do us good to get away. We could be ready in the morning, but we can't leave the place with no one there."

Mac looked at Taz. "What do you think Taz? Can you spare a man?"

Taz hesitated and then snuck a look at Cray Dobbs. "We've been keeping you off the range until this all settles down Cray. How would you feel about caring for their place for a week or so?"

Hiram spoke up. "You'd have to milk one cow, care for the chickens. Feed the dog. Watch over the saddle stock."

Cray hunched his shoulders and grinned. "Kind of like a paid holiday, you mean? Ya, I could do that."

So the decision was made.

The discussions put behind them and a couple of decisions made, the entire group, ladies and all, made their way to the cookhouse for the noon meal. Mac asked the cook to put enough together for the yard crew and the family, to free Margo to sit in on the discussions.

The girls were back from their rides. They joined the family for lunch. Somehow Bobby and Jeremiah found seats beside the young ladies.

Hiram and Della headed for home after lunch while Bobby and Jeremiah started putting a trail package together.

It was agreed that the two McTavish sons would take a week or so and make a round of the area ranches. That would give Hiram and Della time to get to Denver and return. Bobby and Jeremiah gave off an image of toughness and determination that Mac hoped they could dull a bit with Bobby's perpetual smile and careful talk.

Their goal was to see all the ranchers they could locate, leaving them with the message of new and changing times. Surveys, fences, range care, upgraded stock, phasing out of the longhorns. All this, and more, would be required if the country was to prosper into the future.

Mac watched them swing aboard their animals the next morning. Jimbo, mounted on a Bar-M gelding and with his own bedroll and supply cache tied behind his saddle, rode with them. "There's a lot riding on these visits, boys. Be careful of your words and don't make any threats. You can offer the Bar-M's help to the smaller ranchers if any ask. Do more listening than talking. We'll look for you back in about a week."

Bobby grinned at Jeremiah and Jimbo. "Must be an echo in this yard. I do believe we heard all that before somewhere."

Jeremiah touched the tip of his hat. "You take care here big brother. We'll be fine if'n we don't die from our own cooking and if this old reprobate riding beside us don't lead us astray and get us lost."

Jimbo snorted. "Lost? I ain't never been lost. Well, that's except that one time in a snow storm up in Montana but that don't hardly no way count. Why, let me tell you ..."

Bobby kicked his horse into a trot and waved at the gathering in the yard. Jimbo was still talking.

18

FEELING THE NEED TO MOVE around a bit and get off the chair that had been his prison for too long, Mac asked Pepe to harness a buggy horse. He and Margo, with Jerrod and the twins riding beside them drove to the farm, showing Cray the way. The two younger children were settled into a nest of blankets in the back of the buggy.

When they arrived, Hiram and Della were ready to get on the road. Mac was surprised to see the canvas top mounted on the wagon. "I thought you'd take the buggy, Pa. Why the wagon?"

A voice behind them said, "Because I gave them a shopping list, things we need to re-stock the store."

Before Mac or Margo could say anything or even fully turn around, Adam, still astride his horse, blurted out, "Hi, Gramps. Are you going to Denver too? I wish we could go. But Ma says we have to keep at our studies and Pa says we've got chores to do. Don't hardly seem fair."

Ad chuckled, "No, I have to get back to the store. That don't hardly seem fair either but there you have it. We'll go some other time and maybe you'll be able to go along."

Hiram walked Cray around the small holding, introducing him to the work that needed doing. The wagon was soon on the road. The rest of the family enjoyed a short visit with Ad. Before long, Cray was left alone, looking forward to the next few days of easy work and quiet times.

On the ride home Jerilyn rode up beside her father, "How come Grandpa and Grandma were so happy to be going all the way to the city Pa? Seems a long way for old people to be going."

Margo laughed. "Don't you let Grandpa or Grandma hear you calling them old."

Mac answered her question. "I think they mostly wanted to go for a visit. Do you remember that you have an aunt and uncle and three cousins in Denver?"

"I know that Pa."

"Well that aunt is my sister, same as you're Adam's and Jerrod's sister only she's not a twin. Grandpa and Grandma are her Mom and Dad same as they're my Mom and Dad. I have two sisters. One went back to Texas with her husband. We haven't seen them for a long time.

"Jonathon and Nancy live in Denver with the kids. Grandpa and Grandma get lonely for them, so besides doing a bit of work for the Bar-M and bringing some things back for the store, they'll have some time with family."

Jerilyn seemed to think on that for a few moments and then rode over towards Adam. She let out a blood curdling scream and slapped him on the back. "Counted coup on you." She kicked her horse into a tearing run with Adam chasing. They were both doing their imitation Ute war cries.

19

A FEW QUIET DAYS LATER Mac was prowling around the yard, examining the barn, checking out the garden and the corral, stomping through the cookhouse, lifting pot lids and scowling at the cook. He walked in the back door of the ranch house, paused to see what Margo was doing at the stove and left out the front door. She looked at him with a knowing smile. He stood on the veranda and again headed for the barn. Generally, he was doing little more than wearing out his boots and getting in the way.

Pepe watched for a while and then went and saddled Mac's favorite horse. He led the animal out of the barn and over to where Mac was standing, with one arm in the sling, the other hand on his hip, and a scowl on his face. Pepe simply held the reins out to Mac and walked away. Mac looked a question at Pepe and then turned his eyes to the animal. "I suppose it's time. Hold still you horse."

Firmly settled in the saddle, Mac adjusted his left arm in the sling he left hanging loose and unused more and more as the days went by. He turned the animal towards where the herd was held, and the new feeding pens were being built. Jerrod saw him from the veranda and hollered. "Hold up there, Pa."

Mac turned the horse and waited while the young man got his own riding animal. The two McTavish men rode side by side to where the feed pens were being built, neither feeling any need to talk. Mac took a couple of hours to thoroughly examine all the work being done and then sought out Taz.

"Taz, I'd like it if you would pull one of those plows out of the bottom lands for a couple of days. Have a fire guard plowed between all these hay stacks and for a wide swath outside the fence. Let's keep it black all summer. We'd be in serious trouble if we lost that hay to fire."

While Mac and Jerrod were watching the well drillers work, the drill crew let out a collective shout. Water was rising from the piped-in hole with every movement of the drill. It wasn't the first time this had happened. Finding water in the small valley where the stream flowed was proving to be a satisfying venture.

"Shut 'er down boys, we're at water. Shut 'er down and cap 'er off. Then move the rig to the next spot,"

The drill foreman, shouting over the clanking and grinding of the steam driven drilling machine, was all smiles.

The rarely smiling Mac looked over at Jerrod with his face lit up. "Without water the Bar-M, or any other cow outfit, is dead son. Looks like we might be alright down this end of the ranch at least. We'll need a sizable water supply if the feed pens are going to be workable. I'm hoping for some good wells out in the grasslands too. You'll remember that I've explained how walking miles for water or graze walks the beef off an animal. With the white-face animals, it's even more important that water be close by. Those long-legged longhorns can out-walk a Herford twice over and still keep a bit of meat on their bones. The Herford needs more care, but the results are worth it, come market time"

Jerrod nodded. "We'll find the water, Pa."

20

IT WAS TIME TO CHANGE the fencing and survey guards. At the evening dinner hour Taz named off the men that would be going. Early the next morning they set out. Mac and Jerrod were riding the wagon with all the provisions and bedrolls lumped in the back under the canvas cover. Jerrod was handling the team.

The guard riders were hazing a mature longhorn steer ahead of them. The animal would become beef for the camp crew. Mac and Jerrod's saddle animals were running free, pushed along by the riders.

Arriving at the fencing site, Jerrod directed the wagon to the corner post. Mac stepped down and eyed the fence from all directions. It was the first he had seen of the newly completed work. As the wire stringing was progressing Mac was chomping at the bit to get involved but was held back by his inability to ride that far. Just once he mentioned saddling up in spite of the still healing arm. A stern look from Margo that required no accompanying words put an end to that idea.

Mac nodded in pleasure at the sight of the long row of firmly embedded posts snaking over the low rise a quarter mile south.

Climbing back onto the wagon he said, "That's our future Jerrod. These strong posts and those wires you see shining in the sun are the future, along with the water the well drillers find.

"We're not doing it this year, but one day soon I hope to divide all this range into smaller sections. Let the animals graze off one section while the other grass rests and regrows. With good fencing we can do that with just a minimum of paid riders."

The two McTavish men were silent for a few minutes, studying the fence as the wagon rolled past. Mac then turned a bit towards his son. "Jerrod, you'll remember how often I've said God put us in a good land. It is a good land, a wonderfully good land. But it needs caring for. The cattle ain't about to do that themselves. It's us God gave the brains to. We have to watch. Watch and see what we're doing to the land and make adjustments from time to time. I'm afraid of what this land might become if we allow the grazing to continue as it has been."

The wagon rattled over the range while those thoughts continued to simmer in Mac's mind. Usually sparing of his words, Mac enjoyed talking to Jerrod. The young man listened without interruption and seemed to take it all in.

Mac looked forward to the next couple of years when Adam, and perhaps Jerilyn, would put some of their youthful rambunctiousness behind them and start to take more responsibility around the ranch. He doubted as how Margo would be able to hold Jerilyn to the kitchen for long although he knew she'd try.

So far, the best he'd been able to do with the twins on ranch work was to get them helping Pepe with shovel work and feeding the chickens. Margo marched them to the kitchen garden from time to time and passed each of them a weed hoe, but it was a struggle.

In addition to their other chores Mac had all three of the older children helping in the cookhouse, with clean-up, potato pealing and such.

Jerrod graduated from wood cutting and hauling to occasionally helping the cook. The cook seemed to enjoy teaching the young man.

Mac insisted, "Son, on a ranch you're not always going to be at the bunk house, come dinner time. Whether it's over an open fire on the range or in a line shack, you're going to want to know how to put a good meal together. You watch and listen to the cook. You'll never be sorry. You'll never be sorry if you learn how to help out around the house either, when you have your own wife and family."

The twins had been sawing and splitting stove wood for a couple of years, but the cook kept an eye on them. Given opportunity they would be a-saddle again and disappearing over the horizon.

Mac momentarily put the twins out of his mind and again spoke to Jerrod.

"Turning animals loose to roam at large has got to stop Jerrod. Overgrazing and uncontrolled breeding has to stop too. When we turn our white-face beef animals loose on this range in a couple of years, about the last thing we want is for them to be bred back to longhorns. The country has changed. It's still changing. The eastern market is demanding better beef. The ranchers that are able to supply that beef will be the ones that stay in business."

Typically, Jerrod was listening without comment.

The exchange riders followed behind as Jerrod directed the wagon along the strung wire. Mac admired the fencer's workmanship as the wagon rolled along. Again, he spoke to Jerrod, pointing off to the west, repeating information that Jerrod was well familiar with. "This west boundary is the hilliest and rockiest part of the Bar-M lands. Those up-thrusts have a good bit of grass hiding among the folds of jagged rock. But the hillsides are steep, and the grass is near impossible to get at for a beef animal.

"You'll remember when we asked that sheep man to ride out this way to take a look. He came back all excited about getting a herd of woollies working over these hillsides. He promised to find a good flock down in New Mexico that could be bought for a reasonable price. I've never done anything like it before, but I figured since I know nothing at all about sheep I'd give him authority to make a purchase. If he was successful we should have animals on these hills right quick now.

"The fence will skirt around some of the steeper portions, turning inland to outline what we've set aside as sheep range. Rather than fencing that difficult high-up land, the herding and control of the sheep will be done by the shepherds and their trained dogs.

"We'll put up some corrals for lambing and sheering and stockpile hay for winter feed when it becomes available a bit later this summer. We'll put up a few small cabins for the herders too, although I'm told they drag their sleeping wagons along with the moving flock."

Mac knew Jerrod had heard all this before. Mac also knew that the next ten years were going to show major changes in the family, and the Bar-M. He and Margo would be ready to slow down and turn some management decisions over to the kids. If Jerrod or the twins were to be ready for that responsibility it was his job to train them bit by bit as time went on. He hoped he was doing it well.

The fencing crew were several miles southward on the west boundary, with hundreds of posts supporting four strands of shining wire behind them, giving tribute to their work. The camp was moved twice as the wire was strung. Following the line of wire, Jerrod soon rolled the wagon to a stop at the camp site. The peaks of once-white canvas sleeping tents rose above the semi-desert growth.

The chuck wagon and the hoodlum wagon, holding all the required camp supplies were settled under one end of a large tent gone grey and tattered from much use and exposure to sun, wind and rain. A portable sheet iron cook stove, its chimney pointed out the side of the tent, and a work table sat behind the wagons. At the other end of the tent were the dining tables and benches for the crew.

Outside the tent a barrel of water stood beside a small bench holding a basin and dipper. Woe betide any worker who dared enter Hanna's kitchen without washing up first.

Several saddle horses and three heavy teams roamed free where the fence crew could keep an eye on their wanderings. Mac looked twice before he said, to no one in particular, "If I didn't know how unlikely it is out on the range I'd guess that's a milk cow over yonder. Never seen the like. Don't remember them trailing a milk cow when they were at the Bar-M."

Three wagons, with trailers connected in tandem, held posts hauled down the many miles from Denver. A wagon sagging under the weight of shiny coils of barb wire and kegs of staples stood close by the other wagons, all waiting until their loads were needed. The wagons made regular trips between Denver and the Bar-M. They stayed to the two-track trail, bypassing the Bar-M headquarters, only rarely coming to the ranch to fill water barrels.

The fence contractor mentioned cutting fence posts from the hills on the Bar-M, but Mac replied, "No Rocky, I think the land and the hillsides need those trees. They shed a lot of rain and the cattle like to shade up in them, those on the lower slopes anyway, come the heat of summer. And anyway, there aren't all that many trees and I like looking at them. We'll leave them right where they are."

Rocky insisted on a neat and orderly camp. Mac liked that and pointed it out to Jerrod. "Can't work in a mess Jerrod. Pays to take your time and do everything right the first go-around."

Jerrod made no comment. He'd heard that before too, many times. Mac knew all that but felt repetition was a solid way of teaching.

Although Mac met the two women when the fence crew first arrived at the Bar-M, the sight of them working at a ranch-land camp kitchen still made him shake his head.

Looking towards the fence line Mac could easily see that the guard riders were on high alert.

He stepped down from the wagon as Rocky Patterson approached. The two men shook hands. Mac pointed towards the top of a small rise where Chuck Mason, one of his riders, was staring off to the south, with his carbine at the ready.

"What's happening?"

"Heard a few rifle shots a short while ago. Faint. Must be at least a couple or three miles off, maybe more. Our hole diggers are about that far out, and the survey crew are further along than that. I doubt as how we'd hear any shots from as far away as the surveyors, so we're left guessing. But the boys are taking no chances."

Mac immediately called over to the riders that came with him. They gathered around.

"I'm sure you boys could use a cup of coffee. Take time for that if there's some ready. Then I'd like if you would ride ahead and see what that shooting is all about. Ride ready for trouble until you get the truth of those shots. I shouldn't have to tell you to be careful."

The six riders, four long term Bar-M men from Mex Town and two hired more recently gulped down their coffee. They were soon trotting their animals towards where Chuck sat his horse.

Rocky said, "You're probably ready for a coffee too. Come to the fire and say hello to my wife.

"Hanna, you'll remember Mac McTavish and his son Jerrod."

He gestured with his chin, "Hanna and Mable, wife to my foreman Punch McGrew. The last job we were on, up north a-ways, the ladies made up their minds that we were probably wasting away to shadows, longing for the taste of female cooking.

"They talked their way onto the last wagon coming out to the camp with a load of posts. I didn't have the heart to tell them we were managing pretty well, so we let them stay on. Now it seems we're stuck with them. Makes them feel useful I guess, although I already told them I can't afford no additional wages."

Mac glanced at Rocky in time to see him grin widely at his wife.

"Pshaw, you two get your coffee and get away from my kitchen. We have work to do."

Glancing at Jerrod she asked, "Have you taken up the coffee habit young man or can I get you something else?"

"I'd have a cup if you have some milk to soften it a bit Ma'am."

"Fresh every day son. I leave some aside to settle. Skim the heavy cream myself. In the jug sittin right there on that tailgate. It's thick enough you'll need that spoon to dip it with. You help yourself."

Walking away from the cook tent with Rocky, Mac said, "I saw the milk cow back yonder. I don't remember such as that when you were at the Bar-M."

Rocky chuckled a bit. "That's the women's idea. It wasn't with the first wagons. The wife gave orders to one of the drivers. Didn't bother mentioning it to me. Towed it all the way down here behind a post wagon. I didn't even ask where they got it from. The least said the better I figure, less'n I end up milking the thing my own self."

Mac and Jerrod walked along the fence line with Rocky while the fence contractor explained each step in the process. "We put in a gate about every two miles, as you asked Mac."

The McTavish men listened to every word in silence.

A short way from camp Mac stopped, looking outside the fence where a pole A-frame was set up, far enough from the camp site to hold the odors of butchered animals from invading the kitchen area. The camp cook was dressing out a deer. The unhappy man gave Rocky a grim look and went back to his work.

Rocky hunched his shoulders and nodded towards the cook. "Cookies not the least bit impressed with having women in his kitchen. I'm hoping war don't break out."

When he reached the wagon with the rolls of wire spindling off the rear they stood and watched the men work. Mac gave a slight shake of his head. "Hard work, Rocky. Hard work. We built just a bit of fence along one border. You'll run into it a-ways up ahead. We weren't set up like you boys are and we made tough work out of it. We got it done but the work didn't appeal to me or my crew."

He looked further down the line to where the men were scooping out post holes. He shook his head again. "Hard work."

Within an hour the guard crew sent Tyler McCoy back to report. He rode up to Mac and Rocky. "Couple of rough looking boys was all set to cause a ruction with the forward post hole diggers. Must be new to these parts. Never saw them at roundup. The shots you heard were from the guards driving them off. They didn't put up a fight or stick around long. We figure they meant to cause a diversion here while some others were creating mischief with the surveyors."

Mac asked, "Where are our riders now?"

"A couple stayed here with the fence guards but most rode south to find the surveyors."

Mac said, "Ride along and see what's up. If it's all settled out send the returning crew here. We don't want to be too late starting back."

Rocky excused himself and returned to his work.

Mac and Jerrod left the wagon at the camp site and swung into their saddles. They hung around the fencing crew, watching every step of the work. They then rode forward, past the last string of wire and pointed their horses into the higher-up portions of the neighboring range, riding around a few pinion trees and further up, until they were lost to view in the pines that graced the upper hillside. They stopped and looked around. Jerrod asked, "Is this Uncle Bill's land?"

"Just the leading edge of his U.T.E. And a nice piece of land it is. Rougher and wilder than most of the Bar-M. Suits Bill and Little Flower and their Ute family better than the grass-flats."

They let their horses amble forward another hundred yards before Mac spoke again. "What do you notice up here Jerrod?"

The young man was slow to answer. "Pretty country Pa. but not much graze. The grass grows a bit around those spread-out pinions but the pines pretty much shade out the growth."

"That's a good observation son. There's not enough graze to be bothered with. Bill knows that and keeps his animals on the other side of this rise. But the trees shed the rain and hold the soil on these hillsides. Anyway, as you said, it's pretty country. A body needs something pretty to gaze at once in a while. Let's ride a bit higher, see if we can find a clearing. Maybe see the further-out fence crew."

Jerrod was thinking his own thoughts. A young man living on an isolated ranch, dreaming about the day boyhood would be put behind him couldn't be expected to know the ways of the world. He gathered his information in whatever ways were offered. "It's good to have Bobby and Jeremiah home Pa. I've missed them. Do you think they'll stay?"

"Hard to know son. I don't fully understand their ways. Like tumbleweeds sometimes. I expect they'll do whatever they want to do."

"It's kind of like you find this land to be pretty Pa. The boys say they're wandering around the country looking for pretty girls to marry. I figure that's not the whole entire truth."

Mac chuckled and looked at his son. "You figure that about as well as it can be figured. Still, it's a fine thing to find a pretty girl. But some of the best girls aren't always the pretty ones. A man has to be careful. It's no small thing to bring a girl to live on a ranch. Ranching life is not for everyone, man or woman. Pretty is good, but faithful and loving is more important. Someone who will stick with it."

Both men were quiet for a while as they looked over the country from the clearing they'd ridden into. Mac hesitated, planning out his words carefully. Finally, he spoke. "You're coming of age Jerrod. Are you having thoughts about pretty girls yourself? Mighty isolated out here on the Bar-M. Not many folks to meet or get to know."

Jerrod was as slow in answering as his father had been in asking. "Sometimes I think ahead I guess, Pa." He was careful not to mention Rebecca, the young daughter of a farmer from up along the Arkansas. The farm family was making the long trip down to Grandpa Hiram's church services for the past while. The young people hadn't spoken more than a few words together, but every time Jerrod looked over at Rebecca she seemed to be looking his way.

Father and son looked at each other. A small grin showed itself on Jerrod's lips. Mac slapped him lightly on the shoulder. "Let's ride back. Next time we see Bill we can tell him we rode some on his hillside."

21

MAC AND ROCKY WERE TALKING when the report came back from the guards that there was no real threat. The men had ridden down to find the survey crew working without interruption. Three or four warning shots and a show of strength from Shep and a couple of Bar-M men ended the encroachment of a few riders.

With that settled Mac decided to make a long day of it by turning the wagon towards home, feeling that the guard crew could handle the job. He sent word out to the men who would be riding back to the Bar-M. They rode up well after lunch was over and the dishes done.

Mac thought of the headquarters cook when the women showed no concern about preparing a late feed for the men. "Would have heard nothing but clanking pots and grumbling, back home."

While the men were eating, Mac and Jerrod harnessed the wagon team. Jerrod took up the reins as the returning crew threw their bedrolls under the canvas cover and mounted up.

The sky was beginning to cloud over. The men hunched their shoulders as a scattering of dust whorls, blown by an unpredictable wind was threatening to lift their hats and drive a cloud of dust into the tented kitchen.

The loose animals all turned their backs to the wind and continued grazing, their flying tails acting like flags, pointing out the direction of the big blow.

Mac, having a few final words with the fence contractor, stood from his squatting position, turning so he could see the western sky. "If that ain't a soaker coming Rocky, I never seen one. I think before this day is done y'all will be happy for those tents." He called over to Tyler McCoy. "Tyler, I expect you boys are going to get some use from your slickers. Be just like some of those angry ranchers to use the cover of a storm to do mischief. I'm going to have to ask you to stay as dry as you can but keep up the guard no matter what. If it comes to lightening don't be caught on top of your riding animal. You can keep guard from the shelter of a rock overhang or some such if there's one handy."

Rocky spoke up. "You tell the boys to stay away from the wire too. Lightening loves that stuff. It don't do no harm. The charge goes right to ground down a wet post unless there happens to be some brave soul foolish enough to take a grip on it."

Tyler swung aboard his horse. "I'll get the news out boss."

Mac turned to Jerrod. "What say you and I see how many dry miles we get behind us before we need our slickers?"

They were half way home before the storm hit. The wind that was swirling unpredictably straightened itself out and blew steady from the west, driving a leading edge of dark grey clouds followed by a roiling and tossing blanket of almost solid black. Mac was handling the reins. Jerrod stood and turned on the seat to look behind him. "You gotta see this Pa."

Mac swung around and stared, leaning past the bow of the canvas supports. The western sky was black as night. The leading grey edge of the storm clouds was pushed high over the valley while the following storm enveloped the Sangre de Christo peaks in a smear of densest black. Along the bottom edge of the clouds, partially lit by the waning sunlight, was draped a ragged beard of spouts. A solid sheet of advancing rain hid everything behind it. "You're right son, that's a storm to see. It hasn't been hot enough for hail and anyway, the winds aren't right for hail, so I expect it's only rain, but that's a sure enough cloudburst waiting to happen."

The words were no sooner out of Mac's mouth when the grey clouds were parted with a violent streak of lightening, followed by an almost continual display. About five seconds after the first lightening, all sound was blanketed out by the crash of thunder. Although the lightening was several miles away the riding animals shuddered and several of them took a series of hopping steps sideways. Mac and Jerrod's animals, tied to the back of the wagon, shrieked in fear and tugged on their lead ropes. The team, both older animals, plodded along unaffected by the display of heavenly power.

Like the lightening, the thunder continued almost non-stop, some sounding close by but most further out.

Mac pulled the wagon to a halt while Jerrod climbed into the back, digging his own and Mack's slickers out of their rolled bedrolls. The cowboys jumped out of their saddles and rushed to the wagon, where all their belongings were stacked. Soon they were mounted again, each rider buttoning up a waxed or oiled canvas slicker and with their hats tied down tight. The rain was still a mile or two away but coming their way fast. Before the rain reached them, the sky was again blasted apart with several great flashes of lightening.

Mac found a level spot and pulled the wagon to a halt. "Get under the wagon son." Jerrod moved immediately, knowing this was not the time for a discussion. Mac waved the men to the wagon, shouting over the cacophony of sounds. "Hobble those animals and get under the wagon. Quickly now." With that he turned to the wagon team. He soon had the trace chains separated from the doubletree, the wagon tongue dropped to the ground and the docile team tied securely to the side of the wagon.

While he was doing that a couple of the cowboys hobbled Mac's and Jerrod's riding animals, untying them from the wagon. They all dove under the wooden wagon seconds before the storm hit. The first close-by lightening strike was terrifying in its intensity, with the following thunder blotting out any spoken words. After ten minutes of lightening and thunder the leading edge of the storm passed over them, heading off to the east. Then came the rain. Torrents of rain. Not sure about the lightening, the men stayed under the wagon for another half hour.

Mac was the first to impatiently crawl into the open. The rest of the men followed quickly, knowing the action was going to expose them to the downpour, probably for the rest of the trip home. They weren't worried about a bit of wetness, but the lightening was nothing to fool with.

One of the men turned to look for his horse and saw it lying on the ground a short distance away. "Well dang me. I didn't see nor hear anything. But judging by that big burn streak down that horse's neck and shoulder I'm guessing that animal didn't die of old age. Never saw the like."

Mac looked up from where he was untying the team from the wagon box. There was no time for worrying about the loss of one animal, no matter how much it hurt Mac to think about it. "Loose your rig from the downer and lay it on my big black. The coyotes will take care of your gelding. Let's get a move on."

The only words spoken between Mac and his son on the remainder of the trip were, "We surely can use all the rain God sends us son but if He was taking orders to be filled I'd have asked for a bit smaller dump and mayhap a little more next week. The grass will love it though, whatever part doesn't get washed away in some newly forming gully."

Mac passed the reins to Jerrod and slipped his arm into the sling that hung unused more and more as the days passed. This wagon trip was the first real test of Mac's healing.

It was a tired, wet, bedraggled crew that rode into the ranch yard in the unnatural darkness of late afternoon. The rain was unrelenting, first falling in great sheets and then slowing to a simple downpour and then roiling back to sheets again. The lightening moved off to the east, driven by a wind that held the rain to a slanting angle and caused the men to tug their coat collars even higher. The horses were put in the small barn and given a rubdown and a pail of oats before being turned into the corral. The harness team was rubbed down and left stalled in the barn.

Except for the men needed to care for the herd, the work crew made its way back to the yard. The local farmers who were contracting the plowing and seeding job left for home, each riding one big draft horse and leading the rest of their team. They would be back when the land dried enough to welcome the plow again.

The well drillers brought their animals to the ranch yard and turned them into one of the large corrals.

The men whipped as much rain off their hats and clothing as they could, stomped the mud from their boots and moved towards the cookshack.

Jerrod wiped down his riding animal and was helping his dad with the team when Pepe, finished with the animals he was tending, came to relieve the two sodden riders. The young man then went to the house with his soaked bedroll slung over his shoulder and his father's bedroll tucked under his left arm. His mother was watching from under the veranda roof, with a big towel in her hand.

Although he was soaked through, from his Stetson to his boots, Mac went to the cookhouse wishing for hot coffee and a rundown on the day's work from Taz.

Stepping through the door he stopped dead in his tracks when he heard female laughter coming from the kitchen. Taz noticed and strolled over. "That's your big city lady guests. They saw this wet tribe of men gathering in the yard and figured the cook might need a hand. Either that or they were simply acting bored on a rainy afternoon and Margo put the run on them.

I wouldn't exactly say that Cookie invited them or welcomed them. It's mostly that they simply marched into the kitchen and put on aprons. Cookie became tongue tied like he didn't know how to speak, much less know what to say. Howsomever, I'd have to admit the ladies pitched right in like they knew what they were about and pretty soon Cookie quit banging pots around and slamming doors, so I guess all is well.

"The men seem happy to have the ladies here and I must say, the language around the coffee pot has improved considerably."

Mac seemed to consider this and then brushed the whole thing off, There were more important things on his mind.

The cookhouse and bunkhouse were overflowing with men drinking coffee and visiting, waiting for their clothing to dry out. Where the men gathered there was a rank odor of horse, mud, unwashed bodies, soiled clothing and manure-soaked boots. Mac reckoned the big kitchen stove might see heavy use with the heating of bath and laundry water.

He ducked out the door and headed for the house, figuring he could talk with Taz a bit later. No one was about to go anywhere so there was no hurry.

Mac kicked off his boots and went to the kitchen for coffee. He carefully carried the full mug through the house and settled into a rocking chair on the veranda. Margo joined him a few minutes later. "I'm thinking you'd best get out of those wet, filthy clothes before you catch your death. You can have a hot bath just as soon as Jerrod's done with the tub."

22

THE NEW DAY FOUND the rain still sheeting its way across the ranch yard. Before noon, after a night at the Bar-M line cabin, the survey contractor's wagon rolled into the yard, followed by the three thoroughly drenched Bar-M guard riders.

The chuck wagon, with the teamsters gelding trailing along behind was dragging along behind the hoodlum wagon. The surveyors huddled under the flapping canvas wagon top. Shep Trimble, exposed to the weather, held the reins in his cold hands. His sopping and sagging hat tipped rain off the brim with every move of his head.

The Texan spotted Mac standing under the cookhouse overhang. Pulling the rig to a stop in front of the covered gallery and pushing his hat off his forehead he called out, "Suppose you've still got a mite of space to shelter these here delicate townies I saved from the storm? Perhaps we could lay out a feather quilt in the loft and I could sing them a lullaby, come bed time." The soaked and chilled teamster never seemed to stop grinning.

The men gathered beside Mac burst out laughing. The surveyors climbed out of the wagon and moved quickly towards shelter. Lod Anderson looked at Mac. "Forget the feather quilt, boss. I'll take to any place at all to get away from the foolish jabbering we've saddled ourselves with. Time or two I've wished I carried a peacemaker. Not sure what I wished for more though; shooting that big mouthed Texan seemed like the thing to do and then I got to thinking about shooting myself. Anything at all to get a moment of quiet".

When the gathering saw him with the slight smile of his face they all burst out laughing again.

Pepe appeared like magic. He nodded at Shep. Both men had considerable rain running off the brims of their hats. "Bring the rig to the barn Senor, I will help with the animals."

Mac made his way to the house. He pulled off his muddy boots on the veranda and opened the door. The welcoming odor of baking bread met him as he walked in. He hung up his slicker and walked to the kitchen. Backing up to the welcome warmth of the big cast iron stove he watched as Margo helped Jerilyn shape a small wad of bread dough into a bun, ready to join the ones that were already placed in the greased pan, ready for baking.

He stood for a moment smiling at his little girl, with an apron tugged tightly around her and a smudge of flour dusting her nose and cheek. "Is that the way the Ute make buns?"

"Daddy, you're just being silly. Ute don't make buns."

Mac looked at his wife seeking guidance. Getting none, he finally asked, "Why don't the Ute make buns? They certainly eat them by the tub full when they're available."

"Daddy, they can't because they don't know how. I'm thinking I may have to show them how when I'm bigger."

Overcome with this logic, Mac turned to the stove and filled a cup with coffee. He returned to the veranda, settling himself in his rocking chair away from the rain and the noise of the cookhouse.

Margo joined him with her own coffee. "No sign of the boys returning? They've been gone about long enough."

Mac shook his head. "Nothing yet."

23

EARLY THE NEXT MORNING, bathed, dried off and dressed in clean clothing, Shep pointed the covered wagon out of the ranch yard towards Ad's Trading Post. It was time to replenish the stock of supplies that would keep the survey crew fed and working for another two weeks. Now that the surveying gear and bedrolls were stored in the bunkhouse, the teamster had space to rig a seat in the back of the wagon. The canvas top sheltered him from the worst of the still-driving rain.

The well-drilling crew were sending a wagon to Ad's that morning as well. Their cook and a few of the crew toughed out the storm in their tents.

The trip to Ad's was normally a two-hour junket by wagon but with the road wet and soft with rain the going was slow. Slowing the trip even more, the Texan swung off the two-track trail and drove the short distance into Mex town. There he purchased a large supply of corn flour tortillas, carefully wrapped in brown paper and stored in a flour sack. One garrulous visit with the friendly Mexicans led to another, with a lot of poor Spanish being spoken by Shep, along with a lot of laughing and back slapping. Before he got back on the road an hour had snuck by.

He finally pulled the covered wagon past the front door of Ad's store and turned into the side yard where there was a roof overhang offering a bit of shelter for the team.

Mrs. Adkins watched him roll in and said over her shoulder, "Clara, you should probably go hide in the wood shed. That grinning Texan is here again."

"Oh, Mother, be nice!" was all the exasperated young lady could say. Was that a bit of excitement she felt or was it dread?

Ad looked at his two women, wondering again about raising his daughter this far from a bigger town. He could plainly see the feelings the Texan was arousing in each of them; fear of something she couldn't control in his wife, and a bit of interest in his daughter.

The swinging door struck the little brass bell that announced the arrival of a customer. The wind blew in a mist of rain as the door swung open. Mrs. Adkins turned towards the door, feigning surprise, and said "Why, Mr. Trimble, isn't it? Are you needing more supplies? And on such a miserable day too. It seems just a short while ago you were in to stock up."

"Dug a hole and buried the most of that load, Pretty Lady's mother. No other way to shorten the waiting time before I could visit again." His smile was disarming but Amelia Adkins, sensing trouble, thought she'd seen about enough of it. She looked forward to the day the survey would be completed, and the young Texan would ride away, never to be seen again.

Glancing towards the serving counter Shep said, "How-do Mr. Adkins. Good to see y'all looking well. And you too Clara. Of course, I can't picture you looking any other way, Pretty Lady." There was that grin again. Mrs. Adkins had to look away.

Shep strolled over to where Clara was straightening out a stack of shirts that were plowed through by a farmer earlier that morning.

"Good morning Clara. I've been looking forward to seeing you again." There was no privacy in the small trading post, so he ignored the parents and lavished all his attention on the young lady standing before him. He fumbled in his pocket for the list of supplies he needed. "Thought perhaps you could help me find these items."

The lonely young lady took the list from his hand. "Why don't you sit by the stove and warm up while I fill this. Dad was just saying he was ready for coffee. He'll probably bring you a cup and join you."

Ad looked up from his work, surprised to hear that he was ready for another coffee. He just finished one minutes before. But being a man of some wisdom, he moved to the kitchen for the coffee pot and some clean cups.

Clara placed a ten-pound bag of white beans on the counter and reached for another of black beans. While she was mulling over the harsh diet the men were living off, two bags of Pinto beans followed. As she was reaching for the next item she turned Shep's way. "Perhaps you would stay for lunch Mr. Trimble. We're planning on stopping in a half hour or so." She ignored her mother's troubled glance.

Ad arrived with the coffee and took a chair beside the stove. Shep accepted the warm drink with thanks and answered Clara. "I'd be delighted to have lunch with y'all if it's not too much trouble. Thanks for the invite."

The brass door chime tinkled again. The door swung open as another gust of wind blew rain into the room. A worker from the well crew came in. Ad called out, "Welcome. I didn't hear you drive up."

"Tied the team off under that patch of trees out back. Gives the animals a bit of shelter. Need some things."

Mrs. Adkins approached. "I'll take your list if you have one. Or else you can just tell me what you need."

The man lifted his wet hat. "TJ Marpole, Ma'am. With the well crew over to the Bar-M. I'm told ya can charge the account ta the ranch." He held out a crumpled paper.

"Have a seat with the other men and I'll sort this list out for you. It'll just take a few minutes." As Ad was normally busy in his smithy it was really the women who ran the trading post.

TJ Marpole said, "Thank ya Ma'am." He turned and took a step towards the stove. He stopped suddenly, swatted his leg with his wet hat and stared. "Yow'zee, as I live and breathe. If'n that ain't ol Shep Trimble hisself, a-settin there, I'm a doggie calf. What are ya'll doin out here just a settin there like ya've got not a thing in the world to do on a rainy day? News back ta home was that ya were up Montana way, but I see they missed their guess by a mile er two." He thrust his hand towards the young Texan and the two men shared a strong hand shake.

Shep said simply, "Howdy, TJ. Ain't seen you in a while."

Ad glanced between the two men and then spoke to TJ. "I take it you two know each other."

TJ brushed his unruly black hair down and put his wet hat back on his head. "I should smile. Know'd each other since ary a one of us was knee high. Taught him how to ride, I did. And a tough job he made of it. Once we come of age, which happens early in life, down in the panhandle, don't ya know, we 'uns rode many a mile together over yonder on the Double-T, me doin all the work whilst this lazy galoot practiced looking pretty a-settin on his horse."

Shep laughed and glanced at Clara who was taking in the verbal exchange. "Well, now, that ain't just the whole entire truth. Fact is, I was riding the tough ones when this ol' boy was still scampering around the dusty yard riding a broom handle. When he finally got the hang of it I rode along just to see that this make-believe cowboy didn't fall off his horse or find himself a soft piece of ground to lay out on, whilst taking another nap."

TJ grinned at Ad. "Don't y'all be a-listenin to nary a word this ol' boy says. Next thing he'll be a-telling you he's a fer-real cowboy. Dang me if this Texan cain't tell a story."

The joshing went back and forth, with Ad putting in a word from time to time, all three men laughing and comforted by rare fellowship.

Amelia Adkins called over to the men. "Your order is ready Mr. Marpole. Perhaps you want to pull the wagon close to the door and Mr. Adkins will help you load it."

Clara said, "I think that venison stew is big enough for all of us mother. Perhaps Mr. Marpole would like to join us as well." She was eager for answers to some pointed questions that were rolling around in her mind.

The storm and the camping supplies were forgotten while the five adults found their places around the dinner table. Ad gave a word of thanks. With the stew and baked bread dished up Ad turned to TJ. "Mr. Marpole, you say you two men have worked and ridden together. Where was that. What were the circumstances?"

Amelia Adkins held her fork steady, giving her full attention to the answer, anxious to find some flaw in the smiling Texan. Clara kept eating but was intent on every word, hoping that sought for flaw didn't show up.

"Why, I've known Ol' Shep pretty near my whole entire life. You have ta understand that Shep ain't his real name, but he'll throw an awful conniption-fit should I lay ary other handle on him.

"I grew up on a hard-scrabble ranch just a few miles from the Double-T. Pa, he worked hard and all, but somehow it jist didn't come together fer him. Still, he sent me and my three sisters ta school reg'lar. Went ta school nigh onto six years, I did. Shep he stayed in school near twice as long. Pa needed me on the ranch. The Double-T's got themselves thirty or more riders so Shep weren't hardly needed at all. Not that he was of much help even when he was there.

"The Double-T kids mostly stayed ta school. A couple a' the older ones went off to some big eastern university. Never did figure out why. 'Cain't learn much about ranchin at those big-ol schools. The both of them came home ta the ranch, bye'n'bye, one girl a-draggin a husband along with her. She ain't the prettiest girl around. Course you can see she wouldn't be by the looks of this here story telling Texan a-settin beside me. Anyway, she dragged that misbegotten easterner all the way acrost the country and settled him down on the Double-T. Happy to find any kind a' man I suppose. Everyone pretty much jest calls him the Tennessee cowboy. Be a while afore he does much cowboy'n. Pains a man just a-lookin at the way he's a-settin a horse."

Mrs. Adkins broke into the conversation. "What has this Double-T got to do with Mr. Trimble?"

TJ looked troubled at the question. "Why, that's where he was brung up. I jedged ya already knowed that. Him and a passel o' other young-uns."

"Are you suggesting that Mr. Trimble's family own this Double-T?"

"Ain't suggent'n nothin at all. Flat out sayin. Old Boss Trimble, him that's Shep's pa, well, him and his brother, Wyett Trimble, they drove a herd into the Panhandle a-pushin Injuns 'n homesteaders out 'n the way as they come along. Come ta join their pa who was holding down a little chunk of land in a poor-bilt bachelor shack. That was a while back, ya understand. Don't rightly know the truth of all that but howsomever, there they are ta this day, only Wyett, he's dead and buried.

"The story on that is that one of them there Injuns, well he didn't take all thet kindly ta the pushin. Come back, he did, and put a arrer through ol' Wyett's ribs."

The storyteller paused, smiled, looked at the table and shook his head with a small chuckle. "Musta been quite a sight, ol Wyett a-jogging inta the ranch yard, a-holler'n fer help, that there arrer a-bounc'n and a-floppin with every step his horse took."

With another pause and another head shake he continued. "Might be jest as well there come ta be only the one Trimble the way thet old boy took ta fill'n up the country with young'uns. The two brothers together, why they mighta took over the whole entire panhandle."

He smiled and shook his head again. "Anyway, Boss Trimble, he stuck ta the land. Raised him a yard full a' young'uns and a lot a longhorns, with Wyett a-rest'n in his grave.

Clara turned to her mother. "Mother, I do believe Mr. Trimble told us about the Double-T when we first met him." It was not easy for her to hide the small smile.

The two waggoneers were soon loaded, and on their way back to the Bar-M. The rain had slowed to a drizzle and there was a hint of sunshine over the Sangre de Christo's.

Shep and TJ rolled the wagons into the yard and pulled to a stop in front of the cookhouse. They stepped down and went in for coffee, hoping to find a piece of pie left from lunch. Stepping back outside with the coffee but no pie they stood talking on the porch. The rattling wagons put a stop to any visiting on the way back to the ranch.

TJ grinned at Shep. "That there tradin post gal's real sweet on ya. If'n ya want ta stay a free man I'm a-think'n ya needs ta collect your time right this here very day and point yer ride towards Montana. Course, she's a purty enough lady. Might be a pleasant thing, a-comm'n home to find her lay'n out yer dinner fer ya." He slapped Shep on the shoulder, spilling his coffee.

Shep chose to not pursue the subject. "How were the folks doing when you last saw them?"

"Doin fine but they're a wonderin after ya. Near wore out a saddle horse sendin the yard man to town a-lookin fer mail from ya."

Shep scuffed his foot on the porch floor. "I guess it's been a while since I wrote. I'll put something down this afternoon and the ranch can get it over to Ad's. The mail should get it to Texas bye and bye."

24

WHILE THE TWO WAGONS were stocking up at Ad's, on the Bar-M ranch house veranda the rocking chairs and the chairs around the table were all filled. Bobby, Jeremiah and Jimbo were back from their visit to the other ranches.

Margo was silent, but missed nothing, as the riders told their story. When there seemed to be nothing more to say she waited for Mac to speak. When that didn't happen, she looked intently at the story tellers. "So, you're saying that Baxter and his followers are still intent on pushing for Bar-M grass, no matter what?

Bobby answered, "Not just saying. Doing. As we already told you, there's Baxter beef on the Bar-M right now. Baxter and Cox and three, four others. A sizable herd. We're guessing over a thousand head and I'm not sure we saw them all. Baxter's X-O only joins up against the Bar-M for a couple of miles so at first, we thought keeping his herd out wouldn't be a big problem.

"But Fillinger and his Lazy-H are holding to their claim on your south border, He's siding Baxter too, while he eyes up your open plains. So that makes it easy for that bunch to slip their animals onto your grass, claiming it's open grazing country. Jenkins, hard on your south-west line is shouting the same story.

"Baxter has a half-dozen ranchers siding him, and he seems to be preparing to do battle. Both Baxter and Cox have more riders signed on than either one needs for herding animals. When we rode up to the X-O all those riders were just lounging around in the middle of the day. Ain't like a working cowboy to be sittin on the porch when there's work to be done. I don't guess they're there to punch cows. I figure Baxter wanted us to see them."

Mac lifted his head and looked at his brothers. "You saying they've been hiring fighters?"

Jimbo sat silently through the story telling. Now, reverting to the solutions pressed into service a generation earlier he said, "I figure it's time to saunter on down there and slit a few throats, put an end to this thing. Some men just can't seem to learn. Baxter ain't even listening, let alone thinking. He needs to be under the ground."

The group was silent while they soaked in that bit of wisdom, wisdom that was reminiscent of Ma McTavish's solution.

Mac took a long look at Jimbo and then glanced around the table. "That would be easy enough to do Jimbo but all the cows in the country aren't worth a human life. I've been trying to find another way." He fell into silence again.

Mac finally came to a decision. "I need to thank you boys for making that long ride. Seems it might have been for nothing since Baxter wouldn't listen. But you learned what they're up to so that might help us plan. I've been thinking Baxter is the ringleader. If he was gone the others might give it up. Did you see anything that would make me think differently?"

Jeremiah answered. "We talked with them all. There's no doubt it's Baxter. The others are following because they're desperate. Scared and desperate. They know they have too many animals and until this rain their grass hasn't been growing. Even the growth the rain brings on now will be too little and too slow to solve their problems.

"Just exactly why they won't reduce their herds is a mystery to me. Stubborn or stupid I guess. We suggested to several that having the sale money in their pockets would hold them in a good position for upgrading their stock. They simply weren't listening.

"As long as they have Baxter stirring the pot and shouting about unfairness, I figure they'll just follow along. Of course, they're also thinking that reducing their herds will just be an invite for others to push animals onto their grass and nothing will be gained."

Mac took another long time before he spoke again. "The rain's letting up. We'll take the buggy over to the farm in the morning in time for church service. The folks should be back by now. They may have news from the Federal Marshall. We'll make no decisions until we talk with them. Thanks again for taking that ride. Why don't you three get yourselves some food and rest. You might want to see if those lady visitors will put on a pot of bath water for you too."

The two brothers both sat up straighter. Bobby looked at his older brother. "Ladies? In the kitchen? I assumed they'd gone back to Denver when I didn't see them. What are they doing in the kitchen?"

Margo laughed at the looks on the boys faces. "They're still here. Haven't even mentioned leaving. When all the workers crowded in here, escaping the rain, the girls went and pretty much took over the cookhouse, thinking the crowd was too much for one cook. So far, the cook is tolerating them. I'm sure the girls will be happy to see you, but Mac is correct. Y'all need to take a bath before you try sweet-talking them."

25

THE TWO-HOUR RIDE to the farm and the morning service was pleasant in the warming sun. The storm pretty much rained itself out, moving off to the east to dump whatever moisture remained, on the flat prairie grasslands. Mac and Margo again nestled their two little ones in the back of the buggy, comforted with a pile of blankets. Jerrod stationed himself close to his father, keeping pace with the buggy, on his roan gelding. The twins rode a short way ahead. Mac insisted on a quiet ride on a Sunday morning. The twins were given a choice; ride quietly or ride in the buggy. Turning up their noses at the buggy, their decision was quickly made. A large group of riders followed along, led by Bobby and Jeremiah. Shep and a scattering of cowboys brought up the rear, riding guard over the farm wagon carrying the two eastern ladies. The ladies packed a big lunch from the cookhouse.

Jimbo had been riding Bar-M stock as he rested ol Ap, but for the ride to church he saddled his faithful gelding, freshly fed and groomed after his long stint in the horse pasture.

Hiram and Della, just one day home from Denver, waited to greet the family. The trip would be talked about over lunch. It was time for church. Hiram smiled and waved at the large crowd arriving from the Bar-M and then stepped outside the brush shelter to greet Ad, Amelia and Clara. Several farm families from up around the Arkansas River rode the long miles down and were already taking their seats. Amelia looked around for Bill and Little Flower. They didn't make it to every service, but they came as often as their growing family and ranch responsibilities allowed. There was no sign of them this morning.

Hiram stepped to the front of the gathering. "Good morning folks. It's great to be together again. I understand you had quite a storm while we were off to the big city. Well, we can always use the rain and we thank God for it.

"But there are other kinds of storms too. All the storms we're faced with don't lay lightening, thunder and rain on us. Some of the worst storms are in our hearts, troubling our very souls. Some think they can get by in life without God but when those heart-storms hit us we need a shelter. Matthew 23:37 tells us that Jesus wishes to gather us under His wings like a hen does to her chicks and give us comfort.

"I think Mrs. Henderson has a song or two picked out for us, along that line. While we're singing His praises think about His everlasting arms of comfort."

Mrs. Henderson, a farmer's wife from north a way, stepped to the front. With no one to play an instrument the singing was done with voices only. "Let's start this morning with a fairly new hymn, 'Leaning on the Everlasting Arms'. The words are easy. Listen and sing along. We'll soon all have it memorized."

Following the church gathering the visiting started. The men collected firewood before the service. While the singing and preaching was progressing, two large coffee pots hung on wire bales from a metal rod suspended over the flames. Over the years a collection of crude benches and tables had been placed haphazardly around the yard.

A couple of farm families pointed their wagons for home, with daily chores calling them. The ones with lunches brought from home found a place at one of the tables. The cowboys squatted on their haunches or sat with their backs propped against a tree while they ate. Cray Dobbs, freed from his farm responsibilities now that Hiram and Della were home, joined the cowboys. There was much laughing and talking while the lunches were unpacked and shared among the group.

Ad and Amelia took a seat beside Mac and Margo and across from Hiram and Della. They purposely chose a table away from the larger crowd. Their talk would be centered around the Denver trip and Hiram's discussion with the Federal Marshal.

Shep was seeing to the needs of his horse when Clara approached. "I have enough lunch for two Mr. Trimble, if you would care to share it with me."

"I'd love to share it with you Pretty Lady, but you'll have to call me Shep. Else I won't know who your talking to." His smile was as radiant as Clara had ever seen it.

The kids grabbed some lunch and then went running for the double swing Hiram erected in the yard. A couple of the boys were throwing a ball between them. Mac and the older generation sat around the table sharing lunch, ready to hear Hiram's report on the Denver trip. Jerrod, quickly coming of age, was allowed to join the adults.

Before Hiram got a chance to speak, Della told all about their days with Nancy and her family. Mac, usually a patient and family-oriented man, squirmed restlessly while his mother held the floor.

Finally, the subject moved to the Federal Marshall and his response to the gathering problems in the valley. When Hiram was finished telling about his meeting with the Marshall, everyone leaned back and was silent, each thinking their own thoughts.

Mac folded his arms on the table and hung his head, trying to think it all through before he spoke. "So, Dad, you're telling us that the Marshall will do nothing? Have I got that right?"

"He says there's been no law broken yet so far as he could see, and he can't send a man all the way down here because something might happen. He says that something might happen just about anywhere. Who's to know? He can't be everywhere at once just because someone is unhappy."

Bobby looked at his father. "So, we're on our own! Might just as well face it and do what has to be done."

Hiram, always a godly man and a man of peace wherever possible looked at his three sons. "Unfortunately, I don't see any other way. Wish I could."

Jeremiah, needing a bit more assurance from his father asked, "Pa, this might well mean gun business. Not that any of us want that. Are you alright with what might come to pass?"

Hiram shook his head and answered slowly, choosing his words with care. "No, I'm not alright. But we live in a sinful world and sometimes a man must take a stand. I wasn't alright when your brother put on a grey uniform and took up a rifle either. But he did what had to be done by the knowledge of the day.

"Our knowledge today is that there are a few men who wish to crowd others off the range, or not acknowledge the rights of others. That can't be allowed to happen. I know you boys won't do anything to shame yourselves or the name of the Lord. I trust in your judgement."

Della took her pipe out of her mouth and pointed the stem at her three boys. "You were brought up to be men who protected your families and your country. Be men!"

The visiting went on for another hour. The coffee pots were empty. The smallest youngsters were sleeping in the backs of the wagons. One by one the families said their farewells and pointed their wagons for home.

Ad and Amelia were packing up their wagon while Shep led their team out and threw the harness on. Clara was feeling whimsical, clearly reluctant for the afternoon to end. Her mother looked like she thought it couldn't end soon enough.

Just as Ad reached to help his wife into the buggy Jerilyn walked over leading her saddled mare. She held the reins out to Clara. "Aunt Clara, I'm tired of riding. I'm going to go with Mom and Dad in the buggy. Would you take Dolly home for me?"

Clara stood silently while the others, wondering at this girl who loved nothing better than terrorizing the countryside with her wild riding and her Ute war cries, tried to hold back a smug grin. Amelia let out a deep breath of exasperation. Ad held back a laugh. Shep lifted his hat and scratched his head. His smile was about ready to break his face into parts.

Clara took the reins and leaned in to speak into Jerilyn's ear. In hushed tones she said, "Young lady, I will owe you a great favor some day. Thank you for your thoughtfulness. You do, however, know it's not a good thing to lie, don't you?"

The bright youngster whispered back, "You don't really know it's a lie. I might really be tired of riding." She then snickered. "Anyway, it was Mom's idea."

"Alright, thanks to you both. I'll enjoy the ride and I'll see that your horse gets home to the Bar-M." Clara stood back up from the hunched over position.

Jerilyn motioned for her to bend over again. With her mouth close to Clara's ear she whispered, "Dolly will poke along real slow if you want her to."

Clara laughed right out loud. "Get away from here you scamp before you cause even more trouble." Jerilyn laughed and ran to jump on the already moving Bar-M buggy.

Clara turned to her parents. "You go along. Shep and I will be right behind you, provided that is, if Shep wants to ride that far out of his way. Then he can return Dolly to the Bar-M for me."

Ad put the team in motion with a light slap of the reins while Amelia said quietly, "Oh I think the Texan will be willing to take a longer route back to the ranch." She didn't seem to be looking for any input from her husband.

After a half mile in the slowly moving buggy Ad spoke into the silence. "My dear, you pretty near pushed Mac and Margo together way back when, even before there was hardly time to get to know Mac. Maybe you're not giving Clara enough credit for wisdom and common sense."

Amelia was silent for a long time and Ad heard her sniffle a couple of times. Finally, she squeaked out a few words. "She's my baby. My little girl."

Ad put his arm around her shoulders. "I know, dear, I know."

26

THE NORMAL WORK OF THE ranch resumed after the storm, while Mac nearly wore out the yard pacing and thinking. He climbed to his favorite quiet spot on top of the grassy rise behind the house, where he and Margo had discussed the changes required to make the Bar-M successful into the future. This was the one place on the Bar-M where Mac insisted on quiet. Horse riding was forbidden, and the kids knew not to run or shout. This was a place for Mac and Margo, not for kids to play.

There, facing the little pool of water that looked full and fresh and inviting after the storm, the rancher thought it all through again and laid it before the Lord. Mac often sought wisdom sitting on this bench. With his heart heavy at the thought of what lay before him he slid from the bench and went to his knees. 'Lord, I hate what's come upon us. If there is another way...'

A shout from the ranch yard brought Mac to his feet. Two fast-riding vaqueros arrived in a swirling of dust; one horse turning in a complete circle, spooked by the men rushing towards them from the barn and cookhouse.

Mac arrived to hear, "Senor Mac. Senor Mac. Much trouble." He then broke into a long lightening fast garble of Spanish that Mac had no chance of following.

The sweat stained and wheezing animals were still prancing, their hooves, threatening serious harm to the gathered men. Mac shouted over the turmoil. "Get down from that horse Paco. You too Diego." He turned, searching for his yard man. Seeing him arriving from the corrals, he hollered, "Pepe, take these animals and care for them. A couple of you men go and help. The rest of you get back to work."

With the turmoil settled out Mac said, "Alright. Now talk to me. In English, por favor."

"Senor Mac. There is much trouble with the sheep. Many mans, they try to stop thees sheep from crossing the Jenkins ranch. Jenkins, he ride with them. Kill many sheep. Some shoot, some run over beeg hill. Shoot at sheep mans.

"Manuel, he much shoot back. Three mans, they die. Two mans shoot but not yet die. Other mans, they run away."

Mac, his head swirling, took in this information and asked, "When was this?"

"Yesterday senor, it take much time to ride here. Many miles."

"Were any of our men shot?"

Paco was holding his big sombrero in front of his chest like a penitent facing the priest. "No mans die senor. One man is much shoot. We carried heem to Mex Town. For Mama fix. He alive but much sick. We bring other man, shooting man, much sick too for Mama."

"Where are the sheep now?"

"Sheep on Bar-M. Much grass on hills. Sheep, they happy there. Sheep mans, they set up wagons and tents. They make it be home now."

"Alright, men. Thank you."

Jimbo stayed and listened to the report. Mac turned to him. "Jimbo, I'd thank you for taking these men to get some breakfast and for showing them where they can get a few hours of sleep."

Mac and Margo discussed this new information over lunch on the veranda.

About mid afternoon, at a much slower pace than the vaqueros set, two of the Bar-M riders assigned to guard the fence builders trotted into the yard with three securely tied prisoners astride led horses. Mac watched them approach and thought, 'what now'?

"Madison, Ethan," Mac said as they pulled up in front of the cookhouse. "Who are these men?"

Both riders tipped their hats further back on their foreheads. "Shooters, Mac." said Ethan, turning partially around in the saddle and pointing his thumb over his shoulder at the tied-up men. "We were riding the fence line yesterday when we heard a whole lot of rifle fire. Rocky's men were on the alert and didn't really need us, so we rode over that way to take a look. We were just rounding a bend in a little coolie when these three came running right into our arms. Turns out your sheep herd was attacked. When your guards fought back the attackers ran like scared rabbits. These three were trying to find a safer location to save their worthless hides. Ran right into our arms. Gave themselves up with nary a squeak."

Again, he pointed his thumb over his shoulder at the three desperate looking men. "It was late in the day, so we kept our guests at the fence camp overnight. Left early this morning. Figured you might have a question or two for these boys."

Ethan wasn't finished with his story. "Madison, he was all for just shooting them right then and there. I said, naw, let's take them in. Figured we could line them up along the corral fence and use them for target practice, or maybe turn them loose to see how fast they can run. Might even be fun to see how far they get."

Mac ignored the talk of shooting.

Bobby and Jeremiah sauntered out of the cookhouse with toothpicks in the corners of their mouths and with Jimbo strolling along behind. Bobby took a quick look at the three trussed up men and then, walking closer, took a longer look. "Fish Durban! What y'all doin way up here? And all trussed up so nice and tight too. Last time I laid eyes on you was down to Las Vegas. You was just a-settin on the bench in front of the barber shop whittling on a willow switch. Looks like your fortunes have been somewhat reduced."

Mac waved his hand for his brother to leave it alone. "Get them down and seated on the ground over there." He pointed to the side of the tool storage shed. He hollered for Pepe, but the wrangler was already on his way from the barn. The wrangler picked up the reins of one horse and started for the barn. The rest of the animals followed along.

When the men were seated on the ground, still securely tied, Mac said, "Alright, let's hear it." They talked freely, all signs of heroism long gone.

The family gatherings on the veranda were starting to feel like a habit. A habit that was going to have to become action pretty soon if anything was to be done about Baxter and his troublesome cohorts.

Bobby set his coffee cup down and looked across the table. "Mac, I was only a deputy for a couple of years so I'm no expert. But that little bit of experience plus my own common sense tells me that talking on this here porch ain't going to solve the problem. Now, we all been hoping all along to deal with this thing without burning powder. Or not too much powder anyway. But we either have to deal with it or have it hanging over the Bar-M forever. I'm thinking the time for talking is long past."

There was a murmur of general agreement.

Mac was the only one sitting at the table who ever worn a uniform or lived through the carnage of battle. Through all the years since that sad time he hoped and prayed to live a life of peace, never again being forced into doing things as awful as those he remembered.

He looked at Margo. At her slight nod he cleared his throat and spoke to the group.

"Alright, two days from now we move those cattle off the Bar-M and try to reason one more time with Baxter. Then we'll do what we have to do. We'll use the time until then to sort out the men who will go with us. Some will have to stay here to protect the ranch. I'll talk to Taz about the crew. I want you all to understand; I refuse to demand that any man ride with me. That goes for you sitting here. Any man that stays behind will still have his job. His position here does not depend on fighting.

"If I should find one of our riders going over to the other side that would be a whole other matter."

Bobby shook his head. "Mac. Give up your pipe dreams. That talk ain't nothin but dreaming, and you know it. You need to think again. Any Bar-M rider who won't ride for the brand, whatever that calls for won't be accepted by the other riders. You already know that. You need to get past your wishing and get this job done. Your riders will follow you."

The table was silent.

Finally, Mac just nodded his head. "Take the afternoon to see to your animals and your gear. Get a good rest. Each of you pack some trail provisions. Have Paco pick out two pack animals. I'll break out some ammunition tomorrow and every man can lay on a supply. There's a wide range of weapons owned by the riders. I may not have ammunition for all of them.

"Take two canteens each. Work with the other riders to make sure everyone is prepared. We'll be driving cattle so make sure every man has a lariat. Be ready at sunrise the morning after next. I'll talk with Taz; he'll pick out the riders.

"Now I have a couple of riding jobs I'd like volunteers to take on. I want someone to ride to the Flying W to talk with

Wallace, and one to ride to Luke's. They both need to know what we're up to."

Jimbo spoke up. "I ain't seen Luke long enough for a visit, nor Dorit at all, for many a month. I'll point Ol' Ap over that way first thing in the morning.

"Thing is Mac, you got to figure Luke ain't going to sit this one out. His ranch is at some danger too. Besides that, it ain't Luke's nature to sit it out. I expect he's going to have Dorit take the kids to the U.T. E. for safety. The sooner he knows the plan the better.

"How about I take Jerrod along with me. He's been faunchin at the bit for days now. I'll ride along with Luke. We'll ride back to the Bar-M and hope to find your group. Jerrod can drive Dorit and the kids down to the U.T.E. in the wagon. That'll keep Jerrod well inside the property line where he'll be safe and still give him a part in the action."

Again, Mac looked for a silent sign from Margo. When she didn't object Mac said, "Alright. If you see either the fence crew or the surveyors, you tell them to be alert. More alert than normal."

Jeremiah said, "I'd enjoy a ride to the Flying W. Perhaps I'll see if Gail would like to go along."

27

IT MAY HAVE BEEN THE STORM that washed a head-sized boulder out of the hillside. Or perhaps a burrowing animal dug a hole to escape a predator. It might have been that same predator trying to dig the burrowing animal out of it's den, with lunch in mind. But whatever the cause, there was a hole in the side of the slope. It wasn't even much of a slope; just a change in the grade of the land on the faint trail Jerrod and Jimbo were following on their ride to the Lazy L. There were many such slopes on the Bar-M.

A younger horse would have either stepped around the hole or stretched his leg over it. A younger rider would have seen the problem ahead and reined his riding animal in a different direction. But neither Jimbo nor his Appaloosa gelding would be considered young. The long-riding man and his beloved horse had grown old together. Neither man nor animal, if the old horse could think and talk, would have acknowledged that truth any more than they would have acknowledged their failing eyesight.

The incident that changed everything happened so quickly that no correction was possible. Jerrod followed a couple of horse lengths behind Jimbo. He was startled as Ap's left front foot dipped into the hole. The old horse lurched sideways and forward, all at the same time. He watched as Jimbo desperately tried to pull the beloved gelding back onto even ground. He heard the animal's leg bone break. He heard the animal's piercing scream of pain. He heard Jimbo's loud cry; 'no, no' no Ap, no'! He watched as the animal's shifting weight on the collapsing leg, followed by the folding of the other front leg, pulled him head-over-heels down the slope.

The young man screamed a warning as he watched the rider ahead of him trying frantically, unsuccessfully, to kick his feet free of the stirrups. He felt a piercing helplessness as Jimbo rode the crippled animal into the air and over onto it's back, falling with a terrible weight, with Jimbo trapped in the saddle.

Another loud crack told Jerrod that more bones were broken. There was no telling if the broken bones were human or equine. As a final act, an encore to this deathly disaster, Jerrod watched as his friend's head snapped backwards, smacking against the rocky ground.

For long seconds the young man didn't move. In momentary denial of the truth, he watched the horse sag and roll over onto it's side, haplessly trapping Jimbo's leg. He looked at the blood slowly slipping down the rock Jimbo's head rested on. Jerrod would never remember hollering, "Pa, Pa". He had always been able to depend on his father to be close-by. But Mac wasn't anywhere near to hear or help. Alone, in a desperate situation, forcing his emotions down, recognising what had to be done, the shocked young man knew it was up to him. He had it to do.

The grievously injured animal began to thrash, determined to right himself. Jerrod, seeing clearly the mortal danger his friend was in, he reached for his booted carbine and leaped from the saddle. He landed just a few feet from Jimbo, whose leg was still trapped under the horse he had ridden for so many miles over so many years. The young man jacked a shell into the Winchester's chamber, planted his feet and reached across Jimbo. He held the gun one-handed, a few inches from Ap's tossing head, waited a moment for the animal to cease moving, and pulled the trigger. It was one of the most difficult things he had ever done. But worse actions, more needed actions, stared him in the face.

Jerrod tugged Jimbo's exposed foot from the stirrup and climbed the little slope to his own horse. He slid the carbine back into the sheath. He uncoiled his rope, tied the end off on his saddle horn and walked down to the dead animal. He snugged the loop around Ap's saddle horn and climbed back up to level ground. Swinging aboard his horse he urged him backwards, taking up slack in the rope. With the rope coming taut, the saddle pulled hard against the girth strap. The saddle leather squealed as the horn took the weight of the downed animal.

Talking to his horse and urging him backwards, Jerrod watched as Ap rolled off Jimbo, showing just enough clearance to release the trapped leg. The young man settled his own animal and then carefully dismounted and stepped down the grade to his friend. He cautiously reached under Ap and wiggled Jimbo's foot loose. He then stood and pulled Jimbo clear. Walking back up to his own animal he stepped to the saddle and lightly touched a spur. The horse shuffled forward, releasing the weight. Jerrod retrieved his lariat and coiled it.

Only after that was done did the young man kneel beside Jimbo. He was clearly unconscious and unable to help himself. But was he even breathing? Jerrod put his ear to the other man's face and convinced himself that he could hear a slow passage of air.

He had no experience to fall back on, but he knew he had to get Jimbo onto his own gelding. More damage might be done in lifting the old man and draping him across his horse but staying where they were wasn't an option. He led his horse to the downhill side of Jimbo and dropped the reins. Again, he settled the animal, hoping the smell of blood and the feel of an unfamiliar body laid across his flank didn't spook the young horse. He untied his saddle bags and draped them across the horse's neck, in front of the saddle.

Mac had always been extraordinarily strong, as had his father before him. Jerrod was following in that same path, although it would be a few years yet before he would really come into his own. Ignoring the possibility of hurting Jimbo further Jerrod rolled his friend onto his stomach. He then wiggled his arms under the old man's chest and legs. Steeling himself against possible disaster he slowly lifted, talking to his horse the whole time, urging him to stand steady.

With a great effort he slid Jimbo head first behind the saddle. He ignored the grinding noise from Jimbo's spine. With a couple more lifts and pushes he got the old man balanced across the horse's loin and up onto the saddle skirt. One of Jimbo's legs hung crooked but there was no help for that. With his rope he drew a loop around Jimbo's chest, trapping his arms at his sides. Leading the rope along the saddle, looping around the pommel, and taking a half hitch around the horn and then back down the other side, he tied off Jimbo's legs. The tied rope was going to make sitting the saddle difficult, but he saw no other way.

Slowly, with one hand holding the reins and the other gripping Jimbo's shirt he walked the horse down the grade and stopped him when they reached level ground. He re-checked the rope and then swung into the saddle. Reaching back to again grip a handful of shirt he nudged the horse into motion. Jimbo's scalp was still bleeding but it might be slowing down. Jerrod couldn't be sure.

His knew he was much closer to Luke's Lazy-L than to his home Bar-M, so he continued along the trail the two riders were originally following.

For an hour he rode the uncomfortable saddle, with the rope chaffing his thighs, and then got off and walked. The going was slow either way. Three hours later he pulled into the lazy-L ranch yard. Jerrod was walking, leading the exhausted animal with its bloody and broken burden. Dora saw them coming from the kitchen window and ran to help, all the while hollering for Luke.

Luke called one of his riders and the two of them lay Jimbo on an old door that had been removed from the original bachelor's shack. With that done and the vaquero working over Jerrod's horse, Luke turned to the young man. "So, what happened Jerrod?"

Jerrod told the story, using no excess words, as he had learned from his father. He told of the crew preparing for the ride to challenge Baxter the next morning and then explained why he and Jimbo were on the trail to the Lazy-L. He told briefly what happened to Jimbo, closing with, "We were closer to the Lazy L, so I came along. It's a far ways back to the Bar-M. I didn't know what else to do."

Luke gave the young man an easy slap on the shoulder. "You did just exactly right Jerrod. Jimbo could ask for no more from any man. But the old boy's in bad shape. My guess is that he's ridden his last trail. There's no help for him here. I'll harness the team and we'll load him in the wagon. You take him down to the U.T.E. If he's still alive after that Bill can decide what to do next. I doubt if he'd survive a drive to the Bar-M.

"I'll ride to find your dad's bunch. Give them a hand."

Luke turned to his wife. "Dora, I don't expect we're really in any danger here but when these things start there's no telling what might happen. Baxter and his bunch have been on the prod for weeks. If it comes to a head, I don't want you here alone. You pack up everything you need for a few days away. Both for you and the kids.

"If you could dig in the pantry and put a bundle of grub together for me, that would be much appreciated. The cook will prepare a bundle for the men.

"You and the kids will ride the wagon. I'll send Cookie with you. Jerrod will go along too. You'll be safe at the U.T.E. while this whole thing gets sorted out."

Dorit put her hands on her hips and looked her defiance at Luke. "Mr. Black, I finally have the home I was longing for all my life. No raggedy pants, greedy rancher is going to drive me off it. You do what you have to do. Go shoot every one of them if it comes to that. Lay them out where the carrion eaters can get at them. Me, I'll be right here looking after our home. I'll shoot a few of them myself, given opportunity."

Luke took a long study of this mail order bride who had come to mean so much to him. Finally, he burst out laughing. "Dorit, that's a great attitude and I love you for it. You don't at all sound like the city girl who came out here scared of the sound of a coyote in the night. I'd say you've settled in to ranch life just fine. But you need to think differently this one time. I can build another cabin if need be. But I've got just the one wife and mother of my children. I can't risk losing you or those kids.

"I admire your grit but it's not going to be that way. You go pack some gear and get this wagon underway. Move along quickly. I'm thinking Jimbo doesn't have much time. I'd like to think Bill might get a few moments with him before he stops breathing.

"Take the cook with you on the wagon. The vaqueros will come with me. I'll turn the milk cow loose and care for the other animals before I go. Let's move along quickly now."

Dorit stood there staring at Luke, with her balled-up fists pressed firmly against her hip bones. Her lips were moving slightly. No sound came. Finally, she turned to the doorway and called the kids, giving them instructions for packing a few things.

Luke called one of his vaqueros. "You get directions from this young man. Then you ride over and pick up the saddle and gear from that downed horse. Bring it all back here. Quickly. Rapidamente."

While Jerrod ate a sandwich Dorit threw together and a cup of warmed up coffee, Luke and his other vaquero soon had the wagon ready for it's sad and broken burden, with a deep bedding of hay and several blankets laid out. With Jerrod's help they carefully lifted the door carrying Jimbo into the back of the wagon. They propped his head with a folded blanket but left him laying on the wooden door. There was no sound from his lips or sign of life in Jimbo except for his shallow breathing.

Luke lifted his youngest child into the back of the wagon while Dorit's two older children climbed in, being careful to avoid stepping on the old man. The cook threw a small pack in the back of the wagon and climbed to the seat. He picked up the reins and held the team steady as Luke assisted Dorit onto the seat. Jerrod swung aboard his freshly fed and watered gelding.

Luke rode beside the wagon for a half mile trying to think of something special to say. But it was Dorit who broke the silence. "You do what has to be done, my husband. We're here for the long term and we can't be looking over our shoulders in fear of some greedy land grabber. You come get me just as soon as you can. We'll be anxious to return home."

Luke just nodded and tipped his hat back a bit. He sat staring as the wagon rumbled off into the distance.

It wasn't long before the vaquero was back with Jimbo's saddle and gear, having made much better time than Jerrod, who was forced to a walk with the injured Jimbo. With that stored safely in the tack room and the animals cared for, Luke and his two riders rode east, towards the Bar-M range.

It was already late in the day, but Luke planned to ride the evening through, aiming for the Bar-M's south line shack. The three Lazy-L men would start gathering Baxter cattle at first light, moving them south and off Bar-M grass. Mac and his riders would be along soon enough.

Luke often found himself missing the excitement and the challenge of battle. The crashing of the big guns, the bugler pouring coded instructions over the battlegrounds, the prancing of excited cavalry mounts, the sharp whang of the lighter guns, the smell of burnt powder, the shouting of the men. It made his blood run hot and stirred his soul.

Understanding, and sometimes weeping at the cost, he wasn't sorry to have the big conflict come to an end. And yet…

A big part of him was hoping to be the one to locate the Baxter gang. Another charging ride. Another victory. Another battle fought and won. Well, he'd see the situation in the morning.

At daybreak the next morning a rider from the U.T.E. rode into the Bar-M yard on a staggering horse. He was surprised to see the yard a frenzy of activity as nearly thirty riders were rigging out for the raid to the south. When Mac heard the news of Jimbo his mind swirled with indecision. He walked towards the house, meeting Margo half way. "What's going on now? That's Bill's rider. Is it about Jerrod?

Mac explained the situation, assuring the worried mother that her eldest son was fine. "But I hate to think of Jimbo maybe breathing his last without going to him. We've been friends for a long time. I know ranching demands a sizable spread of land but sometimes I regret the distances between homesteads. I don't see how I can get this bunch of men to stand down while I take the full of a day to ride to Bills. And I wouldn't ask them to ride without me."

Margo responded, "There's not one single thing you can do at Bills. Get these men moving while the task is still clear in your mind. If Jimbo even wakes up he'll have lots of friends around him. Go. And get back soon."

Mac kissed his wife on the forehead and turned to leave. Margo said, "That's not much of a kiss Mr. McTavish."

"Ya, well, it'll have to do until a time when there's not thirty grinning cowboys watching."

Mac walked over to the little shack. The three prisoners were still sitting on the ground, securely trussed up. They spent the night there. They were let up to eat and care for personal needs before being bound up again. Mac looked at each one in turn.

"Listen and understand me. If my rider that's over at Mama's with bullet holes in him dies I will hang you. If you try to escape, you will be shot. If you cause any trouble, you will be shot. If I find out you've lied to me I will hang you. I'm hoping that's clear."

None of the three felt it necessary to respond.

Mac swung into his saddle and headed south without a further word. Margo watched him go and the thought came into her mind that a more theatrical leader would lift his hat and holler something foolish like 'move out men.' She knew her husband felt no need to say anything or even look behind him. The men would be following. She turned back towards the house.

The two visiting Boston ladies were standing on the top step with the twins sitting quietly beside them. It was early for the visiting ladies to be up, but they found it impossible to sleep through this important and dangerous morning.

Gail watched the men ride out and then spoke to Margo. "I don't pretend to understand these things, but it appears to me that Mac is a little reluctant to press forward."

Margo was quick to respond. "Don't you be fooled by that thought. Shooting, and certainly killing, is never Mac's first wish. He'll give most men a second opportunity to do the right thing. But when the die is cast Mac will be at the lead of his men and you can pity anyone that gets in his way. I've never known a gentler man, nor a man of more fierce determination. The land grabbers will learn the facts when they push Mac McTavish."

Mac led the men south with his brothers riding close beside him. About ten miles into the ride they spotted a group of six or eight riders approaching from the east. They watched carefully as the two groups closed in on each other. Finally, Mac pulled to a halt. He turned to his brothers. "Hold here."

Mac turned his horse towards the approaching riders, rode about a quarter mile and stopped, waiting for the men to ride close enough to be identified. When the group was a half mile away the lead rider lifted his hat above his head and waved it back and forth. After another couple hundred yards Mac could identify Wallace of the Flying W. He waited while his neighbor closed in on him. The two men shook hands. Wallace looked over at Mac's riders. "Glad we didn't miss you."

Mac nodded. "I'm surprised to see you here."

Wallace looked grim. "You didn't' really think I'd let you fight my own battle for me, did you?"

Mac felt no need to answer. "Good to have you and your men. Let's ride."

28

AT THE U.T.E. BILL and Little Flower settled Jimbo onto a cot on the house porch. It was a beautiful spring day, the air warm and fresh. The recent storm seemed to have ushered in the beginning of summer although the true heat of those months was still a-ways off.

Bill took on the unpleasant task of undressing Jimbo and cleaning him from head to foot. His scalp wound was no longer bleeding, but his hair was matted and stiff with dried blood. Sometime during his wounding his bladder and bowels let loose.

Bill stripped the wounded man's clothing off, cutting some of the seams to make it easier. Little Flower heated water and brought it to Bill. She then bundled the filthy clothing off to the barn, to be burned or buried sometime later.

With Jimbo clean and wrapped in a blanket, Bill watched and waited for the old wanderer to show some sign of life. During the cleaning Bill felt the movement of Jimbo's spine. He didn't know much about such injuries but as he discussed it with Dorit she stated with confidence, "With a broken spine he's not going to ever walk again. Probably not feeling any of the pain either, which is a blessing of the Lord. Depending how high the break is he may or may not be able to move his arms. It would be a mercy for him to never wake up."

Dorit and the kids were settled into a seldom-used back bedroom, welcomed for as long as it took to straighten out the Baxter mess. Dorit spread out the few belongings she had gathered before leaving her own home and then went to the kitchen to see what she could do to help Little Flower.

In the early evening Jimbo opened his eyes. Bill had taken a brief break from his vigil while he looked after some ranch affairs. Dorit was sitting beside the cot reading a book.

Jimbo's eyes opened and he slowly turned his head just a little bit. The movement drew Dorit's attention. She dropped the book to the floor, leaning over the cot to look directly down on Jimbo. "You're back. Can you see and hear me?"

The wounded man tried to nod his head, but his eyes closed in pain at the action. With wetness clouding his vision he struggled to get some words out. "Dorit? We was coming to see you and Luke. Took a fall."

Then, as if remembering more clearly, he said, "Jerrod! Where's the boy? Is he alright?"

Dorit carefully touched his cheek with her hand. "Jerrod is fine. He's around here somewhere. He went to the barn with Bill last I saw."

"Bill? What's Bill doing over here?"

"No, my friend. We're not at the Lazy-L. We're with Bill and Little Flower at the U.T.E. Luke's gone off to join Mac and the others. Luke and our two vaqueros. They're hoping to put an end to the land grab."

Jimbo seemed to be processing that but finally said, "My horse? Ol' Ap?"

Dorit hated to tell him the truth but it didn't seem like the right time to hold back. "The horse was pretty broken up

Jimbo. He was put down. But you're alive. We're thankful for that."

Again, Jimbo struggled with thoughts and words, clearly, deeply saddened by the loss of his horse. "Jerrod? That boy hauled me in? He's a good boy. Going to be a good man. Always knew it. Could tell from way back. Man to be proud of. I need to thank him. Can you get him here? Getting sleepy. Feels like my head is broke."

Dorit patted his shoulder. "Can you hold on for just a minute while I run and fetch him and Bill?"

Dorit stood and ran to the barn without waiting for an answer.

Bill and Jerrod arrived on the run. Little Flower came from the house, took a quick look and hustled off. Bill took the chair, lost for words. Jerrod stood on the other side of the cot.

Jimbo took a moment focusing his eyes before he was sure he was looking at Jerrod. He finally spoke in a voice so quiet Jerrod could hardly hear him. "Want to thank you Jerrod. You're a good man. Like to shake your hand but can't seem to move my arms. Don't know what's wrong. Head hurts. Can't see too well."

There was a long pause as Jimbo took several deep breaths. Finally, he found his voice again. "You follow your dad's footsteps Jerrod. Never met a better man than Mac McTavish. Proud. Proud to call him my friend."

His mumble drifted off and his eyes closed. He lay still for some time before opening his eyes again. He looked around blankly as if he wasn't really seeing things clearly. No one spoke, not knowing what to say.

Little Flower walked quickly across the yard with an old Ute woman and a younger Ute man following in her wake. They stepped up onto the porch and Little Flower pushed Bill out of the way. Little Flower sat in the chair. The two Utes stepped behind the cot. Jerrod moved to stand beside Jimbo's head.

Little Flower leaned over Jimbo and shook his shoulder. "Can you hear me Jimbo?"

Jimbo struggled with the words. "I hear you."

"Can you see these people beside you?"

Jimbo's eyed moved without his head moving. He looked for a long time, showing no recognition.

Little Flower asked, "Do you remember Morning Dawn? That's what you called her many years ago."

Again, Jimbo's face showed his puzzlement. "Mor... Morning Dawn? Dawn, that you? How can that be? Long time ago. Left me. Thought maybe – dead. Loved that woman."

Little Flower showed rare compassion to the old man. "That's Morning Dawn old man. Do you see the man? That's Long Rider, named after his father. Your son."

"Son? Dawn? Son? Never knew. Son?" His eyes filled with tears.

Jimbo spoke to Little Flower. "How do you know? Long time ago."

Little Flower wanted to get the whole story out quickly, before Jimbo closed his eyes for the last time. "Listen carefully old man. Dawn is my grandmother. Long Rider is my father. You are my grandfather."

Jimbo looked completely lost in his thinking. He couldn't move his head, but he moved his eyes from side to side, first taking in Little Flower and then Long Rider and Dawn. "Dawn? Son? Granddaughter? He repeated it all again, like a mantra. "Didn't tell me! Didn't know!"

Little Flower pulled back the blanket and lifted one of Jimbo's unfeeling arms from his side. She tucked the blanket back in and held his hand. "Grandmother recognised you a long time ago. She thought it was best to leave old things in the past."

Jimbo's lips trembled and his eyes misted again. His eyes flashed to Little Flower. "You are a good woman. Good wife and mother. Good woman for Bill. Dawn is good woman. Is my son a good man? Good father?"

Little Flower was weeping a bit herself now, a thing that was unheard of in her life. "Yes, Jimbo, he's a good man. You can be proud of him."

Jimbo was clearly failing. Just the slightest smile showed on his lips. "Wish I -- known. Dawn. Wish I... wish." He stopped talking and closed his eyes. They were not going to open again.

29

ALTHOUGH THE FENCING CREW was spread out over a half mile of grassland no one bothered them. It was clear from a distance that in both numbers and in type, these were not men to fool with. Men with the bark on some would have said. The rebels made that mistake once. After the news of that unproductive raid got back to the ranches, they wouldn't repeat it. Not in small numbers anyway.

Since the disturbance with the arrival of the sheep, the crew worked without interruption. Their carbines were leaned against shrubs or rocks, close to hand as they worked, fighting rock and caliche, with thousands of holes yet to dig.

The fence veered east and then south again to skirt the miles of rocky up-thrusts Mac set aside for the sheep.

After delivering the three prisoners to the Bar-M, Madison and Ethan returned to their patrol duty but there was little to do. Rocky walked over to where Madison was taking his lunch. "I'll make a suggestion. It's quiet here and if something comes up we'll handle it just fine. Why don't you two take a wander over to the sheep camp? See is everything's alright with them. Stay for a bit if you find they need some help. Assure them they can call on us if they have need."

Madison scraped up the last morsel of venison stew with the half of a biscuit and looked up at Rocky. "You sure you're alright here?"

"My boys are getting a little bored with digging and tamping and stretching wire. I don't suppose it's going to come upon us but if it does, a bit of burned power smoke might clear out their noses after breathing dry, foothills dust all this time. You two go ahead."

The two riders threw their bedrolls and a rain slicker behind their saddles, waved goodbye to Rocky and the crew and rode west, into the hill country that divided the Bar-M from the U.T.E. and Lazy L. After less than an hour of riding they saw the wagon and tent camp on the flat bottom of a small valley. The dogs greeted them with a barked warning. Three men stood watching, carbines held down by their legs, ready for instant use. Madison raised his hat and waved it like a flag as the two rode closer. "Hola amigos," shouted Madison, still waving his hat. "Manuel, está bien contigo?" (Is it well with you?)

"Hola Madison, bien, bien."

The two men ground-hitched their horses and shook hands with Manuel. Looking around the small camp it didn't take Madison long to decide that any Baxter rider intent on making trouble at the sheep camp was in for a surprise. Several men rode the perimeter at full alert, all under Manuel's leadership. The traditional image of the gentle, inoffensive, peon shepherd was nowhere to be seen. In its place were hard-nosed, well-armed men on horseback. They would be gentle with the sheep but with little else. The guards were costing the Bar-M money, but Mac figured it as part of his startup costs.

A small band of laborers who drove the wagons loaded with supplies north with the sheep were erecting corrals and a couple of lean-to shelters from lumber and poles Mac sent over. To make up for the shortage of cut boards, the men were using branches cut from the pinyon pine, juniper and whatever shrubs were handy, weaving them skillfully into the structure. They would also be building fencing to protect the stacks of hay that would be arriving later in the summer.

Being ready for the first foothills winter meant there would be little time for resting during the summer months.

The two Bar-M riders weren't yet sure about the sheep business, but they admired these men who were clearly self-reliant, miles from any help. They saw several women in camp and a number of children. They were settling into a small grouping of white canvas tents erected a short distance from the corrals. It looked like the plan was to have a small village built around the breeding and shearing of sheep.

Looking up-slope from the camp they could see hundreds of sheep contently grazing among the boulders. Cattle would have been unable to follow in their steps.

Looking it all over Ethan turned to Madison. "I don't know what to think. Do you suppose Mac is right again?"

30

LUKE AND HIS TWO VAQUEROS, Antonio and Juan, had a half day start on Mac and his riders and a shorter distance to cover. Riding east onto the Bar-M range, it was full dark before they managed to stumble on the southernmost line cabin. Heading for the always well-stocked cabin for their first night out seemed the obvious thing to do.

They might have missed it in the dark but for the smell of wood smoke drifting in the wind. Still, with the wind shifting in the moonless night there was no way to know exactly where to look. Riding slowly, trying to follow the scent, Antonio was the first to notice the dim light that shone through the shading trees surrounding the shack. "Mira Alli", (look there), he said, pointing. Looking closely, Luke could just make out the outline of the trees against the night sky, like black against black. Luke pulled his horse to a stop and gestured with his finger over his mouth for the men to be quiet.

Luke stepped off his horse and motioned for the others to do likewise. Passing his reins to Juan he whispered. "You stay here. Be very quiet. Muy silencioso. I'm not expecting to find any friendly faces in there if the word Jerrod brought is accurate. If there's trouble you come a-runnin. Antonio, you come with me. Bring your carbine but no shooting unless I start it. Quiet, both of you."

The men learned a lot of English after coming to the Lazy-L. Luke picked up only a smattering of the Mex tongue.

Antonio passed his reins to Juan and lifted his Winchester from the scabbard. Juan moved to a sizable tree close by and tied the horses. He also pulled his carbine, waiting until Luke and Antonio moved. He inched his way towards the cabin and then stood waiting in the darkened shadow of a small cottonwood.

Luke moved cautiously towards the cabin. He paused while he listened into the night. Hearing no noise except the natural noise from several horses in the small corral, he motioned Antonio to stand still. Luke cautiously made his way to the lamp lit window. Removing his hat, he slowly moved into position just far enough to allow for a view of the men inside. He recognized one, at least, as a Baxter man. He wasn't sure of the other two. There was talk of Baxter hiring fighters. Luke figured to take no chances.

Luke backed away and then proceeded to the door. Antonio moved like a cat, stealthily and with no wasted motion. Luke, owning no claim on stealthy movements, depended more on speed and surprise than silence, although he did his best to tread lightly.

Stepping quickly to the door, hoping the men hadn't dropped the bar across it, Luke reached for the handle. The hand carved fastener moved easily with the touch of his finger. He lifted the wooden latch to the top of its travel and pushed. The door swung hard against the log wall and the two Lazy-L men leaped inside, their weapons lifted and ready. Luke saw three men, one bent over whatever he was cooking on the wood stove, and two sitting at a table with a deck of cards spread before them.

Holding his carbine at eye level, Luke shouted "Stand fast, all of you. We want no gun play. Put your hands in the air. Now."

Antonio held his weapon on the cook, showing no sign of nervousness.

The two card players looked up in total surprise. They reacted instantly, starting to rise to their feet, lifting their Colts as they stood.

The cook misjudged Antonio, perhaps holding a low opinion of Mexican vaqueros, as many foolishly did. The man pulled his Colt. The speed of the draw spoke of much practice. His weapon was turned towards Antonio when the first 44-40 slug took him just below the top button of his shirt. The second was three inches lower, putting an end to any long range plans the man might have held.

Luke said to wait until he gave the signal to shoot but Antonio saw only blood and death in the wait.

The card players leaped, kicking their chairs out of the way. Luke hollered for them to stop, but the men kept lifting their guns.

Whatever mercy Luke might have felt or been taught in his growing up, fled during his days in the Federal Cavalry. Even years after that grim war the idea of mercy never fully returned.

In the short instant before either gunman could get off a shot he pulled the trigger, levered the action and pulled again. Antonio stood beside him levering his own carbine. The two men never got fully to their feet.

As Luke lowered his weapon, thinking it was over, another shot rang out and Antonio fell to the floor with a groan of agony. Luke dove to the floor himself, frantically looking into the darkened corner where two sets of bunk beds were framed against the wall, beyond the reach of the feeble lamp flickering on the card table. A second shot penetrated the space Luke held just split seconds before, pinpointing the shooter.

Rolling onto his back Luke was struggling to bring his carbine into play when Juan charged through the door, whipping his head about in all directions, trying to sort out the action. The vaquero leaped into the room, holding his Colt in his left hand and the carbine in his right. He disappeared into the shadowy darkness beside the bunk beds.

The shooter on the bunk was concentrating on Luke. He shot again, plowing wood splinters from the floor, plastering several onto Luke's face, and penetrating his cheeks in several places. Although none struck his eyes, the wood fragments and dust from the floor put him briefly out of the battle.

Juan, half hidden by darkness, pressed the barrel of his carbine against the side of the shooter's head. "Senor, life is grand, no? Not so much if you dead."

The shooter's shoulders slumped. He dropped his Colt to the floor as he leaned back on the cot.

Juan poked him in the ribs with the carbine. "Get up, hombre, or I kill. Rapido. Move."

The gunman stood, staring at his three friends crumpled on the floor. He had nothing to say.

Luke was struggling to his feet still wiping his eyes. He looked over at Juan. "Thank you, amigo. Your timing couldn't have been better."

He bent over to see how badly Antonio was hurt. The pool of blood spreading under the man's leg told him there was no time to waste.

Antonio's eyes were open. His teeth were clenched in pain. "Estoy bien," The injured man said, "I am fine. Just my leg shoot."

Luke took out his knife and started opening Antonio pant leg. Juan came closer with the lamp, turning it up as bright as the dirty globe would allow. Luke turned to see what Juan did with the fourth shooter and laughed despite the situation confronting them.

"Never saw anything quite like that Juan. Looks like it will do the job though." The shooter was standing beside the end support for the top bunk. His hands were tied behind his back and around the support. Another rope was snugged around his neck, holding it tight to the upright. For a vaquero with many years experience roping and tying calves at branding time, it was a simple task to secure the shooter.

Juan grinned at Luke. "I think maybe he stay there."

Luke turned back to the bleeding leg. "Set that lamp down and see if there's any hot water. And toss me a couple of those towels."

The bleeding was significant, but it wasn't pulsing or pumping. Luke took that to be a good thing.

Straddling Antonio's leg, his knees resting in the pool of blood on the floor, Luke pressed down with his whole weight to hold the injured man still. He made a folded pad out of the clean towel Juan threw him and pressed it hard against the bullet wound. There was no exit hole.

Juan dipped heated water from the reservoir on the side of the stove and brought it to Luke in a metal pot. Luke carefully lifted the bloody pad. The bleeding had slowed considerably. Luke could see shreds of Antonio's canvas pants protruding from the wound. He pulled out the ones he could get a finger grip on. The rest would have to wait.

He folded another pad and set it aside. Cutting an end off a towel, Luke soaked it in the warm water and carefully washed around the wound. That caused the bleeding to increase but not for long. He pressed the new pad into place.

Turning to Juan, Luke said, "Look in that box on the end of the counter. Should be some salves and stuff in there. Maybe some disinfectant."

The vaquero was soon back with the whole box. Luke flipped the lid off and turned the box on edge, so he could get some light into it. He lifted out a can of disinfectant ointment before he noticed a bottle of liquid. He poured a liberal amount of the pungent liquid onto the folded pad. As the disinfectant fumes rose from the pad Luke turned his head and held his breath. His eyes teared up. After a moment he laid his head to the side, wiping the tears from first one eye and then the other, onto the shoulders of his shirt.

Juan knelt and pushed Antonio's shoulders hard against the floor.

After getting his own sight and smell under control Luke pressed the disinfectant pad to the bullet wound. There was a slight pause and then Antonio let out a blood curdling scream followed by a series of low whimpers.

Luke, still squatting on Antonio's leg, held the pad in place while Juan did his best to hold the wounded rider's flailing, grasping hands.

Luke said to no one in particular, "That stuff gets your attention, if nothing else." After another moment of thought the ex-cavalry man said, "Have to read that label sometime. Maybe it's meant for horses."

When Antonio settled down enough to lay still, Luke reached for the big towel again. Cutting it lengthways he wrapped it around the injured leg, holding the disinfectant soaked pad in place. To be sure it would all hold together he wrapped the other half of the towel on top of the first one, tying it tight with the split ends Luke sliced.

Luke sat back on his haunches, looking down at Antonio. The vaquero was starting at the ceiling. There were just the remnants of a few tears escaping from his eyes. Neither Juan nor Luke thought to mention the tears, allowing the wounded man to hold onto his pride.

The troubling memory of war's heroism flashed through Luke's mind. Times where brave, tough men, wounded worse than Antonio, were back on the line with a rifle in their hands within minutes of first taking a bullet. Looking at the man on the floor, Luke knew him to be that kind of man.

Luke waited a moment and then said, "That's the best we can do here. You think you can ride?"

"I ride."

Luke looked at Juan. "Can you find Mex Town from here in the dark of night?"

Juan nodded his head and looked at his wounded friend. "I can find. I can take Antonio to Mama."

Luke stood. "Good, you bring the horses up to the house. Go to the corral and bring up two other horses too. You can lead them and change off when yours tire out. It's a long ride."

Luke looked down at Antonio, who was trying to rise to his feet. "You can ride that far?"

"I ride."

Juan refilled their canteens and took a small sack of food from the pantry. Within minutes the two men were riding north. Antonio took a firm grip on the saddle horn while his chin rested on his chest.

Luke slowly looked over the mess in the cabin. He spoke to the surviving shooter. "We didn't come to shoot you. You were told to stand down. We gave you a chance to ride away. Now that chance is gone."

He didn't bother explaining what he meant by that. Instead, he straightened up the chairs and grasped the collar of the man closest to the door. Luke was an extraordinarily strong man, shorter than average, broad in the shoulders and thick in the chest. His arms bulged his shirt sleeves.

He dragged the man across the floor, taking up the lamp as he went. Outside he angled towards the small barn, tugging the man behind him. He pulled the dead man into the barn and then went back for the other two. He looked at the blood on the floor and the spilled frying pan and figured someone else could clean up the mess at a better time.

Luke went to the corral and led out a haltered horse. He tied him at the rail in front of the cabin and went to his own horse for a rope. He found a lantern hanging on the outside of the barn and lit it.

Untying the man from the bunk bed he led him outside, his hands still tied behind his back. When the shooter was standing beside the horse, Luke simply picked him up by his belt, balancing him with a grip on one arm, and sat him on the animal. He snubbed a short rope onto one dangling foot and passed it under the horse, so he could pick the end up on the other side.

After snubbing the man securely, Luke led the animal around the cabin into the larger growth of trees, following the yellow lantern light as it opened the way before him. The now terrified man finally spoke. "Hey now, wait a minute. What're you figurin on doing?"

Luke didn't bother to answer.

About two hundred yards from the cabin stood a large cottonwood, surrounded by a group of smaller cottonwoods, a bunch of willows, and various small plants and shrubs, all sucking life sustaining moisture from the little stream. Luke hoped to find a branch at a convenient level.

He held the lantern high to cast light into the branches. Seeing the tree just up ahead he led the horse that way and tied it to a shrub. He took his lariat and threw the end over a branch that jutted from the trunk about ten feet above ground.

The frantic man hollered, "You can't do this. It ain't human. Dang it man, I was just doing a job of work, herding cattle. You can't do this."

Luke stopped what he was doing. "You were herding cattle on another man's grass after you were told clearly to stay off. I was there when your boss was told. And then you shot my friend and shot at me, filling my face with wood splinters. You intended to kill us. There's a price for such as that. You should have considered. Too late now."

Luke flipped the noose towards the man's head. It took three throws as the man ducked and squirmed. With that done Luke tied the trailing end of the rope to the trunk of the tree, leaving enough slack to give a drop when the man slid off the horse, without his feet hitting the ground. Luke was all set to untie the man's feet and finish the job.

With no conscious effort on Luke's part, thoughts of Dorit and the kids and the respect they held for him flashed through his mind. He imagined her saying something like, "A shooting fight is one thing, Mr. Black, protecting your home or your life. A hanging when there might be other options is another thing."

Luke never before considered the thought that he could lose Dorit's respect. Or that he would ever see one of the children looking at him with suspicion. Those brief thoughts, standing beneath the tree with a rope in his hand, brought him up short.

The thoughts of Dorit contrasted with the fact that his friend was riding through the night with this man's bullet in his leg. He looked up at the tethered culprit. With a slump of his shoulders and a great exhaling of held breath, he gave up the silent battle with Dorit.

He untied the rope and dropped the entire spare length in a coil at the base of the tree. Keeping the man's back toward the tree Luke untied his feet. He took a tight grip on the rope, still allowing enough slack for a drop and then whapped the horse with his hat. The horse took three jumping steps and stopped. The shooter slid off the animal and started to fall. As soon as he reached the extent of the slack rope, giving just a bit of a tug on his neck, Luke released his hold, allowing the man to fall to the ground.

All was silent for a few moments and then the half-hanged man choked and started to whimper. The man was so terrified he was shaking, his movements keeping rough time with the sobbing noises escaping his lips. Luke let him lie there for a full two minutes, the time passing as slowly as a glacier's movements.

Luke reached over and slipped the rope from the rider's neck. He then pulled the knotted end of the tie rope, releasing his hands.

Stepping back a few paces Luke said, "Get up. Get up and get out of here before I change my mind. Saddle your horse and ride. Ride just as far and as fast as your animal will carry you. Ride somewhere far away where I'm not apt to ever see you again. You really, really don't want me ever seeing you again."

Having known enough of violence for one night and with no desire to sleep in the line shack, Luke tightened his saddle cinch and mounted. He found a small nest of rocks a mile away. After kicking through the grass and brush, hoping to encourage any slumbering snakes into moving to other resting quarters, he rolled out his bedroll and slept.

31

HAVING GOTTEN A LATE START the first day, the Bar-M crew stopped at the first line shack and settled in for the night. An early start the next morning had them seeing cattle several miles inside Bar-M range. There were no signs of riders, but the cattle were clearly heading south in the slow, plodding manner of animals drifting on their own.

Bobby looked over at Mac. "I'd swear these brutes were started south but I see no riders. Ain't totally natural, a whole herd moving like a drive without any drivers."

Mac just nodded in agreement, watching carefully for approaching riders.

Without being told, several Bar-M men spread out, urging the beasts along at an increased pace.

The Flying W cowboys pushed their horses into the herd and rode among the cattle looking to cut out any W animals the drive might have gathered up.

Mac and the rest of the crew swung to the west to ride past the gathering. Within a mile they saw Luke, sitting on a flat rock, on the edge of a jumble of rocks, holding his canteen in his hand. He made no move to rise.

Mac trotted over. "Morn'n Luke. Would I be guessing right to think you started those animals home? I'm also guessing that you decided to come help with this Baxter thing."

Luke saw no need to explain. He stepped into the saddle. "Let's get 'er done."

The two old friends rode side by side for a few minutes before Luke said, "Got to tell you about last night."

32

A LOT OF THINGS were happening at once.

At the Baxter ranch the neighbors were gathered, those that supported the challenge on the fencing and lease rights anyway. Baxter's cook laid on a big early morning feed. The gathering was the culmination of many evenings of plans, arguments, warnings and doubts, mixed with greed and the fear of failure. Owners rode many miles in repeated trips to sort out the feelings and thoughts of their neighbors. The effort broke old friendships and formed new alliances, if not new friendships. Feelings were running out of control, the men knowing that something had to be done to save their ranches and their pride. They managed to convince themselves that the now unused acres of the Bar-M lands were their answer. They must act this day or not at all. This was the time.

A few ranchers who didn't see eye to eye with Baxter looked at the situation on their home spreads, with the spring grass grazed off and summer's heat still ahead of them and decided that Mac was right. There were too many cattle. As these few men began gathers that would be shipped to market to relieve the demands on their own land, the move showed itself to be hopeless when they found neighbors pushing their starving stock onto their newly vacated acres.

None of the small ranchers could afford enough crew to combat the encroachment. There were shots fired but so far no one was killed. Several cowboys rolled their bedrolls and rode south, having no taste for the pointless violence that was simmering just under the surface.

One angry rancher paid off two of his riders. "I never thought you boys would leave me short handed with my range threatened."

"Boss," said a long-geared, middle aged rider, "I'd stay till the bitter end if this fight made any sense. You know that because I already told you. But what Baxter and his bunch is planning is a pure steal. A land grab. And I ain't no thief.

"Once they start there'll be no stopping. They'll get the taste for it. You think you small ranchers are a part of the Baxter group. You ain't. You don't matter to Baxter. They'll steal from you and others. You won't be able to stop them. And it's a fight they simply can't win. Not in the long haul, they can't. But they can do a power of harm before it's over. The Bar-M is not only big and rich. They're in the right. You know it. Baxter knows it. They all know it."

The rancher slapped his leg with his hat and looked off to the horizon.

"I'm no coward and no quitter boss, but I ain't fightin a purely loosing fight. And one that's in the wrong. You think you can hold Baxter off and get a part of the Bar-M. You can't. Baxter and his bunch don't care about you. We talked this all through, you and me. I say let the fight go right past you and wait for the end. You'll lose some cattle, but you can get more cattle by and by. You can re-group when it's over and save your ranch. I'm sorry we can't see eye to eye, but I wish you well."

33

ON THE U.T.E. SEVERAL Ute men descended on the ranch house. They carried Jimbo's body away on the wooden framed cot he died on, his shrunken body adding hardly any weight to the task. They placed the burden in a small cove of trees a good distance from the Ute tents. The Ute beliefs about the dead were a mixture of respect and fear. The body was approached with a certain reverence, but to take it into the little tent village would have been unheard of.

Little Flower's grandmother insisted on preparing the body for burial. No one questioned her rights or responsibilities on this. Other women stood ready to help but Morning Dawn brushed them aside.

Tradition would have had the body cleaned and wrapped in tanned dear hide. With the killing off of game by both Indian and white hunters, the use of canvas became common for clothing as well as tents. Dawn wrapped the washed body in new, white canvas and carefully sewed it tight. As the sun set she looked over her work, calling it completed. She stepped back and spoke words no one else heard. She quietly chanted old Ute blessings, showing respect to this man she loved and lived with until she tired of his wanderings.

As the father of her first child he held extra respect. The fact that he left her and not returned for a full year was taken as common in such relationships. That she went to the lodge of another man was also taken as common. She remembered those times as if they were just last week.

All those years ago, on a cold, lonely, snowy evening, with a child she told no one about slowly growing within her, and with the firewood supply low, Dawn heard a scratching on the tent wall. At her beckoning Wolf Runner stepped inside. The young man from another village was known to her; a relative, distant enough to avoid the tribal taboo of marrying into family. The young people spoke quietly and before long, Dawn rolled her possessions into her buffalo hide bed. Wolf Runner tied the bundle to a horse he led behind his own mount and lifted Dawn onto the animal. The two new lovers settled into Wolf Runner's village.

At the birth of the child Wolf treated it as his own although it was obvious Dawn was with child before their marriage. She named the child Long Rider. The two stayed together until Wolf fell beneath the trampling hooves of a buffalo he had just driven his spear into. Custom and necessity pushed Dawn into a new marriage before long. She never again lived in her home village and she never saw Jimbo again.

In the morning the men came for Jimbo's body, leading a U.T.E. horse that Bill prepared and loaned for the occasion. As Bill was carefully brushing and grooming the animal he was thinking how appropriate it would have been for his old friend to be carried into the mountains on Ol Ap. Since that was impossible, this grey would suit the purpose. In older times the possessions of the dead were sacrificed or burned, as a part of the burial ceremony. Bill made it plain to Long Rider that he wanted the grey returned.

Bill's Christian stands conflicted with the Ute beliefs in some critical areas. He was careful to not bring offence, but at times he had to take a stand. Sacrificing the horse to appease whatever spirits the Ute believed surrounded Jimbo was not something Bill could abide.

A rider went into the mountains the evening before to find Runs His Horses.

No one from the U.T.E. ranch accompanied the men on their ride to the burial grounds. Bill and Little Flower held hands as they watched the small cavalcade slowly ride from the ranch and wind it's way into the hills. Jimbo, this man who seemingly shirked responsibility all his life, who had amused the men and frustrated the women, who was a fixture over much of the west, would now rest with the people he had respected and lived among for so many years.

His long rides were over. His quiet comings and goings would be no more. For Mac and Bill and a few others it was a sad parting. The old man would be missed.

With the men having ridden away with the canvas wrapped body, Morning Dawn gathered the few belongings Jimbo left behind. Little Flower emptied his pockets before removing the clothing to be burned. The pitifully small bundle was made up of a few coins, amounting to thirty-six cents, an old arrow head, a folding pocket knife, a bar of jerky wrapped in soft dear hide, a faded tintype of a woman no one had seen before and a few other bits and pieces.

Little Flower marveled at how her grandfather could roam the west for decades and end his life with thirty-six cents.

His saddle and other gear were stored in the tack room on Luke's Lazy-L. Jimbo's much loved Green River knife was safe in his saddle bags.

Dawn laid the small pile on the wooden cot, along with the blankets Little Flower wrapped Jimbo in. She then built a fire. As the flames consumed the pitifully small bundle of possessions and the cot that would not be welcomed back in the house, Dawn grieved for the passing of the one she first called husband. She had other husbands over the years, and other children, but Jimbo and Long Rider, the son of Jimbo, would always hold a special place in her memory.

When the men carrying Jimbo on his last ride arrived at the chosen spot for burial, Runs His Horses was waiting. The old chief chanted quietly as his friend of many years was placed in a small hollow in a rock face and covered with gathered stones.

Runs His Horses knew his own time was fast approaching. As he watched the young men reverently burying this white man who had long befriended the Ute, the old chief was pleased that the young men still knew the rituals and that they showed the proper reverence. So much was changed in his lifetime. He prayed the band would be held with strong hands into the future.

34

WITH THE DAWN NOTHING but a thin pink glow on the eastern horizon Baxter stamped his boots on the porch steps, hoping to shake loose the worst of the morning's gather. He pushed into the ranch house where his wife was busy at the kitchen counter.

"The men are saddled up and we're ready to leave out of here. I expect we'll be back tomorrow afternoon, maybe the day after. We just have to push the herd onto new grass and get them settled, along with the bunch that are already there. We'll leave a few more riders there and this will be all over. There's nothing the Bar-M can do. They've abandoned the leases. I have every right to take them up."

He knew nothing of the events already in motion on the Bar-M.

He reached to touch her arm, hoping to turn her around for a hug or a kiss or some kind of encouragement. She responded by shrugging him off and stepping aside.

With her arms tightly folded across her chest she turned, leaning back on the counter for strength. Through tear clouded eyes she looked at her husband. Neither spoke for a moment. Her lips trembled. It was clear she wanted no part of what was happening.

When she finally spoke, her voice was quiet and strangled, rising through a throat tight with grief and concern. "Don't forget to look to the crib. Say goodbye to your son. I don't expect you'll ever see him again."

Baxter thought they'd been all through the issues around the land challenge. Her words took him by surprise. This was her first mention of their son.

"What are you saying Mable? Of course, I'll see him again. I expect we'll ride these miles of range together as he grows into the cattleman I know he can become. Him and his brothers and sisters, as they come along."

Mable struggled to clear her throat. "No. It's not going to be that way. You're wrong in this. You and all those fools shouting each other into false courage out in our yard.

"Herman Baxter, I have long loved you and there was a day I respected you. We have a good ranch. It's all we need. Up till now we've had a good life. We could still have a good life. But you've blinded yourself to the truth. Greed and envy have replaced your common sense. You were told to reduce the herd to what the grass can sustain. That was good advice. But you refused. You're blinded by anger and jealousy. You're setting out this morning to break the law. You're also breaking ranch country tradition of respecting another man's land."

It took her a moment and a couple of deep breaths to gather her words.

"In the process you're breaking whatever is left of us. You're breaking our marriage, our family. Your blindness and greed have turned you into an angry, shouting man that I hardly recognise."

Mable Baxter sniffed and wiped her eyes on the dish cloth she was holding in her hand.

"You can't win this push for more land. This isn't the old, unsettled Texas. You can't just take land here with a gun and expect to keep it. You've been told that time and again.

"You think the Bar-M will simply stand down while others take up their land? They won't. They'll fight back, and they'll drive your cattle off. I fully expect by this time tomorrow you'll be draped over a saddle, you and some of those other fools, all coming home to be buried. If you somehow get home alive, you'll find me packed and ready to leave. I'll stay here to keep the chores done. I'll stay until you return, riding or draped over the saddle, either one. But then I'm leaving.

"I'm loading up a few things this morning. My baby and I will be going to Denver. I'll not live with you after the mess you're making of our lives. I have my own money and I can take care of myself. I'm going home to see my folks before I decide anything else. I'll not be coming back.

"Go chase your dream Herman. But understand me, I won't be part of that dream. Nor will my baby."

Herman said nothing. There was nothing he could say. His shock was complete. Her words were entirely unexpected. He stood there like a school boy, holding his hat in his hands and with his eyes cast to the floor.

Mable turned back to the counter. "Go Herman. Lead your foolish followers out of here. They're stinking the place up."

Baxter wondered for just a moment if he needed to listen to his weeping wife. Did he need to take her words seriously? He waivered for just the smallest fraction of a minute. But a man's pride is a fearful thing. Even set on a path to sure doom a man might charge ahead rather than stop to reconsider. The history books are thick with tales of men, and sometimes women, who fought against all odds, fought hopeless battles, sometimes fighting in the right and sometimes in the wrong, but always with a totally predictable outcome.

Left on his own, Baxter might have thought it through from a different viewpoint. He might have even talked it through with his wife again. But with a yard full of anxious neighbors and cowboys waiting for, depending on, his leadership he couldn't swallow his pride and tell the men to go home. He just couldn't do it.

35

BAXTER SENT FOUR MEN off the day before he planned to move the larger herd onto the Bar-M. They were to scout out the survey crew, forcing them to pack up and move out. He would deal with the fencing gang later.

Why anyone thought the effort would be successful after the earlier try at the survey camp would have been difficult to explain.

Of the men who attacked the survey camp the first time, all but the one Shep Trimble named Black Beard rolled their gear and rode back to Texas. Black Beard, needing his badly shot-up hand treated and bandaged, stayed on at the Baxter ranch. Each day of pain he lived through seemed to cause the growth of his need for revenge. He drew his back-up Colt from his bedroll and spent hours behind the corral, practicing with his left hand. His right hand would never again hold a weapon. With each shot fired his determination to kill the fast-talking survey camp wrangler grew until he thought of little else. He didn't know the wrangler's name, but he would never forget the face.

He was the first to step forward when Baxter asked for volunteers to ride after the surveyors.

With miles to go the men rode well into the night. They rode west, along what they thought must be the line between the Bar-M and the Baxter and Jenkins properties, knowing that the camp would be somewhere on that line as the crew slowly working their way east. Two or three hours before daylight the men saw a low-to-the-horizon glow. Knowing it to be the tail end of a camp fire, they rode closer. Soon the outline of the covered chuck wagon, cutting into the night sky, came into sight. Calling a halt, they whispered their plan. With time to wait they rode into a small huddle of rock off to the south and dismounted. Three of them leaned back against rocks and dozed. Black Beard had no intention of dozing.

As the barest indication of dawn showed from the east the raiders tightened their cinches and quietly mounted their restless horses. They rode towards the camp from three directions, one rider swinging to the north and Black Beard to the south. To come in from the west would have meant riding completely around the camp. They decided that it wasn't necessary to take the risk of being seen or heard.

The camp appeared to be night-quiet. There was no sign of morning activity except a bit of shuffling from the cooped-up chickens who were already starting their day. With carbines fully loaded and the hammers cocked, the raiders charged the camp, coming to a halt in a wide circle around the few, glowing coals still left in the campfire, and the rolled-out beds. They saw no guard on their ride in.

Sly Dumont, the assigned leader of the raiders hollered out, "Hello the camp. Rise and shine boys. The first man to reach for a weapon dies. Get up." He fired a shot into the air to emphasise his words.

When there was no response he again shouted, "Get up." There was still no comeback.

A moment later the response seemed to come from all directions, first a shout followed by the levering of six Winchesters, a sound it was impossible to misunderstand. The drawled-out shout came from the small willow bush beside the stream that attracted the surveyors to set up camp, took the raiders by complete surprise. The racking of the Winchesters came from men lying flat on the prairie grass, hidden by the darkness. The camp crew was out of sight, behind the raiders. The bedrolls seen in the partial light of early morning were nothing more than bunched up blankets.

Again, the shout from the willow bush. "Put them down men. Drop the weapons right there on the ground, the hand guns too. It ain't worth dyin for. Thirty a month is mighty poor wages for dyin."

Three of the raiders dropped their guns, looking all around in the semi-dark for the survey crew. With the dropping of the weapons the crew and their Bar-M guards started to rise from the grass. The raiders were clearly surrounded.

Black Beard held his carbine in his left hand. He held it down by his leg, looking all around. With the last shout from the trees he recognised the voice as belonging to the one who shot his hand half-off.

As Shep Trimble worked his way towards the edge of the willows, Black Beard picked him out of the morning gloom. With a screaming, angry, hate blinded shout he kicked his gelding into action, charging the willows, his Winchester spitting bullet after bullet in Shep's direction. The young Texan dove to the ground behind some willows, which were poor cover at best.

Black Beard, moved beyond reason by rage and his need for revenge, charged the bush. His shots were going wild as he held the carbine in his left hand, supported by what was left of his half-healed right hand. The free running horse was threatening to toss its rider off with its unguided, erratic run, causing the shots to be wild and off target. The outcome was inevitable.

Shep got turned around in time to get off one shot before he watched as Black Beard was literally lifted off the saddle by 44-40 slugs shot from half a dozen carbines. The horse fell to the ground as several wayward shots found their marks in the bay gelding.

Within seconds the camp fell to silence, even the chickens crowding together for cover.

The surveyors and the Bar-M guard riders circled the raiders as they walked out of the dark of the prairie grass into the remains of the camp fire light. They held their carbines at the ready. The three frightened raiders sat their mounts with their hands in the air.

One of the Bar-M men said, "Step down but keep your hands raised." The men did so. "Now sit down. Keep the hands up." There was no question of the raiders doing anything beyond following orders. One of them glanced over at Black Beard who lay crumpled on the ground, one knee folded beneath him, the carbine he couldn't shoot straight lying beside him.

Shep made his way into camp. Looking over the three raiders he said. "I surely don't understand you boys. First you follow the orders of a fool and come to do murder, all the time assuming we wouldn't have a look-out posted. Then you made as much noise as running buffalo. Can't imagine how supposedly bad men could be so stupid. Maybe you drank too much alkali water growing up. Or might could be you were dropped on your heads when y'all were still in yer mama's arms, all the time assuming any of you were ever human babies."

The men were searched for weapons, then backed against trees and tied. Shep and the guards weren't sure what to do with their prisoners.

One of the Bar-M guards stepped close to the tied-up men. "Here's the deal boys. You sit still and keep your mouths shut, you live until we get orders from the Bar-M. You cause a problem and... Well, you figure it out."

The two Bar-M guards threw harness on the wagon team and dragged the dead gelding off into the prairie, far from the camp. One of the surveyors took a shovel and dug a grave with the help of the Bar-M men. Black Beard was soon buried in the unmarked grave, with a jumble of rocks piled on top of the soft earth to discourage scavengers.

Shep was putting breakfast together while the surveyors got ready for a day of work, unwrapping their instruments from the oiled canvas bags that protected them from rain or dew. Shep grinned at the men who hired him for the summer. "You boys ready for a day's work or do you want me to sing you a lullaby to calm your troubled nerves?"

Lod Anderson looked at his survey partners. "It's too early in the morning for this. I'm trying to remember which one of you it was that hired this Texan. Don't exactly know if I should shoot you or him."

36

THE BAXTER HERD WAS JOINED by smaller bunches brought in by Cox and a few neighboring ranchers. Jenkins, coming in from further to the west, was independently driving a herd north, onto Bar-M grass, hoping to get there before Baxter and his bunch had time to spread out. His intention was to stake out the western portion for himself.

The surveyors had worked their way past that point, putting them midway between the Jenkins and Baxter herds. With the distances being so great the surveyors were unaware of either herd.

Jenkins was convinced that having animals in place would put him in a position to lay first claim to a sizable portion of Mac's lease land. With no one there to impede his travels the crew drive several miles into the northern range.

Madison and Ethan were on their way back to join the fence crew after two nights at the sheep camp. Their trail took them a bit south of the fence camp but still north of where Jenkins was pushing his herd. With time to spare they decided to ride some distance east to scout out the land they'd not yet ridden. The Bar-M was a big ranch. There was much of it the men hadn't seen.

A gathering cloud of dust on the south-eastern horizon caused the two riders to pull to a stop. "Now, what in the world?" asked Madison. Ethen offered no answer.

As if thinking the same thought, the two kicked their animals into a lope towards a steep-rising, rocky outcrop a quarter mile to the south. Slowing for the grind up the steep trail, the horses made their way to the top, picking a trail through the scattered boulders. Coming out on a somewhat level surface the riders eased towards the east as far as possible. The two men sat their mounts, studying the movement below them and about three or four miles further east. Clouds of wind-blown dust hid most of the activity.

After a minute Ethan spoke. "Had me a pretty good looking-glass once, some time back. Got it in trade for an extra horse I didn't really need. Man I got it off'n was an army deserter. He figured his chances were more likely to improve with distance, than by looking at far-off places with the use of that glass. Took the horse and paid me a little to boot. Traded that glass off a while later in payment for a few nights in a run-down hotel bed and some greasy meals.

"Surprising what a man down on his luck might do on a cold winter night. Be good to have that glass back about now though."

Madison was rolling a smoke, tucking it inside his jacket against the wind. He said nothing until he was finished and was enjoyed the first drag. "Well, you're right on both counts. Done some things best forgot my own self, time to time. And I expect we'd see more detail under that flying dirt with a glass. Don't really need it though, comes right down to it. What way'd you say them animals is walking?"

His riding partner smiled without turning his head. "Why, I'd say that would be north. I'd also say they're at least seven or eight miles inside the Bar-M. Shouldn't aught to be there I'd say, if you're interested in my opinion."

The two men sat there in silence while Madison smoked his cigarette down to a nub. He crushed the glowing tip on the saddle horn and rubbed the stub between the palms of his two hands until he felt no heat from the little bit of tobacco that remained. He opened his hands, releasing the now cold remnants to the winds. Without a word Madison turned his mount back towards the trail and the two cowboys made their way down onto the prairie floor. Madison turned his head towards Ethan, so the wind wouldn't scatter his words. "I'm thinking we should aught to go and take us a look."

Ethan shouted back, "Never thought no other thing."

The two riders made no attempt to hide themselves, riding towards the herd in full view. It took just a few minutes to close in on the distance. Out of the dust cloud they watched as the point rider loped ahead of the herd. Without warning or any attempt to talk, and far outside the range of a Colt, the point man dragged his weapon from the holster and pointed two shots in the direction of the Bar-M riders. The shots fell far short. The wind whipped away whatever sound the effort made. It was only the sight of two short lived puffs of greyish smoke that told Madison and Ethan that the man had pulled the trigger. It was a fool move by the point man. If he meant it as a warning it showed a lack of judgement on his part.

The two Bar-M men pulled up, studying the herd and the two men gathered around the shooter. One of them pointed towards the oncoming Bar-M riders.

Madison carried a Winchester 44-40 carbine in his saddle scabbard. Although the carbine had a better range than the point man's Colt, he was still considerably outside effective shooting distance.

Ethan casually swung to the ground and walked to the off side of his horse. Unbuckling two hold-down straps and lifting a dust cover off the Sharps 50 cal. single shot buffalo gun he'd been carrying for several years, he drew the weapon. Pulling three cartridges as big as his thumb from a jacket pocket, he stepped to a little rise in the ground, sunk to his knees and then to a prone position. Without conscious thought he calculated distance, elevation, wind. The prairie wind was always a factor with long range shooting. Distance could be guessed with some accuracy. The effect of wind was a gamble.

Ethan spoke out of the side of his mouth with his cheek nestled against the Sharps. "Take ahol't a them reins." The statement was unnecessary. Madison picked up the leathers as soon as Ethan sunk to the ground with the gun. Chasing a frightened horse was no part of the plan, although Madison wasn't exactly sure what the plan was.

Madison hesitated to ask but he finally overcame his reluctance. "You figurin to lay a man down or just get their attention?" He couldn't see that a dead man would make their day go any easier.

Ethan spoke out of the side of his mouth again. "You keep your eye on the black that point rider's a-settin on."

Madison adjusted the sights twice and then settled down, wiggling himself firmly against the grass. He lay still for almost a minute, waiting for the three riders to quit milling around. The herders appeared to be arguing, their arms waving in the air and occasionally pointing at Madison and Ethan. Finally, the point rider turned his horse broadside to Madison.

The Sharps sent its projectile off with a roar and a belch of smoke. Madison immediately ejected the spent shell and stuffed in a new cartridge. It took perhaps two seconds for the first shot to reach its target. The black horse tossed its head and crumpled to the ground. The rider barely had time to kick his feet free before leaping away as the horse fell to its side, thrashing out its final moves.

The Sharps roared again. This time Madison's calculations were off just a bit. A second horse, the intended target, was spared as the animals thrashed around in a panic. Twenty feet behind the three riders a longhorn wasn't so fortunate. The unlucky animal made a frantic leap and turned into the herd, its massive horns clearing a path before the animal staggered to a halt. The brute sagged to its knees and then fell on its side, its legs raising dust as they beat a pattern in the dry sod.

The herd broke into a shambling run, turning into itself, causing confusion before finally lining out to the east at a dead run, away from the dying animal. The drive crew gave chase, leaving the grounded point rider standing beside his dead horse in a cloud of dust. Ethan could see the man waving his arms as if shouting at the departing riders.

Madison ejected the second spent shell and rose to his feet. He put both emptied cartridge casings back into his pocket. They would be re-loaded as time allowed. Showing no particular hurry, he slid the Sharps back into the scabbard and re-fit the dust cover. With that done, he took the reins from Ethan with a nod of thanks and swung aboard. "Let's go see what we've got."

The running herd was a half mile away and slowing to a stop when the two Bar-M riders pulled within ear-shot of the drover with the Colt. Madison was the first to speak, calling out over the steady whine of the wind. "You put that pop gun back into its sack and lift your hands. Else my friend here will be forced to do something unpleasant." Ethan held his carbine with the butt resting on his thigh and the barrel facing the sky.

The angry man put the Colt back and lifted his hands shoulder high. The look on his face said, 'might just turn the tables one day and then we'll see.'

As Madison and Ethan rode closer, Madison studied the man's face more closely and made a decision. "On second thought, don't know as you have enough sense to be trusted. How be you pass that pop-gun to me? Hold it by the barrel. If you point it at me my friend will shoot you dead, and that would be a waste, given the price of ammunition and all."

With that accomplished, Madison spoke again. "Now. tell us your name and what you think you're doing here on another man's grass."

"Name's Jenkins. I own that herd you just scared off. Ranch to the south a few miles. I'm lay'n claim to this here unused land as it's my perfect right to do. You owe me a horse and a fat steer."

Madison, ignoring the comment about the dead horse and steer, lifted his hat off and slapped it against his leg. Chuckling without mirth he said, "Don't much think you're going to get any of this here land. Might get six feet of it if'n you don't get your herd back onto your own grass. The M's about had enough of you land grabbers."

The two Bar-M riders looked at each other, waiting for someone to suggest the next move. Ethan finally said, "Not much more we can do here. It'd be good to make camp before chuck."

Ethan put his carbine away and pointed at the dead steer. "I see you got a belt knife there Mr. Jenkins. How be you make your way over to that steer and carve out the two hind quarters?"

Jenkins gave Ethan an angry, questioning look. "So, first you shoot my steer and now you're going to steal my beef? Even if I can't stop you I ain't going to help you."

Ethan pulled the tie string off his lariat, loosening a loop of rope. He swung it so quickly that Jenkins had it over his head and tight around his throat before he even tried to move out of the way. Ethan gave a small tug and said, "Now, Mr. land stealer, you got you a choice. You carve out that beef and we'll give you a ride to our camp. Or you can walk to camp with me pulling you along with this here rope. Either way, we're taking the beef. What'll it be?"

Jenkins lifted the rope off his shoulders and walked to the downed steer.

Madison grinned at his riding partner and kicked his horse into motion. "Y'all sit tight for a bit. I'll be back shortly"

With just a few well practiced slices the very reluctant Jenkins had one hind quarter off and laying on the grass. Ethan threw his rope around the front leg and rode his horse away, flipping the steer onto the other side. Jenkins gripped the knife with his bloody hand and went to work. Before long the two hind quarters were laying side by side, waiting for the next step.

Madison rode to where the herd was milling around, with the herders trying to hold it tight against another run. As he rode up to the herd three riders pulled together, watching him with suspicion. No one pulled a weapon.

"Well boys, I figure you're all just following the orders of a fool, so the M won't hold anything against you for that. What you have to do now is get these animals off the M's grass before night falls. We'll be coming over this way first thing tomorrow morning. Any animals we find here will be impounded to pay for the M's grass y'all let them eat. Mr. Jenkin's decided to stay and visit with us for a while, so you have it to do yourself. Best get at it."

He turned and rode away without looking back.

When Madison returned the two Bar-M riders were silent for another few moments while Jenkins completed the butchering job, cutting the legs off at the knees.

With a piggin string, Madison tied loops over the two knee joints, creating a sling. Just to be sure the rig would carry the weight he duplicated the sling with a second piggin string. Madison and Jenkins then took one quarter each, laying the burden behind Ethan's saddle, being careful to lay the piggin strings across the saddle's skirt. The horse startled at the extra weight and the smell of blood. Madison figured the beef would adequately bleed out on the ride to camp.

Back in the saddle, Madison kicked a foot free of a stirrup. He looked down at Jenkins. "You pass me up that knife and any other weapons you have. Then you swing up behind me. We'll ride ahead. If'n you make the slightest move with unfriendly intentions my partner there will shoot you in the head. Is that understood Mr. Jenkins?"

The three men rode into the fence camp two hours later. Ethan rode up to the camp kitchen tent. He hollered to whoever was inside. "Got some fresh beef here if'n you want it."

Hanna Patterson and Mable McGrew stepped out of the tent. The two husky women sized up the situation. They walked one on each side of the horse and lifted the beef off as if the weight were nothing. Ethan waited a moment to hear their thanks spoken but when no sound came from the cook tent he finally gave it up with a grin.

Ethan rode his horse to the creek and stepped down. He loosened the cinch, so the animal could drink. Madison was already there.

Ethan asked his partner, "What'd you do with your prisoner?"

"He's tied to a wagon wheel. We'll leave him there tonight and discuss the next step in the morning."

37

MAC AND HIS CREW took possession of the Baxter herd. They started turning it for the drive back south towards its home grass. Mac estimated the approximately one thousand head were about six miles north of his southern most border. He left the driving to Taz and the crew. With Bobby, Jeremiah and Luke, he rode to the west and swung past the herd. Almost immediately the riders saw a haze of dust billowing up on the southern horizon. The grey cloud was obviously made by another driven herd. It could be nothing else.

No one spoke, although every man kept his eye on the roiling grey mass. Once well ahead of the animals already on the Bar-M they began veering to the east to meet the oncoming bunch. Mac welcomed the silence of his riding partners as giving him time to think what his response to this further intrusion onto his land should be. He knew Baxter and Cox, especially, were short tempered and excitable men. Their fear of failure and their anger only complicated matters. He had no knowledge of who might have thrown in with the two leaders or what their reaction to having their plans foiled might be.

At the rear of the first herd the Bar-M riders were tightening the brutes together to make driving easier. The animals were gradually overcoming the confusion, slowly turning as the cowboys pushed them with shouts and swats with coiled lariats. With much bawling and clanking of horns the animals were sluggishly finding their places in the hierarchy of the herd. At the same time the Bar-M men were keeping one eye on the approaching dust cloud.

Taz, Mac's foreman, was in a quandary. He was following Mac's orders. The herd was turning and starting to move, as Mac had directed. But he also saw Mac and the other three riders facing the oncoming herd by themselves and undermanned. Seldom one to question or disobey orders, Taz was slow to do so now. But finally, he made a decision.

Riding over to where Wallace was gathering up a few W animals his crew isolated from the larger herd, he said, "I need you to take charge here Wallace. I'm taking the Bar-M crew forward. I can't leave Mac and them alone to face whatever is under that dust cloud over there. Just do what you can. We can always gather up this bunch later if necessary."

Without waiting for an answer, he rode forward and started calling out the M riders. One man called to another until they all pulled out and gathered around Taz. "We're leaving this herd with the W. We'll ride now to catch up with Mac and them. Don't know what all's coming this way, but I figure to find out. Let's ride."

Taz and the crew were still a quarter mile behind Mac when four riders broke out of the oncoming dust and rode off to the west. They disappeared into a small swale in the land. The strange action drew Mac's immediate attention. From behind the oncoming cattle Mac heard several gunshots and distant shouts. The point rider swung east, running full out to get clear of the path of the now running cattle. The swing and flank riders could be seen shouting and swatting animals with coiled lariats. Clearly, the goal was to drive the herd right over whoever stood in its way.

With the cattle in full run the remaining riders dropped out and made a running dash for the tree lined swale the first riders had dropped into.

If Baxter had convinced himself that being rid of Mac would solve his problems, he came to that conclusion without remembering the earlier warning from Margo.

With less than a mile separating the herd from the Bar-M riders, the stampeding animals were closing the distance quickly. Mac pushed his horse into a run and swung to the west, hoping to get clear of the path of the charging longhorns. The others followed.

Taz made his second major decision of the morning. Splitting his riders in half, he motioned for one group to follow Mac and for the second group to follow him to the east. The men kicked their horses into a full gallop as the herd came charging towards them.

Taz and his followers had less distance to cover than the men riding to the west. They rode clear of the herd and gathered to a stop as the cattle started surging past. Without any warning, shots were heard. Dust blocked out any vision of the shooters. Taz pulled his carbine and looked around at the men riding with him. The men were all pulling weapons as their frightened riding animals rolled their eyes back in their heads. Taz needlessly shouted, "Hold them down and spread out." It was only then that he noticed the rider beside him, a man named Eli Hopkins, was slumped over his saddle with his hands clasped tightly against his stomach. Blood seeped through his spread-out fingers.

As Taz was reaching to hold Eli on the saddle his own horse crumpled beneath him. He frantically kicked his feet free and slid off the rump of the collapsing animal. The horse went down and didn't move. Taz scrambled and rolled until he was behind the downed horse. He stuck his head up high enough to look around. Eli was lying on the grass a few feet away, totally exposed. Taz laid his carbine down and waited for a quiet moment when there was no shooting. With two quick, crouching steps he was beside the wounded man. Ignoring Eli's pained screams Taz grabbed his shirt collar and dragged him behind the horse. He dove for cover himself as the shooting started up again.

Taz wasn't sure where his other riders were but there was nothing he could do about it. He reached over and turned Eli's head, so the two men were facing one another. "You hang on there Eli. We'll get you to help just as quick as we can."

Eli took a surprisingly strong grip on Taz's shirt sleeve. "Known a couple of old cowpokes. Drunks whittling their last days away in some dusty town. Broken bones healed crooked. Teeth gone. Pockets empty. No one left that cared. Never saw the attraction to it." He stopped and took several deep breaths, squinting against the pain. "This, this is better. Ride well, my friend."

Despite the turmoil, charging cattle, dust and shooting all around him, Taz looked at this faithful cowboy who had followed him to his death. He gently reached over and closed his eyes. "Sleep tight Eli. You deserved better than this. I'm sorry old buddy. Sorry!"

Taz turned back in time to see three riders advancing out of the dust cloud at a charging gallop, their weapons spitting lead. Throwing caution to the wind he rose up on his elbows and laid the carbine across the dead horse. Six shots pumped out as fast as he could aim, and trigger had two of the men on the ground, their horses joining the longhorns in their uncontrolled panic. The third rider veered off to the east only to be met by a volley of shots from a pocket of boulders the Bar-M crew took cover behind. With those three men down there appeared to be no further threat from that flank of the herd.

Taz turned at the sound of running horses, lifting his weapon and taking aim at the approaching riders. Before he could press the trigger, he recognized the big black Willard

Wallace rode. He lowered the gun and stood to his feet. The other Bar-M riders were making their way up from their rocky shelter. Every man was looking around, watchful of danger.

Wallace pulled the black to a stop. "Sorry it took so long to get here Taz. Everyone alright?"

Taz turned half around and silently indicated Eli, lying behind the downed horse. No words were necessary. As the other M riders gathered around, Taz counted them off in his head. They were all accounted for.

Taz addressed Wallace. "Suppose a couple of you could catch up our horses? I expect they're scattered from here to breakfast by now."

A quick nod from Wallace was all it took to send his crew after the loose horses. Taz slowly turned and walked to where the downed Baxter followers lay crumpled on the grass. The herd had mostly passed towards the north. The few stragglers were slowing to a weary shuffle and soon came to a complete stop. The wind-blown dust started to dissipate. Where the two herds came together pandemonium reigned. Taz took a quick look and figured the cattle could sort it out for themselves.

As the Bar-M foreman came up to the downed Baxter riders he sensed movement behind him. He turned to see the rest of the men following along, each man carrying his weapon at the ready and with an eye for continuing trouble. He strode up to a dead cowboy and, with the toe of his boot turned him over. Others were doing the same. Everyone was silent. The idea of dying over a few acres of another man's grass was a sobering thing.

One of the W riders was the first to speak. "I've seen every one of these boys at roundups."

Willard Wallace spoke quietly, looking at a man brought down by the Bar-M riders sheltering in the rocks. The man was littered with bullet holes. "This is Cox. Small man with big ideas. Made up to follow Baxter in his hunt for grass." He was silent again for a moment and then said quietly, "Well, Cox, you wanted M grass. How do you like it?"

The horses hadn't run far, and the W riders soon had them bunched. Each man swung aboard and kicked off to the west. Taz was riding a captured Cox animal as his own had gone down in the attack.

With no herd between them they chose the shortest route and angled to where they could see the distant images of Mac's gathered followers.

Although it was now silent in the west, with no sign of the Baxter riders, he figured whatever action would be taken would be at that location.

38

ON THE WEST FLANK of the stampeding herd Mac and his followers barely made it to safety. With their start more to the east, the crew Taz sent to help Mac would have been caught up in the charging longhorns if they had not been further to the rear, giving them a couple of extra, precious moments. They made it to safety with scant seconds to spare. Their terrorized horses milled around in frantic circles before the riders finally got them settled down.

One of the crewmen explained the actions taken by Taz. Mac listened and simply nodded.

There was no sign of the Baxter crew, but everyone knew they were out there somewhere, and they would be coming. They had to. That's what this whole exercise was all about.

Had Baxter cared to find out more about Mac and Luke he would have known his grab for more land could not be successful.

Regardless of what Baxter tried to tell his wife, anyone thinking about the land grab would know it wasn't going to happen without the Bar-M and the Lazy-L fighting back. They had to fight back. Any man not protecting his own holdings would be shamed out of the country.

Mac had never shown himself to be a man of anger or a man looking to pick a fight. Although stern about the things that mattered most to him, those that knew him best thought of him as a gentleman.

Since his marriage, Luke had been on his best behavior, showing a side of his personality that was seldom evident on the drives up from Texas.

But anyone working beside Mac or Luke in the gathering of wild longhorns or who stood beside either of them when they were wearing their uniforms, one grey, one blue, knew what lay just below the surface, and wanted no part of it from either man.

Mac looked all around as the cattle started to slow from their initial hard run. These weren't the same-natured animals as those Mac and Luke dug out of the south Texas brush and taken north. Those animals would fight anything or everything, seeing themselves as the lords of their small pieces of ground. The south Colorado animals were several generations removed from those wild Texas longhorns. They showed their more-or-less peaceful natures by running only reluctantly.

Mac saw no logical place to hole up for shelter. Luke rode up beside him, "What do you think, partner?"

"I think that bunch are hoping to find a way to surprise us. Just can't figure out what it is. We can see a mile to the south and it's all clear. There's some rougher country just beyond that rise, where you see those trees. A pocket of rocks, a stream bed, brush and such. It's not a big area but enough to shelter some men and horses. I suspect that's where they've gone to ground."

Mac took a long look around again. "Trouble is, if we go try to dig them out they might end up with the advantage. I'd rather live to fight another day than lose a man today. What's your take?"

Luke, always bold, and sometimes close to reckless in battle, expressed a different opinion. "Why don't we ride that way? Take a look at the situation. We can't win no battles sittin here."

Mac grinned in spite of the danger. "There was a time a while back, my friend, when you and I both had nothing to lose but our lives, and those not very highly valued by the ones who issued us the uniforms and gave the orders. But now we're both older. We move more slowly. We've got wives. We've got children. We've got ranches. We've got responsibilities. And these men siding us are working cowboys, not government conscripts."

Luke looked away and then turned his face back to Mac with a far-away look in his eye. "Don't you sometimes miss it? Don't you ever just want to pick up and have at it?"

Mac didn't bother answering. Luke already knew what his answer would be.

Bobby rode up to join the two men. "I'm thinking we should spread out and take a slow meander down that way." He was pointing south. "No need to put ourselves at serious risk. But hanging here is not the solution. I'm going. I've got my old deputy badge in my pocket. Maybe I can arrest them." He broke into a cynical chuckle. "Any as wants to come along, now's the time."

Jeremiah rode up beside Bobby. Mac, having needed the bit of a push provided by his brothers, joined them. The three brothers moved south at a slow but steady walk, their carbines held across their saddle bows, each man ready. Luke pushed his horse to the front and closed in on the brothers.

The rest of the crew staked out places behind and to the sides. Each man had doubts. Each man held private fears. Going into battle did that to a man. Each man knew he could die this day. But each man also did his duty without hesitation, knowing that if he chose to hang back he would have to leave the country. No cowboy would ride with a man that couldn't be trusted to stand tall when the chips were down.

Where Bobby and Luke were 'get up and get at em' men, Mac was more the tactician. Riding into what could be nothing less than a battle, where men were sure to die or be wounded, he was trying to see how to turn the situation to his side's advantage. He was convinced the Baxter crew had found shelter of sorts in the rougher land beyond the small rise just up ahead. Leading fully exposed men into that situation was troubling the ranch owner.

Before the riders covered half the distance to the sheltering rise of land, Luke chuckled and pointed off to the east. "Well, looky there! If'n that ain't a site for sore eyes."

Every eye followed Luke's pointing finger. No hoof sounds reached them yet, but they could see that Taz, Wallace and their crews were angling in from the east, pushing their horses to a distance eating gallop. They were angled in a way that would take them to the south of the Baxter hiding place, putting them behind the hidden men, if Mac's figuring was correct. Mac silently wondered if the approaching riders were able to see what they were riding into. He found himself praying they could and that they would not be riding into a deadly surprise.

Mac couldn't know, but as Taz and Wallace drew closer Taz recognised the area. As foreman of the Bar-M he rode the area many times, taking advantage of the little stream to water his horse or to boil a cup of coffee. He quickly saw the rough hollow as a likely hiding place. He purposely angled to be on the downward side from Mac's bunch. The riders followed.

Trying to calculate distances and riding speeds, Mac pushed his horse into a trot, wanting to arrive at the battle ground at the same time as Taz's bunch. There was a lot staked on his belief that the raiders were hunkered down behind the rise. If he was wrong on that he might be leading the crew into a disaster.

Keeping his eye on Taz and calculating when he would close on the Baxter crew, Mac pushed his animal into a slow run. Over the sound of hoof beats he hollered, "Spread out.

We'll ride right over the rise and in among them. We can't stand off and let them stay sheltered. Take all the cover you can find and don't take any foolish chances."

He let another moment pass, then, leaning towards Bobby he said, "Grab three or four men. Stand down here and get ready to shoot any man that pops his head over that bank."

Bobby immediately pulled aside and held his hand up to a group of four men riding close together. Within seconds he had one man holding the reins and three, plus himself, spread out, squatted on one knee, weapons held at the ready, targeting the boulder covered rise two hundred yards ahead. Almost immediately two men pushed rifles over the lip of the bank. With their hats removed only the tops of their heads and their eyes showed. Two carbines from Bobby's bunch, spaced between the running horses, forced them back down.

The timing for the arrival of the two crews was near perfect. Each rider had a weapon in hand and some, finding courage in rebel yells, filled the air with shrill sounds. Most were hunkered down behind their horse's necks. Although the Baxter crew were crouched down and well sheltered, the attacking force was overwhelming. Baxter didn't have as many followers as Mac thought he might have. Nor were the Baxter riders as convinced of the rightness of their cause as their boss was.

Mac rode ten feet in the lead. He swept over the rise without knowing what he would encounter. The rest of the crew followed. On the other side of the little rocky enclosure Taz and his bunch were doing the same. Some of Mac's crew held their carbines in their left hands, along with the reins and pulled their Colts. For close in, one-handed work the short guns held the day. The Baxter crew were confused by the two-pronged skirmish and were overwhelmed by the attacking numbers. The battle lasted less than one minute.

Two Bar-M horses went down, their riders leaping off with weapons in hand, showing a nimbleness that only a young, seasoned rider can show. Once on foot, one man went down with a bullet in his leg. He squirmed around until he was facing the enemy and poured shot after shot from his carbine.

The Baxter crew got only one shot each off, at rapidly moving targets, before the attacking riders were right among them. Hugging the ground and cowing behind boulders as Bar-M horses leaped over the barriers or ran between them, there was little the defenders could do. There was considerable danger of friend shooting friend, so close was the action. One Baxter rider dropped his gun and leaped to his feet with his hands raised high. That seemed to start a flurry of surrenders. Baxter himself rose from behind a rock and ran, frantically trying for a horse. Unfortunately for him, he chose to run right towards Luke. With a single shot Luke laid him down. The 44-40 slug took him high in his chest. He was lifted off his feet, dead before he hit the ground.

With the death of Baxter, whatever fight had been left in the raiders disappeared.

39

THE BAXTER CREW WERE DISARMED and gathered in a loose circle up on the open plain. Taz sent a couple of men back down the line to re-load and bring up the pack horses that were staked out a few miles back.

Bobby and Jeremiah put a fire together in anticipation of the arrival of the packs, where there would be coffee and some simple food available.

Wallace sought out Mac. The two men shook hands. "We'll be leaving for home now Mac. This get-together would appear to be about over. I'm wishing you luck my friend and thanking you for standing up to these others. You know you can call if ever there's need."

The W crew were mounted and ready to ride for home. They would pick up their loose cattle along the way. Mac went among them, shaking hands and thanking each one. Taz did the same.

Luke ambled over to Wallace. "We're a fair few miles apart, you and me, but I'd enjoy getting to know you better. My wife always looks forward to a bit of company too. You ever find yourself over west you come by the Lazy-L. You'll be made a welcome."

Wallace nodded his thanks.

Wallace swung aboard his big black gelding. "By the way Mac. You never asked, and we've never talked about it but I'm expecting to pay my half for the fence down this east boundary. The fencing and the surveying too. You do the numbers and we'll square up."

"Well, that's good of you and I thank you. But it's not necessary from my point Willard."

"It's necessary from my point though. You've started this entire country on a new life and I want to be a full part of it. Can't be a part if I don't pay my way. See you soon." For Wallace the matter was settled. With a tilt of his hat he turned north, and the men rode for home.

Taz and Mac rode over to the other battle ground together. Three crewmen rode along, leading horses to load the dead cowboys on. As they were nearing the site they heard the crunching of wagon wheels and the clatter of trace chains. A quick look showed a team-drawn wagon rising over a slight grade.

Mac pulled up and stood in his stirrups to see who was coming. He recognised his wagon and team but couldn't make out the two people riding the box with the horses shielding them from a clear view. The wagon was escorted by a rider on each side. He waited where he was, watching the approaching wagon. Before long he said, "That's Cray Dobbs riding the black. Looks like Ezzy Hannibal on the bay."

Taz looked at Mac before speaking, waiting to see if the boss had more to say. Mac didn't. Taz quietly said, "I do believe that's Margo and Mama riding the wagon. Mama has the ribbons. That woman truly loves driving a team."

Mac was all set to grumble about his wife putting herself at risk. Taz's comment moved him to another direction. "Not always. When we first met Mama, she preferred horseback. Wouldn't cross even the smallest stream on a wagon seat."

The men riding with Mac were gently laying Eli Hopkins over a saddle, ready to tie the dead Bar-M rider down. Mac waved a hand. "Put him back down boys. We'll use the wagon." With that he stepped to the ground and waited while the wagon pulled up beside him. Margo leaped off the wagon like a young girl and threw herself into Mac's arms, nearly bowling him over. She gave him a long hug that embarrassed Mac in front of the other men, before asking, "Is it over?"

"It's over." His tired voice held no sound of victory or joy.

"Tell me," said Margo.

Mac pushed her off just a little and turned her to where the men were laying out the bodies. Margo looked, shuddered and began weeping. "Who."

Mac continued in his solemn manner. "Of our bunch, just Eli. One injured over there." He indicated the other battle site with a nod of his head. "A few others from the Cox and Baxter riders are down. I don't know how many or who they are."

Margo continued clinging to her husband while she wept. Mama went among the dead, confirming that there was nothing to be done.

Mac called Taz over. "Taz, I'd appreciate if you'd pull this wagon over and load those men. Gently, with respect."

Taz took hold of the bridle of one horse and led the team the fifty feet to where the bodies lay. The box was piled partially full of hay with a few folded blankets on top. Mac could see where the outline of sleeping forms pressed the blankets into the hay. Mama's medical box was settled carefully into a corner. A bag of oats lay beside it.

Margo saw Mac examining the wagon. "We've been on the way since yesterday morning. Drove all night. Mama and I got some sleep on the hay last night, but these men have been up and riding for too many hours. Men and animals are all exhausted. We should let the men sleep some and unharness the team while they graze."

Mac nodded in agreement. "We'll do that but not here. We'll load up and go over to where the rest of the crew are."

It took but a few minutes for the crew to load the bodies and pick up the downed weapons, lost hats, and whatever else they found on the battleground. The saddles and bridles were pulled from two dead horses.

The solemn procession made their way to where the Bar-M crew were drinking coffee and eating cold biscuits. The Baxter riders were seated in a group off to the side. They held empty coffee cups in their hands, waiting for the next pot to come to a boil.

The wounded Bar-M rider lay on a blanket with his leg raised over a saddle, his bloody pant leg split and folded back. Mama climbed off the wagon and immediately went to him.

No one spoke as Margo stepped to the ground. No one seemed to know what to say. As if expecting the men to understand her meaning she put her hands on her hips and said, "How many over here?"

No one spoke for a few moments. Finally, Bobby said, "One of us with a hole in his leg. One of theirs dead. That's Baxter. A few scratches and close calls."

Mama took charge of the wounded while a couple of men started placing Baxter's body into the wagon.

Mac strode over to the wagon and spoke to Luke. "Take Eli out of there and hold him off to the side.

"Roll the wagon over to the lip of that swale where the battle was fought. Lay the bodies out there and bring the wagon back."

There was nothing in the mood of the day that would indicate that questioning Mac would be a good idea.

The bodies were laid out and the team watered and turned loose to graze. Cray and Ezzy cared for their animals before turning them loose and finding mugs for coffee.

Mac gathered the men beside the five laid-out bodies, Bar-M and Baxter crews standing together. With a paper and pencil taken from his shirt pocket he said, "Names. I need the names of these men."

With no further instructions he looked at the group. No one spoke for a while. Finally, Cray stepped foreword. "I know them all Mac. That's Baxter at the far end. Cox is beside him. Then Carman Solara, Toya Hernandez, Billy Willoughby."

Mac carefully wrote the names down. Looking up from that task he said, "All of you take a good look. These men were alive an hour ago. They should be alive now except for foolish pride. Take a look and remember the next time someone comes up with another foolish idea."

There was not a sound from the gathered crews.

Mac got their attention again. "If anyone wishes to say something over these men now is the time." No one spoke until Cray stepped forward, removed his hat and said. "A couple of minute's silence will say the words for us." With that he held his hat in front of his chest and bowed his head. One by one the men followed his pattern. Not a sound was heard. Finally, after what seemed like a very long time but was, in fact just over two minutes, Cray put his hat back on and cleared his throat. "Thank you, men."

Mac spoke again. "Now listen men. All of you. Bar-M? You're to saddle up and ride for home. You should make the close-in line shack before dark.

"Now, I need three of you others to volunteer to grab that shovel off the wagon and dig some graves in this hollow. Keep them back from the high water mark. Who will it be?" Every man, Bar-M and Baxter, together, raised a hand.

Mac said, "Thanks men, we'll change the plan just a little then. Someone grab that shovel and you can take turns.

"Then you Baxter's will ride home together. You can gather up that herd and take it with you. I'm making the assumption that you men know it's over. There'll be no more fighting over land. Do you all understand that?"

A few half-raised hands and a lot of unintelligible mumbles acknowledged the truth of the matter.

Mac spoke again. "Most of you were just riding for your brands, working for wages. None of this will be laid at your feet. Go back to your ranches and work hard. There's two widows that are going to need a lot of help. A couple of you are small owners who never should have been here in the first place. Put this all behind you and take care of your own ranches."

The men waited while Mac seemed to be gathering his thoughts.

He finally spoke again. "You might not believe it right at this minute, but you can call on the Bar-M if you need anything. Baxter and Cox were never our enemies and I'm truly sorry they saw it differently."

With that he walked over to where his crew were readying themselves for the long ride home. They would be ready when the digging was done and the bodies covered.

Mama had the injured rider comfortably stowed in the back of the wagon.

Mac pulled Margo over to the side where they could talk. "I'm riding down to Baxters. We're safe enough now and I'd like you to come with me. Mable is going to need a woman beside her right now."

Margo asked, "Can we borrow a horse from one of the men."

Mac called Taz. "Taz, can you pick out a good horse and saddle for Margo please? We're riding down to Baxters and the wagon will be going home. A man or two can ride the wagon to free up a riding animal. And Taz, we'll be a couple of days getting home. Give the men a full day of rest. More if you think they need it. Then put the crew back to work.

"Mama tells me our wounded back at Mex Town are recovering alright, so turn those others loose with a warning. Then we'll call this shindig done."

Taz nodded in agreement and added, "Luke told me about the mess at the line cabin. We'll deal with that too. You have three extra graves dug here and I'll see that the men from the cabin get buried. I got their names from one of the Baxter riders, so we can mark the graves."

The five bodies were soon in the ground and a map made to show where the bodies lay. Their pockets been emptied into their kerchiefs and kept for whoever might claim their belongings. Eli was laid out separate from the others.

Taz and the Bar-M were saddling up to start north. The Baxter riders were readying to go after the cattle. Mac spoke to the group again. "Men, it's been a long day for everyone. No one's in the mood for any more trouble. You've been given your guns. They're all unloaded. You can load them after we're all gone. I'm hoping you all understand that I'm taking you at your word. The fight is over. If any of you start it again there will be no mercy."

While the men were breaking camp, someone shouted and pointed to the west, where a small group of riders were trotting towards them. Several Bar-M men picked up their weapons and stood to repel the riders if that became necessary. One of the oncoming riders spurred ahead and waved his hat, the universal sign of friendship. Taz studied the approaching men. "That's our boys. Two of them anyway. Don't know the others."

As the men rode into camp Taz said, "Thought y'all was guarding the surveyors."

The rider who had assumed the lead grinned and tilted his hat back a bit before saying, "We were, and we did. One man down. Buried him. These here are the last of them. Hated to waste any more lead shooting them so thought we'd bring them to headquarters. Let someone else decide what to do with them. When we heard shooting out this way we turned and set out to find what was going on. Judging by who's standing and who's sitting I'd guess we're on the winning side."

Mac spoke for the first time. "There's no winners in such as this. We're about to break camp. Step down and grab a cup before someone pours the last of the coffee on the fire."

The three new prisoners were added to the others who would be heading south with the cattle.

40

IT WAS EARLY EVENING when Mac, Margo and Cray Dobbs rode into the Baxter ranch yard. Mable Baxter saw them coming and was waiting at the yard gate. The three riders held their animals twenty feet back. No one spoke. Mable Baxter was fighting tears. Her bottom lip and chin were trembling.

Margo finally swung to the ground and slowly made her way towards the new widow. She stopped a few feet away and spoke very quietly, gently. "The news is not good Mable. I'm so very sorry. This all seems so foolish when the price is counted up. We came because we wanted you to hear it from us. Please believe me when I say we never wanted this to happen."

There was no response from Mable Baxter. She stood silently, but now there were tears running down her cheeks. Her chest and shoulders were heaving in an effort to hold back the sobs.

A new voice spoke from the veranda as the door opened and another woman stepped outside. Margo had met Mrs. Adel

Cox just once, but she remembered her well enough to be sure who she was seeing and hearing.

"And what about the others?" She already knew the answer by the fact that Mac and Margo were standing there.

Again, Margo said, "I'm very sorry."

Mrs. Cox simply turned and went back into the house.

Mable Baxter was beginning to get a grip on her emotions. That she expected and predicted this same outcome made the news anticlimactic. She looked at Mac and Margo. She wiped her tears with a scrunched-up handkerchief she held in her hand. And then, for a long time she looked at Cray.

She finally spoke to Mac and Margo. With her hands held before her, wringing her fingers, she said, "You've only confirmed what I knew the outcome would be. That doesn't make the hurt any less, but I thank you for coming yourselves. And Cray, thank you for coming too. I know you were treated horribly on the X-O."

She paused and caught her breath before continuing. "I'll have some decisions to make now and no one I trust to help me make them." She looked like she had more to say but finally dropped her hands to her sides and her chin fell to her chest. It was as if she was embarrassed by that short outburst and didn't know how to proceed.

Mac stepped to the ground and strode to stand beside Margo. "If I may suggest, Mable, you might ask Cray to take up his old position with the ranch. There's no better or more level-headed man you could have standing beside you on ranch matters. If you were to take your time and sort it all out with Cray's help I'm thinking you'd find yourself headed in the right direction."

There was silence for a long minute. Finally, Mable raised her head and spoke to Cray. "Cray, would you come back as foreman until I can figure this all out?"

Cray nodded his head. "I'd like nothing better, Mable."

Mable looked back to Mac and Margo. "Adel will be wanting to sell. She's talked about it. She always hated this west country. She never stopped longing to be back in the big city. There's no chance that she'll stay on alone."

Mac looked up at the house hoping to see Mrs. Cox, but there was no sign of her. "You tell her to hang on for a week or two. We're not looking to add to the Bar-M, but I know a couple of men who might be interested in establishing themselves. I'll send them on down in the next short while."

Cray stepped down and started to lead his horse to the corral. Mac spoke again to Mable Baxter. "We'll be leaving now Mable. I hope you know you can count on us for anything you need. And again, we're all truly sorry this mess ever got started." He turned for his horse with Margo beside him.

Mable said, "We have room and it's late. Won't you stay the night?"

Mac answered, "No, you need the time alone. We'll be fine. But thank you just the same."

Mac and Margo stepped aboard their horses. Mac trotted to where Cray was working over his animal. The two men spoke quietly and shook hands.

Mac and Margo left the Baxter ranch at a slow walk. A few hours later, wrapped in a single blanket and a ground sheet, they made a cold camp somewhere on the south-east corner of the Bar-M.

41

IT WAS THREE DAYS BEFORE the men were rested and the work around the Bar-M was back to normal.

Mac and Margo were several days returning. They rode into the yard looking rested. They offered no explanation for their absence.

The well drilling program was completed at the new corral and feed yards. Mac laid out a rough map of where he hoped to find water on the range. The well diggers were left to their own wisdom on how best to locate and pull up that water. They were pointed to the far west side of the holdings as the place to start. The sheep would be the first to need water if the summer sun dried up the small streams.

The hay was growing and would be harvested within a few weeks. The new grain fields were plowed. It was late in the spring season for planting, but Mac figured there might still be enough frost-free days to get off a crop of oats if the rains came at the right time.

The same farmers hired to plow and harrow, breaking open the virgin sod, were hired to get the seed in the ground. Other crops would be tried in the years to come.

Jerrod returned home with Bill siding him as an escort on the long ride. Leaving out no detail, the two men told Jimbo's sad story.

Luke and Dora were back on the Lazy-L. Antonio would need another bit of time under Mama's careful attention before he would be riding again. Juan was back at Luke's side attempting to do the work of two men.

Knowing the fence would remain a controversial matter, perhaps for years to come, Mac rotated the guards assigned to Rocky's care. Madison and Ethan rode into the Bar-M ranch yard two days later.

Mac saw them coming and waited for them beside the corral. "How goes it men? Everything well?

Ethan tipped his hat back and grinned down at Mac. He slowly stepped from the saddle and turned the horse loose. "Well, Mac. That all depends. If'n it's you or me we're talking about or is it rancher Jenkins? As for me and Madison, I expect we're doin' just fine. As for rancher Jenkins, he just could be hungry and foot sore by now. Or perhaps one of his crew found him walkin and doubled him home."

Mac looked at his two riders. "You better tell me about it."

When the cowboys completed telling the short story Mac asked, "So what did you do with Jenkins?"

Ethan grinned. "We kind of figured he needed time to contemplate. To consider, you might say. So, we gave him back his unloaded gun, a sack of grub, a full canteen, and pointed the way to his spread. He left out walking yesterday morning in no happy frame of mind. We explained the choices to him; get shot or hung or take a walk. He made his choice. And a good choice it'll be too, if'n he learns anything along the way."

Mac shook his head and looked long at his riders. "Well, I'm glad you didn't shoot him. Take care of your horses and go get some grub. Taz will detail you off to the next work. Thanks for looking after the fence crew and the Bar-M interests."

After his return from the big land battle, Mac was in a melancholy frame of mind. His arm was hurting, and the sling was put back into service. He found it difficult to be enthused about much of anything. He was deeply troubled by the graves newly dug on the south end of the Bar-M. That he hadn't been able to find a peaceful solution to the land grab was keeping him awake nights.

For the first time ever, he left important decisions to Taz while he saddled his horse. He rode for several hours each day, going nowhere in particular, just letting his mind wander at will, seeking silence. He prayed until he didn't know what else to say to God.

Many miles north of the Bar-M he found himself sitting on the low bank of the big river, trying to sort out what it was all about. The slowly flowing stream had a calming effect on his mind.

Why were men willing to tear their lives and families apart, fighting and dying for something they couldn't have? Something that belonged to another. Something that would add very little, if anything, to the betterment of their own lives if they did somehow succeed in gaining it.

Why were otherwise sensible men, who's only rewards were day wages, willing to follow a fool into battle, putting their own lives at risk?

He knew the indelible memory of those bodies lying on the grass, waiting to be buried, would be carried in his mind all the days of his life.

He hadn't experienced that melancholy emotion since the couple of days he spent sitting beside another slow-moving stream in East Texas, after the war.

In both cases he was left with no answers. The twists and turn of human nature escaped his reasoning.

After a visit with his dad in the farm smithy, sitting on a stool made from a cut-off tree trunk, as he'd done so often during his growing years, and a similar talk with Margo in the quiet of evening on top of their private hill, he finally decided to accept that all of life's issues don't provide clear answers.

There was a family to raise and a ranch business to run. He finally thanked God for the little bit he did know and tried to put the rest out of his mind.

Stepping out of the house in the pre-dawn light, planning on an early start to the work day, his few days of melancholy wanderings put behind him, it was as if he could hear Jimbo say, "Welcome back friend. Best to take life just like she comes."

He was going to miss his old pal.

42

MARGO ASKED PEPE TO SADDLE her horse. Jerrod and the twins saddled their own rides. With Jerrod showing a leap in his already serious, responsibility-accepting nature, brought on, no doubt, by the Jimbo matter, and with the twins back to their old, boisterous selves, the four of them rode to Ad's store for a day of visiting. Margo found it worked well to have one of the grandmothers from Mex Town care for the little ones when she needed more freedom, either for ranch business or for time with the older children. She'd been doing that more and more lately. Margo got her freedom; the kids were kept safe and well and the grannie took home a few coins. They were both satisfied with the arrangement.

Clara and Margo went for a stroll along the creek bank. The age and experience difference between the sisters had a way of making Clara feel awkward when they were together. Most of what Clara hoped to do in life, her older sister had already done. Clara tended to hold her silence. Margo was equally awkward, not knowing what Clara's thoughts and dreams were and being unsure how to approach the subject of love and men.

Stopping in the shade of some scrub bush Margo said, "I'm thinking you have feelings for the young Texan working for the survey crew." She left it at that.

After a moment Clara said, "Shep. His name is Shep. Mr. Trimble. He hasn't been in for a while. Should be due any day now. Mom worries, but I like him. Dad seems alright around him too but if the situation was to get more serious I'm not sure what his feeling would be. I'm not even totally sure what my feelings are."

The two sisters returned to their slow stroll.

Margo took a chance on nudging the topic along. "Do you think there's solid stuff under all the smiles and curls and nonsense talk?"

Clara chuckled, "He is full of nonsense, isn't he? Still, I've seen a seriousness there when the need was upon him. When the survey crew was attacked and needed help he was all business. And then, when he had the opportunity to shoot the attacking men, he didn't. He just drove them off.

"He's very purposeful about the supplies he lays in for the surveyors. I don't know how well he can cook but he chooses good provisions to work with.

"And then, that man from the well drilling crew, Mr. Marpole, spoke very highly of Shep and his family."

Margo let a bit of time go by before saying, "Those are all good things. But what about when you're alone? You rode home from church with him. I'm not asking what you talked about. But did you get the feeling that you could love this man? Live with him?"

Clara was even longer than Margo had been in speaking, as if she was choosing her words with great care.

"He was a perfect gentleman. I don't think it was an act either, although I have nothing particular to compare to. He did ask if he could come calling even if he didn't need anything from the store. I told him I would like that. I guess all that means something. But living out here away from anyone except family and a bunch of passing-through ranch and farm workers, I've never been faced with anything like this before."

Both girls were silent as they strolled along. Then, into the silence Clara burst out with, "I like him Margo."

Margo said nothing. She simply smiled at her little sister and gave her a hug.

The two girls turned and started back to the trading post. Margo was still concerned about interfering in matters best left alone. Yet, opportunities must to be seized when they presented themselves.

Margo cleared her throat and said, "There's a ranch that's going to be for sale. That doesn't happen all that often around here. There were only two small places last year.

"A couple of ranchers gave up and moved off the land. You might remember that.

"Both those ranchers owed loans to the Bar-M. Mac took the land as payment. The ranchers sold their cattle for 'starting-again money'. We've done nothing with the land except collect a small bit of rent from neighbors who are grazing the range. Bobby and Jeremiah could have those places, but they've shown no interest.

"Now, with Adel Cox being a widow, she's determined to sell and go back east. It's not a large spread but it's big enough to support a fine herd of quality cattle. And it's a nicer place than either of the two that starved out last year."

She let a half a minute go by before saying, "It's a pretty place, nestled into a background of wooded hills, with an active stream close by. I've only been there once but I think you'd like it."

She paused again, almost afraid to go on. Finally, she said, "So I got thinking…..."

She was interrupted by light laughter from Clara. "That's good thinking, big sister. But how would I get Shep to know about it without sounding obvious?"

Margo laughed along with Clara. "Well, Pretty Lady. I think that's what he calls you is it not? Some things you will have to do for yourself. Perhaps you need to do something like ask if he ever thought of ranching around this area, or is he stuck on returning to Texas. Men are very easy to lead Clara. I can almost guarantee he'd walk to the Cox ranch carrying his boots in his hands, for one of your encouraging smiles."

The sisters walked into the trading post laughing. Amelia Adkins looked up from where she was putting an order together. "Now what in the world are you two up to this morning?"

"Just girl stuff Mom."

43

TEN SHORT DAYS AFTER the land fight Mac was surprised to see Cray Dobbs riding into the yard. Mac waited for him at the corral where he was working with a young gelding he hoped would take the place of the black he gave to the Nez Percé chief.

"Good morning Cray. What brings you way over here on a warm summer morning? Step down and rest yourself."

Cray stepped to the ground and turned his horse loose. The animal immediately went to the water trough.

"For sure, it's a beautiful day Mac. It's good to see you looking well. I need to get back, so I'll get right to the point. You made an offer of help if it should be needed." He paused to allow Mac to answer.

Mac nodded his head. "I said it and I meant it. What's up?"

Cray absently scuffed the ground with his foot before answering. "I've found myself wishing many a time that this had happened a month ago, but it didn't. What a world of hurt could have been prevented.

"Anyway, Mable has decided to clear her range of longhorns, every last one. She calls them giant locusts. She's decided to let the summer go by while the grass greens up. She'll consider everything else in the fall. She had me fire all the new hands that were brought in for the fight. That leaves us with just four men for cattle work.

"Adel Cox is selling out. All her animals will be going to market too. She has only two riders.

Then four or five other brands are cutting way back. I expect more ranchers to see the light and follow suit. All in all, there's enough animals for two big drives now. I don't know how long it will be before another drive will be put together."

Mac took all of this in without comment, just watching Cray intently.

Cray finally spoke again. "Anyway, what we need is riders. Cowboys. I got to wondering if that New Mexico bunch were still on the payroll or have they ridden back south?"

"They're here and still drawing pay. I don't need them but decided to hold them over until the end of the month to make their ride up here worth while. My guess is they'd jump at a chance to put down their post hole digging tools and chase cows for a while. Maybe see the big city at the end of the chase.

"I'm thinking that we could spare four or five additional men if you needed more. Why don't we ride out to the feeding grounds and have a talk with Taz?"

Two hours later Cray was ready to head back to the X-O with fourteen seasoned hands. With bedrolls behind their saddles, and saddle bags bulging with left over biscuits, beef sandwiches and a can of peaches each, they were well prepared for the two-day ride.

Mac went to the safe in his office and came back with a box of mixed bills and coins. He counted out the pay for each man, adding in the rest of the month as a small bonus. He thanked them and bid them well. "Don't spend all that in the city, fellas. You're better off keeping some for seed."

The men walked off laughing. Mac figured they'd be flat broke before they were back in New Mexico.

With the yard quiet again Mac went to the house for coffee with Margo. During a lull in the conversation he said, "I have to figure out when to make a trip to Denver. There's banking to do and I want to find out if the telegraph wires are being strung out this way. I heard some time ago that the wires were going to reach the town over east of here sometime soon. Should have been here years ago but we didn't push for it. Seems foolish now that we think more about it.

"Then, I have to make a report to the Deputy Marshal. We're past the time when a range war can take place, and everyone just forgets about it."

44

THE SURVEYOR'S HOODLUM WAGON, with its rolled-up canvas top flapping in the breeze pulled into the shade of the adobe trading post. Shep leaped off the seat and immediately went to care for the horses. Ad strolled over and watched for a minute.

He finally spoke. "It's good to see you again Shep. I'm glad to see you always caring for that team so well too. Never could abide a man who abused good horseflesh."

Shep lifted his head and smiled at Ad. "Good afternoon, Mr. Adkins. I've made a rushed trip on account of those pilgrims I'm saddled with are all alone out there. No Bar-M guards anymore. You never know, those city boys might fall into a prairie dog hole or some such a thing and I'll never find them again.

"Anyway, these horses have stepped right along with nothing but this empty wagon dragging along behind them.

"Heading back, it'll be a different matter by the time you load us up. This pair are in need of a breather. I'd like to give them a couple of hours now and then start back. We'll camp out somewhere when darkness hides the trail."

He straightened his back after checking the horse's hooves. "As to caring for these beasts, only once in my life did Pa take to teaching me a lesson with a cut-off length of tug strap. I was still pretty young, but he figured I was old enough to have listened when he spoke. Seems I pretty much sweated up a riding pony and turned him out to pasture, wet and uncared for. Never did that again. It's a caution what a boy can learn from the end of a length of leather."

Shep chuckled and shook his head. "Remember that like it was yesterday. As far as that goes, there never was an animal rough treated on the Double-T. Any man who couldn't learn that the first day didn't stay on to enjoy a second day."

Ad said, "I assume you have a written down list. If you want to give it to me I'll get the women started on putting it together. Then I've got to get back to the smithy."

Shep fished in his shirt pocket and lifted out the paper. Ad could clearly see that the young man was hesitating, but he said nothing, just waiting.

Finally, Shep pulled all his courage together and said, "Mr. Adkins, I'd like to ask your permission to call on Clara. I'm hoping she'd welcome my visits. I have no experience at all to look to, so I don't know if this is the proper way or not, but I thought to ask you anyway. I sure do admire her. I'd like for us to get to know one another better."

Ad waited to see if Shep had more to say. When it was clear the young man had said his piece, Ad looked Shep full in the eye. "I've seen nothing to suggest that you are anything but honorable Shep. I'm hoping you don't do something that would make me rethink that. If Clara welcomes your visits you have my approval."

Shep was somehow smiling from ear to ear and looking bashful all at the same time. He squared his shoulders and said, "Thank you Mr. Adkins. I promise you can trust me."

He passed the shopping list to Ad and turned back to the horses.

A while later, Shep and Clara were strolling along the same stream she and Margo had walked beside. Ad was at the smithy. Amelia Adkins was putting Shep's order together, stacking it on the counter, ready. The loading could wait until Shep pulled the wagon up to the door after the horses were more rested.

Amelia couldn't resist taking periodic peeks out the front window. Shep and Clara were turned so only their backs were visible. The frustrated mother went back to storekeeping.

Shep told Clara about his talk with her father. The two young people were both a bit bashful about the matter. While it was true that most women were married and many of them were already mothers at Clara's age, neither she nor Shep had any experience in the matter of courtship. Still, the conversation was going more smoothly than Clara imagined it might. And Shep was sparing with the nonsense talk, telling about the Double-T and his family.

When it was nearing time to harness the team, Shep cleared his throat and took a big breath. He plainly had something important to say. Standing in the shade of a willow bunch, the young people facing each other, first Shep's lips moved with no sound coming out. Finally, he found his voice.

"Heard about a ranch for sale. Widow woman named Cox wanted to sell out and leave the country. It's about a short day and a half ride south of here. That puts it pretty close to due south of where we're doing survey work, by maybe a three-hour jaunt." He glanced at Clara, trying to read her reaction before continuing.

"Couple of days ago I laid out some lunch, ready for the boys when noon came, and jogged down to have me a look at the spread. Wanted to take a look-see before someone else puts their hooks into it."

They were both silent. Shep was making wishful plans in his mind while Clara was saying to herself, 'that Shep knows about the Cox ranch sounds like Margo somehow got into the act."

Clara gathered her boldness and asked, "Working way out there on the survey line, how did you hear about a ranch for sale?"

Shep chuckled and kicked his toe in the sod. "It was the doggondest thing. A big bunch of cowboys riding south to drive a herd from the X-O stopped by for coffee a few days ago. Drank three pots before they all had their fill.

"Well, we got to talking and the next thing you know this foreman from the X-O comes up with this bit of information. He allowed as how it wasn't often land became available anywhere near here.

"We talked some more, and I figured I'd better get down there right quick.

"This Mrs. Cox, she was real anxious to sell out and head back East. Her cattle are going to market so it's just the land and a few head of horses, some haying machinery and such.

Nice house and a great location among low hills on the west side. Flowing stream."

The young man took another deep breath and blurted out, "So I bought the place. Wrote a check on the home bank, which they'll honor with Pa's say-so."

The look on Clara's face showed her astonishment.

Trying to recover his thoughts, Shep jumped back in to say, "Course, I'd not be the least bit interested in the place if you were to tell me you want to spend your life behind the counter of the trading post, and that you'd probably not be interested in ranching. Or that there was someone else taking up your thoughts. Or that you wouldn't be interested in me, no matter what."

Clara laughed and put her finger over Shep's lips. "Shep, you're rambling."

Shep sucked down a big breath. "I'd imagine you're right on that. Anyway, to get down to it, I just felt the need to make this here trip today to kind of sort out the situation."

When he stopped talking there was a very awkward air between the two.

The young man tried again. "I realize that's all rushing things a mite. I wouldn't no way do that to you if it weren't for having seen that ranch. That kind of pushed my thoughts forward. I'm hoping you don't take offence."

Clara had no idea what to say. Thoughts were scrambling through her mind, crashing into each other and leaving her a bit dizzy.

The two stood in silence for a few moments before Shep said, "I apologise Clara. Now that I think on what I just said, I know I have no right to blurt something like that out. Of course, what I did was lay out my private thoughts. Thoughts best kept inside my own dreaming mind."

He offered a sheepish grin. "I know this will surprise you some but from time to time I've been known to speak before my thoughts are really all put together. But not this time. In this case my thoughts are very much put together, have been for some time, but I still should've kept my peace. Again, I apologise."

Clara knew she had to say something to keep the conversation going without getting into water any deeper than they were already in. "Did you intend to run a cattle ranch here? What about the Double-T?"

Shep's smile was coming back. "Oh, I love the folks and all but the last thing the Double-T needs is another body or two hanging around. No, I set out looking for greener pastures. Found them too."

Impulsively he picked up her hand and held it. "Clara you would love the place. Pretty house, good outbuildings, nestled in a few wooded hills, running stream."

He paused and let go of her hand, seeming to be unaware of his actions. "Anyway, none of that matters. It's not totally what I have in mind."

Clara knew this time would probably not be repeated. They had worked their way through the initial awkwardness without either saying anything that they could not back away from. She had to speak now.

"Shep, you'd best tell me exactly what it is you have in mind if you bought a cattle ranch and don't figure to ranch."

He picked up both her hands and shone another smile at her. "To put it plainly, what I have in mind is raising and training horses. I've seen about enough years of living miles from other folks. I figure to breed and raise horses on a ranch. A couple of horse savvy men can manage the ranch and look after things for me.

"I plan to move the yearlings closer to town for the months of training that good saddle stock needs."

He swung his arm around the land the little stream was flowing through. "A place like this. Maybe fifty acres or so. Maybe a quarter section. Enough for a house and yard, a barn and corrals. Just a bit of pasture."

When Clara didn't immediately respond Shep deflated a bit and said, "Well I thought I'd tell you about it anyway. Kind of find out your thinking on the subject. If you were to laugh at me I would just finish up my surveying job and then probably ride back to Amarillo. Put the ranch back on the market.

"If you showed some interest I would put on a search for another piece of land close around here.

"You could probably plan on me calling on you regular too, now that the survey line is getting closer."

He left his thoughts there hoping the young lady would respond.

Again, the two of them fought the silence. They finally turned and started slowly strolling back to the trading post.

Finally, Shep spoke again. "You and I were both raised in far away places Clara. Seeing the same folks day after day and longing for a new face once in a while.

"TJ was chuckling about my sister dragging a husband home from that eastern school. But who's to blame her. She'd never seen more than fifteen, twenty people her age all her growing years and some of those were her own family. Closest neighbor ten miles away. Maybe a dance once a year. She must have looked at all the choices on the hoof running around that school and thought she'd died and gone to heaven.

"She's a pretty girl too, no matter what TJ says. Her husband is an alright guy. He's judged hard because he's not a Texas cowboy but he's learning just the same."

To ease the conversation Clara said, "Your friend TJ is an interesting man. He thinks highly of you and your family."

"Well, I think highly of him too. There's more to TJ than he lets on. He's one of the smartest men I ever met. Not much schooling, like he said, but smart. Always wanting to know. Wouldn't surprise me any if he were to own that well drilling outfit by the end of summer. He would be a great partner in the horse raising business."

Clara gathered up all her courage and said, "Shep, you come here working as a cook and wrangler, but you talk of ranching and cowboying and knowing cattle and of a family ranch. But no one here has ever heard of this Double-T ranch or knows anyone from the Texas Panhandle except for you and TJ. You'll understand that my folks are just a bit nervous and, quite honestly, so am I."

The two stood quietly for a while, looking at each other, before Clara said, "I like you Shep and have welcomed your attention. But we really don't know much about each other."

Shep somehow found another smile. "I know you're right on that Pretty Lady. I don't know what the solution is, but I'll try to come up with something. Truth told, it's only about a long three or four day ride down to the Double-T. Shouldn't be too big an obstacle. I'll work on it. And I'll see you again soon.

"I'd better load up and get along. I've got to be getting back to my job, else those surveyors are liable to do something foolish and then I'll have to fix that too. I'll be back just as soon as possible.

As Clara watched the loaded wagon head off across the Bar-M she was wondering how much to tell her folks.

45

MAC RETURNED FROM HIS TRIP to Denver with much news. He and Margo took their comfortable chairs on the veranda. All the children gathered around them. Mac brought gifts for everyone. He passed out a package to each child and waited while they opened them.

Jerrod opened a pair of deer hide chaps tanned almost white. The twins each opened a new hat. Margo helped the smaller children open their packages of new clothing.

Mac then passed Margo a carefully wrapped box. She opened it and exclaimed over a matching Navaho silver and turquoise ring and bracelet set.

Everyone was delighted with their gifts, thanking husband and father enthusiastically.

The kids then went off to leave the parents to their talk.

Mac explained about visiting the bank and showed her the balances from the three banks they dealt with.

Margo's only comment was that she hated the idea of Mac riding alone with the payroll money in his saddle bags. This was an old discussion.

Mac smiled and said, "No such a thing this time around. The entire payroll is safely stowed under a pile of fenceposts on one of Rocky's wagons. It will be here in a few days. Anyway, with the costs of all the contractors that need paying I'd have needed two pack horses to carry that weight of coin."

Margo said, "Did you see the marshal?"

Mac nodded and looked grim. "I saw him and I'm sorry I didn't just hold my silence. Turns out he'd rather not have known. Strange way to uphold the law, is my opinion. The fool pushed paper around his desk and growled under his breath while he studied me and listened to the story. He finally asked if it was finished. I assured him it was. I was all set to remind him about being warned before it started but decided that might complicate things.

"He talked a bit about asking the court for advice but finally said he'd have to come down and look into it personally. Then he told me how busy he is. Said it could be some months before we actually saw him out this way. I expect we'll never hear any more about it."

Mac poured another mug of coffee from the pot on the table and spoke again. "Saw Nancy and them. They're talking about visiting out this way, come summer. Doing well, I guess.

"Nancy had a lady visiting with her. Woman named Kathleen Keeler. Seems she recently graduated from a horticultural school up north somewhere. Knows about trees, plants and such. Seems nice enough.

"Nancy got a bit pushy, acting like we were all still kids again, making like a big sister. Told this Miss Keeler the Bar-M could benefit from her coming down and providing advice. Long and the short of it is this Miss. Keeler said she'd find a way to get down here. Wants to ride around and look over the land, water and such. Tell us what trees will grow best. Never heard of such as that before. I figure what would grow best is probably already growing but then I didn't graduate from no horticulture school."

Margo laughed, "Are you sure she wasn't talking about fruit trees, garden vines and such. You know, growing food? Or maybe she was talking about shelters you could plant around the new dug-outs you're planning when the well drillers bring up some water."

Mac had no response.

The two sat in companionable silence for several minutes. Mac then looked across the table and asked, "Where are the Boston ladies? Haven't seen hide nor hair."

"Gone," Answered Margo. "Three of Rocky's wagons came in to fill their water barrels, setting out on their return trip. The girls saw it as a good opportunity to have an escort to Denver. Mattie was talking about seeing California. They were packed in just a few minutes and drove out with the fence crew."

Mac nodded his understanding. "The boys go with them?"

Margo shook her head. "The fools, you mean. Your idiot brothers. No, they were off to see the sheep operation. They might be some surprised when they get back. Fools."

Mac didn't argue about Margo's assessment of the situation.

46

HIRAM AND DELLA LEFT THE FARM in the care of a neighbor boy. They drove their buggy on a leisurely course, taking advantage of the beautiful summer weather to visit with Ad and Amelia, planning on a further visit at the Bar-M before returning home the next morning. They were greeted like the old friends they were.

Working together through the indescribably hard times of the early years, learning the wild cattle business, suffering through the Texas northers in poorly built jacals, crossing the continent on horseback or wagon, eating trail dust for thousands of miles and, generally pushing the boundaries of human endurance, as well as sharing grandchildren, made for lifetime friendships.

The land grab fight was thoroughly talked through in the past. There was nothing to gain by delving into that matter again.

Range conditions and cattle prices were always ready topics of interest. The latest antics of the children held the foursome enthralled for a while also. But the big news had to do with Clara.

Sitting on kitchen chairs dragged from the living quarters to the store veranda, to join the rocking chairs that were a fixture on the shaded porch, the friends were enjoying the warm, early afternoon sun along with their after-lunch coffee. Being outside, Della was able to light up her old pipe. Amelia frowned on smoking in the store, although she tolerated it. The practice was absolutely forbidden in her attached home.

When the conversation came to a pause Ad cleared his throat and said, "This will be news to you. In fact, the news was only confirmed to us yesterday."

Amelia let out a long sigh. Neither Hiram nor Della knew what the sigh meant but they both glanced at Amelia, noticing her far-away look, and then back at Ad, waiting for the story.

Ad lovingly patted his wife's knee. "It's all fine dear. You knew what was coming."

Ad turned to the two visitors. "Well, the story is that Clara seems to have found the young man of her choosing. You met him once. He came to the church service the day after your arrival home from Denver. He's a young cowboy from Texas. Been working as cook and wrangler to the survey crew. Shep Trimble. He's been here several times buying supplies. Family own the Double-T over in the panhandle.

"The young people were attracted to each other right from the start. Although Amelia still holds some doubts about the cowboy's claim to her youngest daughter, neither of us has been able to find any direct cause for concern. Shep is a pleasant young man, showing considerable responsibility, and according to the surveyors, a hard worker.

"At my asking, Bobby and Jeremiah rode down to Texas and found the Double-T. It's only a short ride. There and back in just over a week. They report it's quite the operation. One of the biggest spreads in the Amarillo area. They met Shep's folks and three, four brothers and sisters. A framed photo of

Shep was on the fireplace mantle. The family was anxious for news of their son.

"The boys got back yesterday. They confirmed everything Shep told us. I expect our concerns are dealt with. It's all up to Shep and Clara from here on."

Della asked, "Where will they make their home? I always somehow thought Clara would take over the trading post when you felt you'd done enough work for one lifetime."

Ad told them about the Cox ranch and the horse raising. Then he said, "As to the trading post, I don't think it'll even be here ten years from now. That town over east is growing fast. There's a couple of places opening up along the big river. We'll probably just shut it down when we've had enough."

Amelia let out another big sigh. Big sighs were becoming a habit with her. She turned from her husband to look at Della. "So now everything around here is in a tizzy while the girls plan for a wedding. Margo's taking the lead but not because she has any particular knowledge of how a wedding should go. You'll recall that she and Mac got married on the run so's not to interrupt the cattle drive. No, she's mostly leading because Clara knows even less."

The four grandparents were all silent for a bit before Hiram asked, "So where is the young man now? Is he still working with the surveyors?

Ad answered, "No. The fencing still has a way to go but the surveying is complete. Just as soon as the boys brought back their report on the Double-T, Shep and Clara went for a walk along the river. They were back within an hour with their decision made.

"Shep left almost immediately. He's gone off to gather some quality mares and a stallion from the Double-T. He plans to drive them to the Cox ranch and make a start at horse ranching. Should be back in a couple of weeks."

Idly, as if she'd given the fight her best and was now resigned to the future, Amelia said, "Oh, I expect it will all somehow work out."

47

THE HOT SUMMER WAS FADING into the cooling breezes of early fall. The surveying and fencing was complete.

The well drilling crew was still hard at work. Some of the drilling brought up water. Some simply brought up more dust and rocks.

The sheep were settled in. Mac spent some time with the shepherds, learning from them, growing more fascinated with the animals and their herders every time he went there.

Shep and Clara's wedding was planned, with the date fast approaching.

The range recovered better than Mac thought it would, showing considerable green growth. One more summer without the trampling of hooves and the grazing of beef animals should have it back, ready for regular use. The main concern now was prairie fire. If the maturing and dying grass wasn't pretty soon wetted down with rain there could be a real problem.

A large group of neighboring ranchers, families and cowboys were gathered. Mac sent riders out to invite the people in. It was a solemn group, the reason for the gathering making it so. Many there were fighting personal memories. Although some were smiling as they greeted seldom seen neighbors, it was done with dignity and respect.

Mac spent days fussing and re-thinking, praying that he was right in calling the gathering. He had no desire to set old fires aflame again. His belief was that gathering and visiting and remembering might prevent another land grab battle or anything like it in the future. A look at the stark cost of the confrontation was very sobering to Mac and he was sure it would be to the others as well.

Everyone stood quietly while a late arriving buggy wound its way across the Bar-M sod, accompanied by four outriders. Mac was surprised and pleased to see Jenkins and his wife step from the buggy. He was especially surprised to see Jenkins approach him directly. Mac was steeling himself against possible problems, but Jenkins stopped a few feet away and held out his hand. Mac gripped it eagerly.

Jenkins tipped his hat back with his thumb. "Are we alright?"

Mac gripped more tightly, "Couldn't be better neighbor."

Mac had long believed that not every issue should be discussed to an end. Some things you just let go.

The two men studied each other for a few moments and then Jenkins turned to walk to his wife.

The four Jenkins riders tied their horses and joined the large gathering of cowboys who were standing on the fringe of the crowd.

Mac and Margo walked arm in arm and stopped before the metal gate Ad built in his blacksmith shop. The gate was firmly mounted into an adobe wall constructed by a few men from Mex Town. The wall surrounded the little hollow in the land that became a burying ground. No cattle would tromp on these graves.

Each grave was marked with a simple plaque ordered from Denver.

The land didn't show any difference. It was all as it was before. The trees still grew. The grass was green and growing. The scrub brush wove its tangled web. The little creek tumbled along, escaping through an outlet left under the adobe fence. Birds nested where they wished. No doubt, prairie dogs would build their dens and never give the wall, or the graves, a thought.

Everything was the same as before and yet everything was different. The graves of fighting men who paid the price for their beliefs made it different.

While the crowd was silent there seemed to be an expectation growing, an expectation that Mac should say something. He finally turned to the crowd spread along the fence. What he said, he meant as strongly as anything he ever said before.

Looking from one face to another he seemed to gather resolution, if not courage.

Speaking against the never-ending wind he said, "I pray never again. I am resolved, never again. As for me and my family and the Bar-M, never again. Never, never again."

Someone started singing a hymn. It had to be Bill for that was Bill's way. He sang three verses and choruses, although few joined him.

When the crowd was again silent Mac and Margo walked away. Someone opened the gate and folks strolled among the graves. A few women brought along picked and gathered prairie flowers to lay across the head stones.

Several people made a point of speaking to Mama, thanking her for her help.

Mac walked over to where his brothers were tightening their saddle cinches. "You're loaded for bear boys. You didn't need all this truck for a ride down here."

Bobby grinned at his big brother. "We figured to take a little ride out to California. Man never knows what he might find until he goes looking. You take care big brother. We'll see you come spring."

Their way of saying good bye was to wave their hats and kick their horses into a run.

Ground sheets were being spread out and food hampers were being opened. The mood of the morning was gradually lifting as people turned from the graves and sought out neighbors and old friends. Folks were visiting and finding places to sit together.

Mable Baxter came over to Mac and Margo. Cray was walking protectively beside her. "Thanks for doing all this Mac. It's more than most of those men expected. Herman was still wrong, and most of this lays on his shoulders. But being here just this once will make the memory a little less harsh."

The widow and her foreman walked away together.

Margo looked at them, turned to her husband and said, "Do you suppose…?"

"Ain't none of our affair."

"Our only affair is the Bar-M and the folks who depend on it. We look after that, we'll have enough to do."

He held his hat in his hand as he turned and looked at the land once more. As far as his eye could see there was green. Green leaves on the trees. Green shrubs of many varieties. Green cactus, somehow looking pleasant in its spiny naturalness. And over it all a clear blue sky with an early fall sun shining on grass waving its new growth in the continual breeze.

Taking it all in with thankfulness the rancher spoke silently, 'Lord, I asked for your help and I made you a promise to care for this land. I could ask for no more than what I see at this moment.'

He sat, joining his family on the ground sheet Margo had spread out.

He picked up a plate of chicken sandwiches and passed them among the children. Then he and Margo each took one.

"Jerrod, do you want to give thanks?"

A Look at Mac's Law (Mac's Way Book 3)

Best-selling author Reg Quist brings you book three of the Christian western series – Mac's Way.

Mac McTavish is called upon to assist the Federal Marshal in dealing with a murder case in a remote corner of the state. Not only have there been murders, but rustlers have also been working in the area, which Mac takes a personal interest in.

In order to unravel the crimes, Mac recruits his deputy sheriff brothers, Bobby and Jeremiah.

When the crimes are finally solved, everyone is surprised to learn who is behind it all.

Mac's Law is a captivating page-turner that has something for everyone – action, humor and romance!

AVAILABLE NOW

About the Author

Reg Quist is the grandson of homesteading pioneers. From the soddy that was home to his grandparents to the farms and ranches of the modern era, the Quist family has had an attachment to the land.

Quist was always an avid reader with the desire to write. The responsibilities of work, business and family had to take precedence but now in retirement, the stories that lay dormant all those years are being put on paper.

Although Quist's writing talents have led into many genres, it is the Western that has become primary.

While recognizing that there was a certain amount of confrontation and violence in a lawless West, it is the basic goodness of the pioneers, their brutally hard work, their sacrifice, the looking to the future, their spiritual soundness and their hopes for their children and their grandchildren that Quist tells about. Having witnessed these very attributes in his own family and, as much as humanly possible, has lived them himself, Quist is able to bring his characters to life.

Find more great titles by Reg Quist and Christian Kindle News at http://christiankindlenews.com/our-authors/reg-quist/

Reg Quist is the grandson of homesteading pioneers. From the soddy that was home to his grandparents to the farms and ranches of the modern era, the Quist family has had an attachment to the land.

Quist was always an avid reader with the desire to write. The responsibilities of work, business and family had to take precedence but now in retirement, the stories that lay dormant all those years are being put on paper.

Although Quist's writing talents have led into many genres, it is the Western that has become primary.

While recognizing that there was a certain amount of

confrontation and violence in a lawless West, it is the basic goodness of the pioneers, their brutally hard work, their sacrifice, the looking to the future, their spiritual soundness and their hopes for their children and their grandchildren that Quist tells about. Having witnessed these very attributes in his own family and, as much as humanly possible, has lived them himself, Quist is able to bring his characters to life.

Find more great titles by Reg Quist and Christian Kindle News at http://christiankindlenews.com/our-authors/reg-quist/